BOUNTY

KALIYA SAHNI BOOK ONE

K.N. BANET

Copyright © 2020 by K.N. Banet

All rights reserved.

No part of this book may be reproduced in any form or by any electronic or mechanical means, including information storage and retrieval systems, without written permission from the author, except for the use of brief quotations in a book review.

This is a work of fiction. Names, characters, businesses, places, events, locales, and incidents are either the products of the author's imagination or used in a fictitious manner. Any resemblance to actual persons, living or dead, or actual events is purely coincidental.

1

CHAPTER ONE
SEPTEMBER 2018

It was late on a Friday when I walked out of the airport and breathed in the dusty, overbearing hot air of Phoenix, Arizona. Cars drove by in the dark, trying to dodge each other and pick up their families, friends, or whatever.

I never much liked airports, but I loved Phoenix.

Home sweet home.

"Kaliya! Welcome back!" someone called out.

I turned, wind kicking around my white hair, causing my braids to begin coming undone as said wind pushed through the concrete tunnel. A smile bloomed on my face at the sight of my friend—curly blond hair nearly to his shoulders and a casual look that screamed beach bum.

"Carter!" I called back, waving as I picked up my only bag and started walking toward him. "Thanks again for the ride home. I didn't like the idea of leaving my car here for who knows how long."

"It's no problem. No one wants to leave their car at the airport."

I quickly tossed my backpack into his trunk and jogged for the passenger's seat, sliding in as he got behind the wheel.

"So, what was the emergency business trip about?"

"Oh, you know, the Tribunal wanted me on standby," I answered, sighing as he hit the gas and started to swerve dangerously through traffic. "Please remember, I would die from a car accident, Carter."

"I've never been in an accident," he retorted.

"You're immortal, so you've got plenty of time to fuck it up," I countered. His driving didn't really scare me, but giving him a hard time normally kept him from getting the inevitable

speeding ticket I knew was waiting on him one day.

"Sure," he said, chuckling. "So, what did the Tribunal want?"

"I was just on standby," I repeated.

"For the werecat thing?" When I didn't answer, he sighed. "You aren't going to tell me anything, are you?"

"Nope." I was generally close-mouthed about my business trips. "Do you really want to know how a business trip goes for a Tribunal Executioner?"

That shut him up quickly. I leaned toward the window, knowing I made him uncomfortable. I just wanted to be glad I was home.

"Nothing happened," I finally said. "No execution. The werecat was allowed to walk, and a small loophole was addressed in the werecat portion of the Laws."

"No shit," Carter said with a gasp. "You have the coolest job, getting to see all that. I wouldn't have found out until my Mistress was told, and she decided to tell the nest."

I smiled, looking at him. "Thank goodness you have better sources than your Mistress."

"Yeah, just don't ever tell Imani that. She likes to control what we do and don't know."

"Then act surprised when she tells you," I said, shrugging. Carter's vampire problems weren't mine, and I tried my best not to meddle. The last thing I needed was a vampire nest to get pissed off at me, and knowing his Mistress, the leader of the nest, they would if they found out I was feeding information to him that wasn't carefully worded or put in the right light.

"She won't tell me. They'll put out some memo."

I chuckled again, nodding.

"So, are we taking you home, or do you want to stop somewhere?" he asked as we got onto Interstate 10.

"Take me to The Jackalope," I answered, watching us fly past other cars. For a moment, I was glad that Carter didn't have the AC on. It was over eighty, just past sundown, and I loved it. The dry heat the area was known for didn't feel hot to me; it just felt like home.

"Really? Jumping into it the first night you get back?" Carter seemed surprised, and I looked over at him again, raising an eyebrow.

"How long have you known me?"

"Ten years."

"How many short, stupid trips does the Tribunal send me on?"

"Probably one or two a year, though not always for actual trials. Normally, they just send you out to kill someone who was convicted in absentia." He shrugged.

It might say something about me that he said that so nonchalantly.

"And what do I always do when I get back?"

"Go to the Jackalope. Yeah, yeah. I just figured for once in your life, you would take a break."

I snorted, shaking my head. "You just need to drop me off. I know how your Mistress feels about any of you hanging around there. It's where the rogue vamps are." With one more look at him, I reminded him of the last important reason I was going to the hidden supernatural bar in Phoenix. "I left my car there."

"Yeah, that's right."

He pulled off the 10 and got onto the 17 that ran straight through Phoenix. We weren't on it long before he pulled off to take me to The Jackalope in Downtown Phoenix.

On the corner of 2nd and McKinley there was a strange abandoned building, surrounded by several small lounges, a parking lot, and other little pieces of the Phoenix nightlife. The roadside parking was full, and so was the parking lot. On a Friday night, everyone was out and about. I smiled, blinking several times as I saw the building come into view. The glamor recognized me as a supernatural and revealed its secrets. Humans were turned off by the building—no one wanted to go near it or thought to try to buy it. It was just there, standing the test of time with the bustling city around it.

To me it was The Jackalope, the only supernatural bar in Phoenix worth visiting. Even with the glamor gone from my vision, it wasn't much to look at—black walls, sealed windows, only a single story tall, with a neon sign with its name and mascot. There was even a warning posted on the door to ward off trouble and trespassers. It was considered *the* seedy bar for supernaturals in Arizona, *the* place to go to get drunk and do something stupid. No self-respecting supernatural would come here, nor would they let anyone they were responsible for come near it.

Carter pulled up to the front door and smiled at me.

"It's good to have you back, Kaliya. Call me sometime, and we'll go have drinks at my place. It's a lot nicer than The Jackalope."

I made a face. "Your place sucks. Literally. I'll see you soon, though. That's a promise."

He didn't stop laughing as I got out, pulled my bag from the trunk, and slammed it shut. I knocked on his car with my knuckles to let him know I was done, and he hit the gas, screaming down the street and going back to his own Friday night destination, probably the blood club that his nest ran.

Wasting no more time, I strolled into the bar, throwing my pack over my shoulder. I couldn't go home if I didn't get my keys from the owner, who knew me well enough to keep my car from getting towed while I was gone. He also kept it from getting broken into. The amount of favors Paden and I owed each other was uncountable, so we'd stopped trying years ago. We had a set of rules we followed, and one of those was I could leave my car at the Jackalope for any reason at any time, give him the keys, and leave with the expectation everything would be fine when I got back. He never failed me.

"Hey, look who's back!"

I waved silently at the bartender, not stopping for chit chat. Glenn was cool, but I was just trying to get home. I couldn't get caught up in a round of drinks, not upstairs.

"Who's that?" someone asked softly. My sensitive hearing couldn't miss the exchange, so I listened in as I walked through the bar.

"Oh, that's right, you've never seen her. That's Kaliya Sahni, Tribunal Executioner."

"The naga?" someone else asked in a gasp. "I heard she's like the last of her kind or something."

"She's the last female, a nagini. Don't get in her way, she'll fucking kill you. They've taken bodies out of this place before when someone has tried to fuck with her."

I knew the last voice, gritting my teeth as I realized Martin was around. What the scrawny werewolf was doing upstairs wasn't my business, but it was unusual. Upstairs was for people just looking to drink, but types like him were never in The Jackalope just looking for a drink.

Then again, neither are types like me.

I ducked into the back hallways of the bar, trying to control my temper about what he was telling people about me, and found the bouncer in the back. It was hard walking away. If there was one thing I hated, it was being the topic of conversation, especially that conversation.

The last nagini. Like anyone really needs the reminder that my kind are going extinct.

"Welcome home," the burly fae said, nodding at me. Before I could say anything, he touched his ear and spoke into a mic on his shirt. "Kaliya is back, boss, and on her way down."

"Any reason he needed a warning?" I asked softly, looking around to see if anyone was listening. I also noted Deacon didn't move to open the door to the Underground yet. Normally, I got in without a worry.

"There are some new players in the city. A lot of them showed up the last week or so. He wants to make sure there isn't anyone you might take offense to."

Ah. He wants to make sure there're no criminals with open warrants on them from the Tribunal. Smart move, Paden. I'd have to act and take them out, even if they aren't my assignment.

"He didn't vet them as they came in?"

"You know we do, but sometimes they bring friends faster than we can get information," Deacon answered. "You know how the underground clientele is."

"I do." I was one of them.

It took a few minutes, but Deacon received an all clear and opened the door for me.

Already, my return home was strange. Paden had never done that before, meaning something had him uncomfortable, worried about the safety of his establishment, especially with me roaming around in it.

I walked down the narrow staircase quickly and breathed in the unique mix of magic, alcohol, soil. This was the secret of The Jackalope I didn't tell Carter about —The Underground. This was the reason I always came back.

"Well, if it isn't my favorite bounty hunter," Paden said, greeting me from the bottom of the stairs.

I grinned. Only Paden.

"I'm a Tribunal Executioner. You know that," I reminded him softly when I reached the bottom of the stairs.

"Everyone knows. It's an open secret that you are also a bounty hunter with your own agenda when you aren't on the Tribunal's dime," he countered. "Come on. Have a drink with me before you drive off into the desert."

"You going to tell me about the new faces Deacon mentioned?" I inquired, falling in step beside him.

"In a minute. It's a little weird. I know you just landed, but I want to pull you aside for this one."

As we walked into the Underground's main bar, I ran my tongue over my lips. Everyone probably thought I had a bad case of chapped lips, or I was playing with my lip piercing, but I was a naga. I pulled in scents from the air with my tongue that my nose couldn't pick up. In the room, there were five werewolves, over six types of fae, three vampires who smelled like the humans they had recently fed on, and a witch. Of that group, the only one I was worried about was the witch. They always had too many tricks up their sleeves for me to be comfortable around them. They didn't have the same consistency as the rest, every one of them different from the next.

It wasn't just my unusual ability to 'taste' scents on the air that helped me remain aware of my surroundings. If I closed my eyes, I could map the room out based on thermal information. Werewolves ran hot; vampires were cooler than any human; fae fluctuated in strange ways, depending on how much magic they were doing. The witch only read as human thermally, another reason I didn't like them. They could hide in the crowd.

I followed him to his back office, knowing every set of eyes in the underground was on me. It was actually a light night. The underground was three times the size of the bar above and hosted the worst of the worst from the state of Arizona.

They watched me because I played both sides. Bounty hunting wasn't illegal because it was a way for the supernatural world to police itself, but it was frowned upon that I did both, Bounty Hunter and Executioner.

"What is it?" I demanded once Paden shut the door.

"A new bounty. Ten million U.S. dollars."

My eyebrows went up. "That's serious money."

"It is, and has gotten everyone's attention because it's probably going to be easy, but it's also going to get a lot of them in trouble." Paden seemed uncomfortable as he picked up the printout for the bounty.

We all recognized the deep yellow parchment that

bounties were printed on, one of the few things consistent in the world of supernaturals. There was a simple system. A bounty was put out publicly, giving any of us a chance to go for it. It guaranteed the backer would get the best work, and there was a competitiveness that was normally friendly. There were only two stipulations for bounties, two very simple rules.

"Why?" I had a sneaking suspicion this wasn't a normal bounty.

"It's for a human," Paden answered.

"Oh. Well, that's bad," I mumbled, taking the bounty from his hands. Reading it over, I shook my head. "Idiots. There are two rules for the bounty hunting world. No humans and no killing. Bounty hunters have to take people in alive and let whoever put out the bounty deal with it. This breaks one of those rules." I put it back down on his desk and shrugged. "It happens all the time, though, Paden. Why does this one bother you?" I didn't take bounties on humans, considering it was a conflict of interest. Anyone else was fair game, but it left me confused why Paden showed me this one.

"I did a little background on the guy like I do when any human comes through. He was in college and set to join the human military once he graduated. That was ten years ago, over in New Mexico. The bounty came out seven days ago."

"What happened in those ten years?" I asked, looking at the name on the bounty. Raphael Alvarez—who had he pissed off?

"No idea. He didn't exist."

That made me look back up at Paden, frowning.

"Excuse me?"

"You heard me. They put out a bounty on a ghost. No one has seen or heard of him in ten years, and his name doesn't come up in any records across the United States, Canada, or Mexico. I know you hate bounties on humans and won't do them, but I want you to look into this one. It seems off. There's more to this story than someone looking for a human who might expose supernatural secrets."

I sighed, giving Paden a look that would normally put the fear of the gods into someone. He just met my stare evenly.

"I'm an Executioner, not an Investigator or a human detective, Paden. The Tribunal has people for that—"

"But you're here, and I know you. I'm just asking you to look into this. You don't need to catch him and take him in yourself, just look into it. I don't like that this brought a truckload of new people to Phoenix to hunt him down."

"Has anyone gotten any leads?" Paden heard things, and if he wanted me to look into this when I had just gotten back from a business trip, he needed a damn good reason and needed to tell me everything he knew.

"Not yet. A lot of people bitching how they came to Phoenix, expecting to find something, but it's a cold trail."

"I'll look into it, Paden, but you owe me big for this one. I mean it. This is one I'm holding you to." I picked up the bounty and folded it quickly, sliding it into my back pocket. "Let me have a drink and settle in. I'm not going to make this a priority. I do have a life."

"Still dating that Tribunal Agent?" he asked casually, an obvious change of subject.

"Cassius? No, we ended that five years ago. I never told you?" Frowning, I looked at Paden in confusion.

"You still hook up with him," Paden pointed out. "When he comes through town."

"And? The last time he came through town was three years ago." I shrugged. "Last I heard, he was flirting with a possible engagement to some fae Lady, politics and shit. I knew Cassius wasn't a forever thing, Paden. Let's not pretend otherwise."

Cassius was a good fuck and an afterthought in my life most of the time. Another one of the string of men I had been with in an effort not to deal with the problems only I could have.

"True. You were both pretty mean to each other."

"I'm mean to most people," I reminded him, smiling. "Now, I'm going to get a drink and kick my feet up. The business trip was a bust."

"Yeah, I heard about what happened. They didn't need you or the Kitsune in the end, did they? Also, strange of them to call two Executioners to a Trial. Thought protocol was only one."

"It was a werecat. There was a chance she could have killed an Executioner before the job was done, so a backup had to be around," I explained, starting to walk out of the office. Werecats were powerful and not to be toyed with. Everyone knew it, and most of us respected it.

I only knew two personally and sitting in a meeting with either always made me a little jumpy. "Hasan popped his head out of whatever hole he's been hiding in and put a stop to it. Some stupid loophole that needed to be closed, a small change in Laws. Considering he was one of the original writers, I don't think anyone was in the mood to give him a real fight over it."

"Hasan, eh? Old werecat and one of your bosses, right?"

"Yup. One of the two Tribunal werecats," I said as we entered the main area of the Underground again. "He's never taken an active role with the Executioners, though. He was long gone by the time I joined up, off to sulk about his daughter dying. If I remember right, my parents knew him, at least in passing."

"You know many interesting people, Kaliya." Paden chuckled as we made our way to the bar.

"And yet, I find you my favorite," I said with a smile. "Now, get me a scotch," I ordered as he went behind the bar and tapped his bartender on the shoulder. Henley looked up from his phone and rolled his eyes when Paden pointed at the cell.

"One scotch, coming right up," Henley said. He was one of two werewolves who worked in the predominantly fae run bar. "I was just reading about that werecat thing. The Tribunal Trial you were just at. My Alpha put out an email about it."

"It's not a big deal," I said patiently as he poured me a drink.

"It's not," he agreed. "I remember the war my kind

had with them. Luckily, I was in the Americas already and could stay well out of it. Stupid fools. Only good thing that came of it was the Laws."

I nodded. I hadn't been born yet, but I knew my supernatural history. Before the werewolf-werecat war about eight hundred years ago, there had been no governing force over supernaturals. Deciding it was a bad idea to let every species of supernatural do whatever they wanted, a group got together, brokered peace, and created the Laws. The Tribunal, that original group, ruled over everyone, enforcing the Law.

"My Alpha is taking it as a big deal," Henley mumbled, shaking his head as he slid the drink to me. "We'll see how it goes. Not that you care," he said, looking up at me.

"Not that I care," I agreed, lifting my drink.

I sipped on it slowly as the Underground moved around me, different patrons coming up to order another round. No one spoke to me, keeping their eyes off me. Generally, when I disappeared for a few weeks, I came back with another name on my list of confirmed kills. It made the local lowlifes a little edgy for a couple of weeks. A stark reminder of who and what I was. I was the only sanctioned killer in the bar, the only one in Phoenix. Hell, I was the only one in the state of Arizona. Were there assassins out there working illegally? Certainly, but I could kill anyone and walk away without facing retribution in a way they couldn't.

I worked hard to become someone that couldn't be

trifled with, and in my home state, there wasn't a soul who didn't know me or my reputation.

"Paden, Deacon said there were some new faces," I mentioned after a moment. "Any I should worry about?"

"Not yet, but a ten-million-dollar bounty and a cold case tend to bring out the *best* in everyone," he answered, looking around the Underground. "I made sure none of the new faces here tonight would be a problem for you or you a problem for them."

I nodded in thanks. That much I knew, but he was right. Even if I didn't get involved in this weird bounty, there was a chance I was going to be an Executioner before it was over. Paden tried his best to keep me and his other clientele satisfied, but most bounty hunters were also criminals. They ignored human crimes. The supernatural and the Tribunal didn't care if one robbed a human bank as long as it wasn't in a way that could expose everyone. They didn't care if someone mugged a little old lady or committed fraud. Well, we all committed fraud on a regular basis, trying to hide our fortunes, so we could survive for another century.

Bounty hunters also had some legitimate criminals, ones I had to worry about. If one of the Wanted List showed up, I was required to take them down- capture or kill, it didn't matter.

I finished my drink and picked up my bag. Paden slid my keys across the bar, knowing it was time for me to go.

"Paden, if I learn anything interesting, I'll give you a call or stop by," I promised as I grabbed my keys.

"I'll email you what I found. You might be able to dig deeper than I could."

I headed back upstairs and went to find my Aston Martin Vantage out in the parking lot. Getting in, I sighed happily and pulled the bounty out of my back pocket, throwing it onto the passenger's seat with my bag.

It was good to be home.

2

CHAPTER TWO

I drove well out of Phoenix to get home. Off Eagle Eye Road, west of the city, there were several dirt roads. One of them was mine. I lived in the shadow of Harquahala Mountain, on a desert property that kept neighbors from moving too close. I enjoyed the desert, and it was safer to live outside the city, being what I was.

I got home in the pitch black of night, my headlights my only source of light, grabbing my bag from the passenger's seat as the garage door closed behind me.

"Honey, I'm home," I greeted the empty house sarcastically. No one answered. No one ever did since I lived alone and had for most of my adult life.

Maybe I should have stayed at my condo in the city tonight.

I dumped my bag on my dining room table and got to my chores, the same things I worked on every time I came home. Going into my office, I made my way to a small fridge and freezer, grabbing the pair of tongs off the top. I used them to grab a thawed dead rat and took it to the large enclosure behind my desk on the wall opposite the door.

There were three feeding spots in the enclosure, small spots that only fit the rat and tongs, and needed to be locked up when I was done. I picked the one closest to me and wiggled the thawed rat.

With a lightning fast move, the female Indian cobra inside the habitat struck the dead rat and took it from me. I watched her massage her fangs into the flesh and smiled.

"Good, Naksha. Maybe you can go home soon now that you're eating properly."

About six months before my little business trip, I had taken her on, sick and weak. The vampire who owned her didn't know what was wrong, and neither did the vets he coerced into seeing her. I was his last hope, and I was grateful he brought her to me. Snakes were something of a specialty for me. I got her well again, and now we were just waiting for upgrades at her permanent home to be done.

"Hopefully, his new habitat for you is done soon. You'll enjoy having more space."

I didn't know why I talked to her. She couldn't understand. Normally, there weren't any snakes in the habitat except me, so maybe I was just grateful for the company.

Maybe I just like talking to snakes. I should see someone about that. A therapist or maybe a zookeeper.

With Naksha eating for the first time in over two

weeks, I was glad to see my new habitat system had worked well for the trip. I recently installed a state-of-the-art camera system that let me remote view her, a new filtration system for her running water feature, and a remote temperature control that also controlled the intensity of her heat lamps. I had been hoping it saved me from needing someone to check on her while I was away. I didn't like having people in my home while I wasn't around. Truthfully, I hated it. As long as there were no emergencies, I didn't want anyone near her or in my space.

In the end, it all worked out, so that's one less worry.

I went back into the living room and dining area, letting Naksha enjoy her meal in peace. My house was large, but no mansion—one story, four bedrooms, two of them converted into workspaces, a large living room, a dining room, and a kitchen. It was all I needed. I had a second building, but it was only a gym. I didn't want to live with my equipment.

I grabbed my bag off the table and started pulling everything out of it. First, clothing I dumped into a nearby hamper so I could make sure to wash it. Then came tools of my trade. I only needed one bag, but I had to fly commercial like all the humans. I spent a pretty penny, making sure my one bag could carry everything I needed without getting me arrested. The front pouch was spelled. I opened it and reached my hand in, going nearly to the elbow. I sometimes wished I hadn't gotten it spelled to be so deep, but as long as security missed it, I knew I shouldn't complain.

I pulled out a variety of weapons. The sai were my standard defensive weapons of choice, and I placed them gently onto the table. Next, I carefully pulled out my shuriken, especially careful with the edges, even when they were in their carrying case. Nearly everything I owned was treated with poison, generally my own venom. While it couldn't kill me, it would cause some unwanted side effects I wasn't in the mood to deal with.

Trying to dismiss the idea of accidentally hitting myself with my own venom, I grabbed the two guns I kept in the bag, a Beretta M9 and an M4 carbine. I laid each gently on the table, wondering why I forgot to put them in their carrying case.

Oh, yeah. I was attending a Trial. I needed them ready to go at any moment.

I unloaded them and broke them down, readying them for cleaning.

Next came the weapons I was raised to use since birth, owned by my family for centuries. I used these when I was feeling particularly nasty or sentimental. The kirpan seemed like an ornate dagger for ceremonial purposes, but I knew how to kill someone a thousand times over with it. The talwar was a saber my father taught me to use. Two pieces of home I rarely used anymore, but I hauled them around for when the mood struck me.

"I carry too much shit," I mumbled, beginning the long process of cleaning everything and putting them away. It would take me most of the night, but I didn't let that dissuade me. There was plenty of time to relax now that I was back in Phoenix. I cleaned off my venom from the blades, rendering them just sharp steel again. I put everything away in different display cases around my house. The dagger, I tucked under my pillow, always ready to protect me.

Just in case.

I yawned and checked the time, groaning as I saw it was past one in the morning. I wasn't tired enough to sleep and realized I was probably going to pull an all-nighter. Feeling restless, I went onto my back porch, looking out over the desert that surrounded my home. The night was eerily quiet, and the stars dazzled overheard. I could see the fuzzy outline of cacti on the horizon, and Harquahala Mountain loomed over me. My actual address said I lived in a town called Aguila, but I always pointed people to the mountain and said, 'there.'

It was a hot night, over eighty. The dry heat made me feel rejuvenated, waking me up and giving me a dose of energy that had been missing while I was inside my carefully temperature-controlled home.

As I stood out there, I remembered Paden's request and resigned myself to dealing with it. I checked my back pocket for the bounty and mumbled incoherently as I realized it was probably still in my car. I went inside the garage, grabbed it and my laptop, then went back onto my porch, setting up to work under the stars. I wasn't in the mood for cloistered, constricted rooms. Working under the stars was one of my favorite things to do, especially during the end of a hot summer. Winter was going to come soon, and I was going to be slow on my feet. I had to enjoy the heat while it lasted.

"Who are you?" I mumbled, looking over the bounty as my laptop connected to the internet. "Raphael Dominic Alvarez. Who are you?"

Starting simple, I went with a web search, looking for any reference of this Raphael Dominic Alvarez. The picture was old, that much was clear as I looked through different hits. If he's been missing for ten years, it had to be a picture of when he was younger. He looked like he was in his early twenties.

I grew bored quickly and reread the bounty. It was put out by Mygi Pharmaceuticals. Strange since they were a supernatural pharma company, dealing in ways to help different species control difficult aspects of their lives. They were the lead researchers behind medication to potentially curb a vampire's bloodlust permanently. They also tried to develop drugs and remedies for werewolves and werecats, giving them a break from their curse.

Frowning, I was beginning to see what Paden meant. There was no way the guy in the photo was old enough to be a problem for Mygi. They were a powerhouse of a corporation and one of the few companies on the planet that successfully brought different species of supernaturals together to work on a large scale.

Someone like Mr. Alvarez stood no chance against a company like Mygi. Why would a human be worth a ten-million-dollar bounty?

I kept clicking through search results, and it took

nearly forty pages to find something interesting. The headline read 6 *People Dead: Military Involvement?*

Wow. Paden said something about this guy almost joining one of the human militaries. Maybe...

I clicked it and hit a small jackpot. The face I was looking for was right there in a buried, old article dated just under ten years prior. In 2009, Raphael Dominic Alvarez was partying with his friends, graduation right around the corner. Come morning, someone went to check on the party animals and found six young men and women dead. Raphael was long gone.

"No fucking way," I mumbled, realizing that was it. There was no other information on the case. I checked the location and raised an eyebrow—Albuquerque, New Mexico, one state over.

My email dinged, and I realized it had to be the information Paden must have already dug up. He had the exact same link in his email I was reading. This human, for whatever reason, either killed six of his friends or watched six of his friends die. Paden also had links and attachments for his birth certificate, social security number, and any official documentation from schools, the American military, and more.

None of the documents were dated in the last ten years.

"He's right. This is an odd bounty." I tilted my head as I tried to think about what Paden hadn't done yet. Whatever feeling he had about this one was pretty on the money. Ten million, one human, six dead people, and who knew what else because the man hasn't existed for the last ten years. We didn't even have a current picture.

I sent Paden a quick text, asking why everyone decided to start their hunts in Phoenix. Maybe that would offer me a clue what this was. I added that if I didn't find anything in a week, I was done.

I'm not going to lose sleep over this. Not my job to deal with these types of things, and I don't like messing with bounties that deal with humans.

He didn't text back, so I clicked around, falling into endless searches and different directories, wondering if I could stumble on anything he hadn't found.

The sun started coming up, casting a warm glow over the world. My back porch faced west, so I couldn't see the sunrise or feel it. I enjoyed the hotter afternoons, lying out on my porch under the intense sun. Mornings were always cold, and seeing the sun come up, I decided it was time for me to get some sleep. Closing the laptop, I grabbed the bounty and took all my things back inside, dumping them on the coffee table in my living room without breaking step.

I fell into my bed and closed my eyes, letting sleep take me fast.

∽

MY PHONE WOKE ME UP, blaring with my midday alarm. I groaned and fumbled to get it, hoping to turn it off before it woke me up completely.

If I get it soon enough, I can get back to sleep.

I was too late. By the time I was able to figure out how to hit the button properly, I was wide awake. My white hair was in my face, a reminder of complicated problems and things I didn't want to deal with. Stumbling into my bathroom, I grabbed a brush and tried to get it out of the way, glaring at myself in the mirror as I pulled it up into a ponytail.

"Why am I awake right now?" I asked my reflection. "Do you know? Why do I keep that stupid alarm?"

My reflection said nothing in return, only offering me a good look at myself, exhausted from a lack of proper sleep after long flights and late night researching because I was too antsy to relax. At that point, I realized I should clean up and get my day moving.

An hour later, I was out of the shower, my hair was dry, and I was ready for a day dedicated to nothing. Well, it should have been nothing. I was off duty, and there were no bounties out I legitimately cared about enough to do for extra cash.

I knew what that meant for my day.

Walking down the hall to my second office, I punched in the keycode and stood still as the retinal scan read my eye. When the lock disengaged, I walked in and locked it behind me. My second office was my sanctuary and one of two safe rooms I had on the property—both necessary. I had lost count of the number of people who had tried to kill me decades ago.

Considering the whole Raphael Alvarez thing was a dead end, I wanted to work on something important.

I stopped at my secondary desk and turned to see the

wall by the door. There, my pride and joy and eternal nightmare, *The Board*. I'd lost dates, friends, and colleagues because of *The Board*. At some points in my life, I'd lost nearly everything, thanks to it.

Dozens of photos were thumbtacked on with strings and small bios written of different people under mug shots or crime scene photos. Companies and shell companies. Phone numbers and addresses from all over the world. It stretched over the entire wall, slowly building up over the years as new pieces came to my attention.

After two weeks of not seeing it, I felt almost relieved it was in front of me again. Even though I'd had no real breakthroughs in nearly five years, The Board and the information on it kept me remembering, kept me on task. Every day I was home, I came in and looked at it, wondering if I would see something new, something I missed that I had tacked up years earlier but didn't think was important.

Today, something was bugging me.

I started on the left, looking through different people and places. Whatever was bugging me wasn't apparent, but I had a need to look over everything, carefully analyzing small things I wrote and clippings of articles. I subscribed to every supernatural publication possible, always on the hunt for more information, more connections.

I lifted a piece of the picture and read what I had underneath, frowning. Was this what had stuck with me?

Five years ago, I had read about a rich vampire

bragging about her snakeskin bag in an article on a supernatural dark web fashion site. To most people, it was innocuous, innocent. Snakeskin was readily available for most people, and they hadn't paid her love for the bag much attention. I had paid attention.

I knew naga skin when I saw it.

I had broken into her home and stolen the bag, leaving a note—a warning—that owning parts of other supernaturals was illegal. She never went public with the theft, and when others noticed the bag was missing and she no longer spoke about it, she had claimed it had been ruined. She had known what it was, which was why she had loved it so much.

She was lucky I didn't kill her, and she knew that too.

I had put her face on The Board, along with any possible ties she had in the supernatural world.

"There it is," I murmured. "Her brother is a high-ranking board member of Mygi Pharmaceuticals." I sighed. *Doesn't help me any. I'm not chasing down this human. I did what Paden asked, and I have a feeling there's not much more information to find.*

Unsatisfied, I sat down at my desk and stared at The Board, wondering if there was anything I could do. What if the human was somehow connected to it all? I knew better than to go down rabbit holes—they always sent me spiraling—but there I was, staring down the dark hole that accounted for most of my worst choices in life.

I haven't even been back for twenty-four hours. Do I really want to jump into this?

It was an addiction, the need to connect the dots and

discover the secrets behind it all. An addiction, like many others, that destroyed my life every time I dabbled in it.

I can't get answers if I don't follow every lead.

I texted Paden again. He should be awake by now or getting up soon.

Kaliya: What do you have on Mygi Pharma?

Then I pinned Raphael Dominic Alvarez's bounty to The Board.

CHAPTER THREE

I walked into The Jackalope that night with only one thing on my mind. Paden had texted back, saying he could have something by the time business opened, and I was resolved to be there. I didn't much care about the human who was in trouble with a large bounty out on his head, but I did care about anything he might know or his connection to The Board. He wasn't my problem, but what he potentially knew was.

"Paden!" I called out as I walked down the stairs into the Underground. "Do you have anything for me?"

It was early for a Saturday, and the Underground was practically empty. Licking my lips, I caught the species of the six supernaturals who were around. Henley was there, working the bar as he always was. Two vampires talked in the back corner, their heat signatures cooler than everyone else's, and three fae were commiserating over pints at one of the tables in the middle of the room.

I saw Paden walk out of his back office, and he waved me back without a word. I walked fast, ducking into his office, and let him lock us in.

"Mygi Pharmaceuticals," he said, picking up a file from the top of his filing cabinet and dropping it on his desk. "That's all public information. If you want to break into their backend systems and steal information, you'll have to do that on your own."

"I looked at all their public shit already," I said, feeling a bit peeved. "I was hoping you could hunt something down I couldn't."

"You're good at finding things most never could. I'm not going to risk my security to look into a giant like Mygi." Paden shrugged. "Last night, you were barely interested in this. What got your attention?"

"Nothing," I answered softly. Paden hated The Board. He figured it was going to get me killed one day, and he was probably right. "You wanted me to look into this, so I am. Mygi put this bounty out. They didn't even bother with a shell company or a subsidiary, which is bold. It means they aren't worried about Tribunal backlash. Doesn't that seem strange to you?"

"It was strange to me the moment it went live. Information is more valuable than gold, and I deal in information when I'm not running this bar. This came out of nowhere, and whatever this human might know about Mygi is obviously worth something if they're willing to give up ten million to get him back in their grasp." Paden crossed his arms as he sat down. "Would it surprise you that I don't want you looking at it because I feel bad for this guy? I want to know what he knows."

"It doesn't surprise me at all. Humans are easy and vulnerable targets for anyone looking to strike at a weak point in a company or who needs blackmail information. Or you could expose something and watch the world burn. What's your agenda on this, Paden?"

"I hope you learn something that will help me," he said, smiling. "I don't really care about Mygi, but someone might, and they'll be willing to pay me a pretty penny for the information you could get from this human."

"Yeah," I said. "Poor thing is stuck in the middle of forces he probably has no business being involved with. Did you hear anything last night after I left?"

"Yes, but you won't like it," Paden answered. "Mygi hired a private guy to come in since the public bounty isn't getting them results fast enough. A lot of people are going to be pissed, thinking Mygi is going to try undercutting everyone, so they never have to pay out the ten million they promised to whoever finds and catches this human."

I frowned, considering that. "The bounty has only been up for a week, maybe eight or nine days, tops," I said, finding a seat in his office. This obviously needed more thought. "And if they've hired a private bounty hunter or worse, a hitman or assassin, they're definitely paying him more than ten million. That skyrockets the worth of this human. By double, at least. They want this fixed, and they want it fixed right now."

"I came to the same conclusion. Whatever is happening is big. Very big, Kaliya."

"It's going to get messy. Are you sure you want me digging deeper into this?" There was a line I had to draw. This was the loosest connection I ever had on The Board, and it was a company name that could be pure coincidence. Mygi was huge; of course, some of their members would have hands in different pots. Raphael could have nothing to do with my personal investigation.

But I wanted to chase it anyway. That's why I was asking Paden to pull me back, to tell me to leave it. I could feel the call of the hunt, beckoning me to go after another dead end, lose more friends, and risk my life.

"I think you don't have an option anymore," he whispered, his light grey eyes boring into me. "Do you?"

"There was a name on The Board. I saw it this morning. Five years ago, naga skin bag. Her brother was employed at Mygi," I answered, swallowing.

Paden shook his head. "You have to let it go, Kaliya. Chasing the answers to those questions is going to get you killed."

"Easier said than done," I reminded him. "So, yeah, there's a tenuous connection between Mygi and my...my personal case. It's got me sniffing for a better one. Maybe this human knows something."

"Gods..." Paden groaned. "I should have known you would find some way to connect it to that fucking board of yours, you paranoid bitch."

"I have to try," I said, steeling myself for his words.

"If you think Mygi is part of *that* world, you are in for a battle you cannot win, Kaliya." Paden shook his head again, hitting his hand on his desk. "How many times has this obsession of yours nearly gotten you killed? Are we going down that road again? I thought it ended five years ago when everything went cold."

"It never ended," I snapped. "I'm a patient hunter, and I'll get what's due to me in the end, even if it kills me." I stood up and started for the door. "I'll look into Mygi. If there's any information I think you'll be interested in, I'll send it to you encrypted."

I marched out of his office and went to the bar. Henley looked up and sighed, pouring me a scotch before I had to ask. Once I had it in hand, I realized I forgot to ask Paden if he had any idea on who Mygi hired to clean up their human problem. Turning to look at the bar, I realized I didn't need to ask. He was walking in.

Oh, for fuck's sake.

Five hundred and thirteen years old, Sinclair was the vampire everyone called when a dirty job had to be done. He lived in and practically ruled Las Vegas but stayed away from Phoenix. I tried to keep him out of Arizona, but that was impossible. He was too good at what he did and too dangerous for most to toy with.

He saw me from the bottom of the stairs, and the cold smile he gave me would have terrified others. For me, it was a daring challenge. He knew he was in my space, in my city, and there was nothing I could do about it. Three times in eighty years, Sinclair had stood in front of the

Tribunal and walked away, declared innocent of all crimes. Everyone knew he was a monster. He made no attempt to cover it, but he found loopholes. He exploited situations and let others take the fall for him.

And each time, he laughed in my face as he walked away. There was more than a small rivalry between us. I wanted him dead. He wanted me to know I couldn't kill him—not legally.

If I did, everyone would know it was me. I would find myself on the same chopping block he walked away from so many times.

"Kaliya," he crooned, walking toward the bar. "It's very good to see you."

"I bet," I snapped. Of all the faces I wished was on The Board, his was the one I could never find any connection for. Maybe this was finally the chance I had to connect him to everything else.

"Now, now. I'm only here on a short trip. Mygi said the locals weren't helpful in their pursuit of an errant human."

"I figured you were the guy they hired," I said, sipping my scotch. He was taller, but I was never intimidated by Sinclair. I had run into him too many times over the last eighty years to be afraid of him. I knew him, understood him, and he knew and understood me.

"You know, I always wondered why you never go solo, get out of the Tribunal's grasp. You could probably find this bounty in a few days. You might be an Executioner, but you have the mind of an Investigator. The Tribunal doesn't know what they're wasting with you, do they?" He was complimentary, sounding innocent, but the look in his eyes told me otherwise. He was looking to get a rise out of me. He always was.

"I don't pretend to assume what the Tribunal does or doesn't know. I think you missed out on a good thing by never trying to join up with them."

"What do they pay you? A million a year? That's not worth my talents," he retorted. "It's not worth yours, either, but if the last nagini wants to sell herself short, then what business of it is mine?"

"Exactly. It's not," I replied, hating how he brought up what I was. Some days, I felt like I couldn't escape the fact I was the last female of my kind. I sure as fuck didn't need Sinclair reminding me. I didn't need *anyone* reminding me. "Get your business done, if you can, then get out of my city, Sinclair. I don't like your kind here." I finished my scotch and started toward the door. I only made it two steps before he and I were shoulder to shoulder, looking in opposite directions.

"And what kind would that be?" he asked softly, leaning down to invade my space further as I tried to pass. "The kind that wins?"

"The kind that makes me want to sink to your level," I hissed back, stopping to face him again.

"We both know you already have," he taunted. "I'll be out of Phoenix soon enough, though. Mygi gave me some private information they weren't willing to share with the public. I'll be out of your hair before the week's over. Stay, enjoy your little shithole bar, and have another drink. I'm not staying."

"Why did you even come here?" I demanded, not moving.

"To see how my favorite Executioner was doing," he said with that cold smile he was known for. "I figured if you saw me here first, you would be less inclined to try to kill me on the streets and lose your job. Consider it a courtesy call. I'm in Phoenix for work and would like to finish it and leave as soon as possible." He turned and walked out of the bar, leaving me standing alone, everyone watching me.

"Kaliya..." Paden's warning tone came out. "Maybe you do need to just head home and stay out of this."

"Funny. I was thinking I needed to join this little hunt for a stupid human. Ten million is good money." I grinned over my shoulder. I *never* gave Sinclair a free pass. He was in my city, and I was going to win this time. Less than twenty-four hours back in Phoenix, and things were getting interesting. This seemed like it was going to be the most fun the supernaturals of Phoenix were going to see for at least a decade.

Sinclair, The Board, Mygi Pharmaceuticals, and one human stuck in the middle of it.

"You could lose your job," Paden reminded me, walking close to say it under his breath. "Kaliya, they warned you off Sinclair fifteen years ago, the last time Cassius was able to get him to stand in front of the Tribunal."

"He's in my city," I reminded my friend. "He wants to play? We'll play."

I walked out. I didn't intend to follow Sinclair, but I

needed to get home so I could start hacking into Mygi's system. I needed to know what he knew if I had any chance of beating him to the prize. If this Raphael Alvarez knew anything important to my personal case, I couldn't let that fucking vampire make him disappear.

CHAPTER FOUR

Once I was home, I locked myself into my secure secondary office and booted up my rarely used work computer. It was a beast of a machine that could crack damn near anything, and I hoped it was up to the task of helping me get into Mygi's private servers. I was half decent at breaking into email and bank accounts when I needed to fish for information about a bounty.

Sinclair was right in a lot of ways. I was suited to the role of an Investigator. The Tribunal had two divisions, Investigators and Executioners. One division was both a cop and a lawyer, building a case and bringing a supernatural to trial. The Tribunal was the judge and jury. And then there was my job, the Executioner. It was an open secret that I was good enough for both divisions, but it was against Tribunal policy to allow someone to be both. What I did in my free time was my business, but any case I tried to build was usually handed over to tasked Investigators to finish. I was normally fine with that unless it was personal.

"All right, Mygi. Let's see what you're hiding," I said to the screen as several programs began to boot up.

It didn't matter what type of security they had, I had an answer to it. I tried to stay on top of technology, and being my age it was easy to keep up. Everyone had some fatal flaw in their system; it was just a matter of finding it. My system was far from secure—that's why I kept it off when I wasn't using it. I used a variety of techniques to keep someone from getting into my data. I also kept my personal data off this computer and didn't hook up any of my household security measures to it.

I began typing, considering ways I could find a weakness. Normally those were emails, and I had some very good places to start. Since I knew they were in touch with Sinclair, I decided to start there. As something loaded, I grabbed an empty USB stick and popped it in. I needed a place to dump any data I got in a place I could find later.

Sinclair's email was well known, his normal business contact. I figured he had more hidden email accounts, but anyone starting initial contact would only have the public one. I hissed at Sinclair's two factor identification and decided I would hack into the email provider directly. With a few more clicks, I was in Sinclair's email through the host company. If he ever found out I could do that, he would delete the email address, so I didn't leave any evidence as I went through his things. I didn't read unopened mail or leave him a snarky note, no matter how tempting the idea was.

I found his Mygi contact and quickly copied and saved the email into the USB's folder before disconnecting from the internet. I hoped that would keep whatever security features the email provider had from finding me via my IP address, even though I used a VPN to cover it up. I was done with Sinclair's email in less than a minute.

Cassius would be impressed. He's better at this. Maybe I should give him a call and let him know what I'm getting myself into before I get in further.

I went to make a drink, watching the time, thinking about the idea of contacting Cassius as my coffee brewed. It was nearly ten at night, and I knew he would be awake, working on something. Or maybe he would be with the woman I'd heard about. It didn't matter.

I can't tell him. He would take it off my hands and foam at the mouth that I was getting into this again. I would be lucky if he didn't tell our bosses.

Coffee done, I poured myself a mug and went back to the computer. The hunt was too good to pass up. I sat down and reconnected the computer to the internet, waiting to see if I had any security concerns. When none arrived in the twenty minutes it took to drink my coffee, I got started.

I checked the email that contacted Sinclair and grumbled at the lack of useful information. It was the standard request for a meeting, dated three days ago. I knew I could search that person's name to find more. A

Miss Amanda Ziegler. She was probably going to be fired soon, thanks to me, but I didn't let it bother me. I couldn't find a way into her email, though. I tried several different websites to Mygi and its subsidiaries but couldn't find an opening.

Frowning, I began to realize if I wanted the same information that Sinclair had, I was going to need to take it from Sinclair.

"Great. I guess this is where I have to decide if I want to jump off the deep end," I mumbled, looking over the monitor at The Board. "Do I really think this is related, or am I just fishing?"

Does it matter?

I started my search, finding out where Sinclair was staying during his trip to Phoenix. He once owned a property in the city, but after tangling with me twice, he sold it off and stayed in Las Vegas and left me alone.

He was a vampire, which meant he would be up all night, but he had to have somewhere to go once the sun came up. Instincts would force him to sleep. He wasn't old enough to stay awake while the sun was high. That worked in my favor—as long as he didn't already have Raphael and was leaving the city with him, which was unlikely. He'd been at The Jackalope not long after dark, which meant he had just arrived in Phoenix, probably using a body bag while he slept to get transported into the city. He obviously had at least two people he trusted with his life, and they were in the city with him.

When nothing came from my search, I gritted my teeth. I was going to have to do this the hard way.

"Time to go hunting," I said, grabbing my leather jacket off the back of my chair. Pulling it on as I walked out of my office, I considered the places I could find Sinclair at this time of night and figured I needed to give Carter a call. He picked up after the second ring.

"Kaliya. I didn't think I would hear from you so quickly," he answered, not even giving me a chance to say hello. "Yes, I know he's in town. No, I don't know why."

"Do you know where he's staying?" I asked, hoping he might have an idea.

"Not with the Nest or in any of our hotels. Our Mistress hates him with a burning passion. He makes the rest of us vampires look bad. You probably don't need me to say it, but none of the legit werewolves, fae, or anyone else would hide him either. Everyone in this city knows who and what he is and that you two have history."

"At least the city knows whose side to be on," I commented lightly. "Look, if you hear anything, let me know. Oh, and try to find the names of anyone working for him while he's in Phoenix."

"Kaliya, what are you doing?"

"Digging where I'm not supposed to."

"You've only been back for a day. You can't be serious—"

"Just let me know if you learn anything and give me a call or text back," I said quickly, cutting him off. "Have a good evening!" I hung up on him. I didn't need to be told to let it go or relax. Paden made the mistake of giving me a scent, and I intended to track it until I figured out what it was and how it might connect to The Board.

Considering Sinclair was also a hunter on the job only raised the stakes.

There's no turning back for me now.

To pass the time, hoping Carter worked on my requests as soon as he could, I went back to trying to break into Mygi's shit. They had damn good firewalls on the backend of their websites. They had no logins available to the public and considering their public pages were only a cover, I knew I had to find a better deep web version of their site if I wanted any chance to get into them.

Every supernatural knew tech wasn't secure. They all had the best that could be done, but any practiced supernatural tried to stay on top of the game. I personally wasn't on top of the game, not like the way real Investigators or professional hackers were. Mygi's systems were top-of-the-line. Only the best could break in, and I was wary of making too many attempts and getting exposed for my activities.

I'm stuck.

I hated it. It was like a worm of an idea in the back of my mind, wriggling and annoying me as I stared at the monitor, wondering if there was any way I could get the information I needed. There were options— all of them even more illegal than what I was already doing—like breaking into Mygi's headquarters, which were located in Georgia in the middle of nowhere. That wasn't convenient, and Sinclair would definitely have the human before I even tried that.

Frustrated, I turned off the computer and left my

office to refill my coffee. There was also the option of stalking Sinclair around the city.

That...might actually work. I know Phoenix much better than he does, and if he leads me straight to this human, I can get the drop on him, take custody of this guy, and find out what I need.

Too bad it's illegal for me to turn him in. Ten million is good money.

I drummed my fingers on the counter while I sipped coffee with my other hand. That was a very, very good idea. Risky, but not impossible. I would have to be careful, which meant I needed to prepare for the task. Hopefully Sinclair wasn't getting Raphael tonight, because I needed to prepare and find a place to start.

My phone buzzed, and I looked down to see who it was. Paden or Carter were the obvious choices.

Carter: He just came to Midnight Reverie. Thought you should know.

I grinned.

Kaliya: I guess tonight is going to be a good one for you. I'll be there, asap. Keep an eye on him.

My phone dinged several times as I rushed to get ready. Grabbing my bag, I threw in whatever weapons I figured I may need. It took me close to an hour and a half to get into Downtown Phoenix on a good day. Saturday night while everyone was running around to party? I checked the time and hissed. It was already eleven. I could speed and maybe get there by midnight, but I had to go fast.

Did I remember to get the fae to refresh the Look Away charm on my work car?

I couldn't remember, but I was going to test it anyway.

When I hopped into my work car, a black BMW M6, I was ready for anything. It had taken less than fifteen minutes for me to get ready, even picking out an outfit that would help me blend in. I knew my roads well enough that I didn't care about the high speeds or staying in my lanes. Once I was on Interstate 10, I put the gas pedal to the floor and let the car skyrocket to over one hundred and thirty. If I made good time, I could be there right around midnight.

I flew through Phoenix and proved the Look Away charm still worked as I passed by several police officers patrolling the streets. I knew where Midnight Reverie was, the blood club run by the vampires. They attracted lots of young people to go clubbing, then took advantage of what too much alcohol and drugs could do to an early twenty something. They kept a witch and a fae on the payroll, in case any memory tampering had to be done, even though vampires were generally good at keeping their secret. They weren't one of the 'out' supernatural species and probably never could be, considering their diet.

I parked in a back alley a block away from the club, making sure there were no warnings against it. Pulling out my phone, I saw Carter had messaged me a couple more times while I was driving.

Carter: Kaliya, you can't come get into a fight with him.

Carter: He's talking to my Mistress, but I can't hear about what.

Carter: It seems like he just wants to enjoy a night at the club. He has a couple of people with him, but I haven't heard their names. Why am I doing this for you again?

I CHUCKLED AND REPLIED, typing fast. Carter was a young vampire, thirty, turned only a decade ago. I had been there, and he had looked up to me early on. I was the one who set him up with the nest in Phoenix. He was a good kid and I enjoyed his antics, but I was glad I put him with the nest. He always proved useful when I got into something and needed eyes on the city's vamps.

Kaliya: Are either of his people guys? If so, ask one of them to dance. Maybe something will slip.

Carter: Are you fucking serious?

Kaliya: Do I joke?

Carter: They're both dudes. The fae, though...he's cute. Are you going to come inside?

Kaliya: Are you crazy? Of course I'm not going to go inside, especially if Sinclair is around. He'll know something is up. He doesn't know you, though. I don't think he's dug that far into my personal life. He and I keep it professional for the most part.

Carter: 'Professional' meaning you want to kill each other for strictly business reasons.

Kaliya: Pretty much.

I SHOVED my phone into my pocket and leaned against the driver's side of my car. My laptop was in my bag, and I was hoping for one of two things—the names of Sinclair's friends or the place they were staying. Carter liked sex and flirting, so I had no doubt if he could get one of them to dance, he could get them talking.

My phone didn't buzz in my pocket for nearly an hour. I stood there, guarding my car, waiting for word, and resisted the urge to leave and find out if Carter had gotten into trouble. Hopefully, he was really hitting it off with the fae guy, not getting hit *by* the fae guy. With Sinclair's type of crowd, either was a possibility.

He's a big boy. Carter wouldn't go into a dark alley with a stranger...

Right?

Pulling my phone out of my pocket an hour and a half into my waiting, I started texting him when my phone buzzed in my hand.

Carter: Cutie's name is Tom Lennon, not very fae, but I'm guessing it's a human name to blend in. You know how the fae are. Out but not out and all that.

Kaliya: Thank you. Be safe.

I should have said it earlier, but I said it now, hoping my vampire didn't run off in the middle of the night with a fae he barely knew and worked for the bad guy. I knew what Carter meant. The humans knew fae existed, but fae still didn't live openly. They continued to keep disguises and kept their business to themselves. No fae was technically 'out,' even though the species was. It was kind of the werewolves' faults. A fae died after they went into the open, and they just confirmed fae were real before the fae had much of a say in the matter.

Carter: So, Tom told me I should go by this address any night this week to hook up. It's booked under his name. The witch's name is Jeremy. They're all talking a lot of shit about you.

Kaliya: Please don't actually go fuck him. He works for Sinclair of all people.

Carter: They're picking up a guy named Raphael soon, probably tomorrow night. They came to town a day early to enjoy Phoenix since they don't get to often.

My blood ran cold. Sinclair was moving a lot faster than I thought. How much information did Mygi give him that they didn't release to the public? Why go public with the bounty at all when they wouldn't give up what was needed to catch a single human?

Kaliya: Did he say where?

Carter: No. Now I got to go quiet. He mentioned me being on my phone so much and not paying attention to him. Kaliya when you get the chance tell me what the fuck is going on. I'll tell you when they head out.

How about I don't and say I did?

I looked up the address and found the large home where they were staying. A private residence, of course, in Scottsdale, a nicer area of the Phoenix metro area. As long as they stayed at Midnight Reverie, I could get away with this.

Sinclair can talk all the shit he wants. I'm going to win this one.

5

CHAPTER FIVE

I pulled over two blocks away from Sinclair's address. He needed to watch what his people said because it had been comically easy to find. Then again, I didn't think he cared if people knew where he was. He had an ego the size of California, and there was no doubt his people did as well, thanks to him. They were probably used to ruling over everyone and being unafraid.

There was also a chance they had two places in Phoenix for their mission. I knew how criminals worked. Get a public address, somewhere safe that would throw everyone off their trail. A secondary address would be used for all the illegal things they planned. I just hoped this address had something I could use. If they were planning on picking up Raphael tomorrow night, I had less than twenty-four hours to get the information they received from Mygi and find him myself. It was already nearing two in the morning, and I would be lucky if Sinclair and his friends stayed out close to dawn.

BOUNTY

I do love a time crunch.

I found their house and stood down the quiet street from it, wondering what sort of camera security they might have. Deciding I wasn't willing to take the chance getting caught going in, I left the sidewalk and ducked between two houses once I was certain they had no security cameras watching the area. I pulled gloves on preemptively—I knew better than to leave fingerprints. I flattened my hair out as best I could and made sure no strands would come loose. I wouldn't be able to do this later.

Then I shifted. The shift took everything I was wearing with it, not leaving a pile of clothing or any of my weapons. Magic was cool like that. I slithered in the grass, lifting my head to look around. In snake form, I was an eight-foot-long unclassifiable mix of a pit viper and a cobra. It was the standard naga snake form, though the colors were unique per individual. I was mostly a black cobra with a pit viper's triangular head, red-orange eyes, and an orange to red underbelly. When I first shifted into the form, my mother had told me I looked beautiful and deadly. I had been a foot long and seven years old, thinking I wasn't pretty because my colors were boring.

It took a few decades, but there came a point when I agreed with her. I was beautiful and deadly, and I was only getting bigger.

Slipping through holes in the fences to get to the yard, I lifted, looking around to check for predators or humans before continuing. At this point, there was no way I could contact Carter or vice versa if anything came up. I had to get in and out quickly.

I made my way around the presumably rented or borrowed home and tried different windows, annoyed as I found them all closed and locked. I resigned myself for the impending annoyance of climbing up to the roof and trying to find a way into the attic. I used the side paneling, different windows and the gutters to get on the roof, then found a hole into the attic. I dropped onto an unfinished wood floor and found my way to the attic door. Checking for cameras before I did, I shifted back into my human form and took a deep breath, relaxing. Shifting to and from snake form always got my heart rate up, normally from adrenaline—something about it was exhilarating.

Pulling the attic door open, I reminded myself that most homes didn't have security cameras in every room. I was one of those paranoid people, but as I climbed down the attic ladder, I realized I was right. This house didn't have security cameras in every corner.

"Cassius would kill me if he found out I was doing this," I muttered as my feet touched the floor gently. When no motion sensor alarm went off, I counted my blessings and got moving. Licking my tongue over my lips, I tasted the air for different scents and couldn't discern anything out of the ordinary. Three people had been through here recently—a vampire, a fae, and a witch.

Let's hope this keeps going as expected. I don't want a bunch of trouble tonight. I just need Sinclair's intel.

I moved fast, checking rooms, deciding to ignore the bedrooms unless I needed them. Wandering into the dining room and kitchen, I found files laid out on the dining table. They had gotten their hunt started before going out for the evening. They were overconfident, making no attempt to hide the information after they were done looking through it before going to party.

And it was definitely partying. Sinclair would stretch his trip in Phoenix for as long as he could to annoy me and everyone else who lived in the city, most of whom hated him as much as I did. His activities in Las Vegas, only five hours away, were too close for us to ignore on a good day.

I pulled my phone out and started taking pictures. I couldn't steal all the papers and wasn't green enough to try. He would know who to start looking for if the intel went missing, and Sinclair wasn't afraid of a bloodbath. He would kill every possible suspect until he got what belonged to him. I was unafraid to shuffle the papers around, though, knowing I wouldn't leave fingerprints. The likelihood any of them remembered exactly how they left the papers was incredibly low.

I stopped as I stumbled on a report written by Mygi about possible aliases Raphael kept. Taking a quick photo of it, I decided to give it a read through.

"'He's been known to live in towns for a very short time, posing as an illegal alien from a South American country, and gets paid under the table,'" I recited from the printout, raising an eyebrow. "He's smart and knows Mygi is looking for him..."

It continued on with how they had been trying to capture him for five years, but he was slippery. The moment he caught wind someone was looking into him or acting strange near him, he vanished. He was also very good at escaping from brute force measures and disappearing again for up to ten months. I remembered Paden's intel on how Raphael had been about to join the military and wondered if he had already received some training or if this was something he picked up, trying to outrun Mygi.

One thing was becoming apparent, and I wasn't sure how I felt about it.

This guy was a victim of something. Of what, I had no idea, but he obviously thought he was running for his life. He murdered a bunch of his friends, then a supernatural pharmaceutical company took an interest in him? He *escaped* five years ago? He wasn't running from human law since humans had no idea where he had been for the last ten years.

The good people at Mygi had him for five of those years. Holy shit, Paden, you had good instincts on this one. This guy is probably a gold mine of information and blackmail you can make millions off of.

I took more pictures, knowing I was in for some interesting reading once I was out of there. Then my phone buzzed in my hand, and I saw Carter's name.

Carter: They just left, probably headed home. I know I am since dawn is only a few short hours away. Whatever you're doing, don't get killed, please.

. . .

BOUNTY

I QUICKLY TOOK pictures of the last stack, thanking my lucky stars Carter knew I was going to need the heads up. Shoving my phone in my pocket, I made my way back to the attic and closed it up. Once I was shifted into my snake form, I took the same route out, carefully climbing down the building. I had to move fast. I forgot to check the time before shifting, but if dawn was coming, people were going to be waking up. My car wasn't in a good spot, and I couldn't get caught shifting back into my human form where people could see me.

I found a quiet place between two houses and shifted, then jogged to my car. Sinclair and his friends didn't have a long drive to get home, and I needed to get out of the neighborhood before they had a chance to see me. One of them being fae was inconvenient. He would be immune to the Look Away charm.

I was able to make it out of the neighborhood without seeing any of them and breathed a sigh of relief as I jumped onto the 101 and headed toward home.

"If I play my cards right, I can find Raphael before they're active tonight. Sinclair's little minions won't move on the human until he's ready, and he can't do anything until after the sun goes down."

My phone started to ring, and I picked it up, not paying attention to the caller ID.

"You never came back last night after you ran into Sinclair. Am I going to assume you aren't going to drop this?" Paden sounded tired and annoyed. "I know I gave it to you, but I don't want you out there doing something stupid."

"I actually just got a load of good intel you're probably going to be interested in, Paden." I grinned. "He was running from Mygi. They had him for five years after he killed all his buddies that night, and he escaped. Been running ever since."

"Wait, so they made him not exist? They're the reason he disappeared completely?" Paden seemed as intrigued as I thought he would be. "Well, that is interesting."

"Oh yeah. I highly doubt this is a case of a human employee gone rogue. This feels more sinister, without a doubt." I was amped up. This was the kind of thing I lived for. Not so much the saving the human thing, but the dirt. I loved sticking my nose in the business of the dirtiest, most underhanded pieces of shit in the supernatural world. It gave me a rush and kept me going, day in and day out.

"I might need to bring Cassius in or some other Investigator, but I'm going to wait until I have Raphael in hand. I have to find and get him today because, apparently, Sinclair has plans to grab him after he sleeps."

"Well, your new information makes mine seem light and stupid," Paden mumbled. "You're moving a lot faster with this than I thought you would."

"I'm moving a lot faster than *I* thought I would. Tell me what you got."

"It's nothing. Stupid personal shit."

"Paden, that's the best stuff. If you give me a way to

make him emotionally vulnerable, I might get him to hand over information willingly."

He chuckled in my ear. I felt bad for his wife—Paden's chuckle was like something out of a porno, meant to get women worked up. His wife probably had to beat those women off with a stick. I had only met her a handful of times, but once she realized I didn't see Paden like that, she was an easy acquaintance to have.

"His parents called him Raphael. His siblings and friends called him Raph. His girlfriends all called him Dom," Paden informed me, and I could hear the smirk.

"Kinky." I laughed. "I'll have to figure out which one I can use without pissing him off. Raphael is too cold. Raph might be too friendly. Dom is definitely too friendly."

"I don't know, looking the way you do, you might be able to get away with Dom."

"Paden!" I was laughing harder, trying to keep my eyes on the road. "I have white hair."

"You don't look a day over thirty, and you know it. You don't even have the beginning of a wrinkle on that face."

"I'm one hundred and seventeen. He's, what, thirty-two now? I think I might be a little old for him." Snorting, I shook my head as I drove. "I haven't done the whole 'act sexy and gain their trust' schtick since I was a kid, like ninety years ago," I reminded him. "I'm not sure I could pull off the act now."

"You know you could. This is absolutely going to sound

old-fashioned, but you have that exotic look, and the white hair only adds to it, not detracts. My wife is oftentimes jealous of you." Paden snorted. "Ever since those silver-grey looks came into human fashion, she's been bouncing back and forth with the idea of changing her hair color for her human form. She wouldn't stand out with it nowadays."

"Yes," I said with some acid. "Exotic is an incredibly old-fashioned way of putting it. I'm Indian. Let's just call it like it is. I'm Indian, and not the type that Columbus misidentified. Just like every naga."

"I'm not trying to be...insensitive, but this is a thirty-two-year-old man who probably hasn't had companionship in a decade or more..."

"I get what you're saying," I snapped. "Change the topic. It's not going to happen." There was a reason I didn't play that act anymore. There was a dark, terrifying, nightmare-inducing reason.

The last time I did, it went way too far.

"Fine. Tell me your intel." His tone went back to professional, the friendly teasing and compliments evaporating. We knew each other well enough to know when a button was pushed.

"I haven't read through all of it. I'm driving home from breaking into Sinclair's place and taking photos of everything I could find there. He's got a couple minions with him, and one of them rented a house in Scottsdale."

"You...KALIYA!" Paden roared into the phone.

Since it was coming through my car's speakers, the audio distorted, and I reached out to turn it down before he continued. I barely made it in time before my ears started ringing.

"ARE YOU MAD?"

"He taunted me. He explicitly told me why he was here. Did you really think I wasn't going to make this personal?" I demanded, huffing in annoyance. "And it's interesting. There's something fishy going on here, and I might have a connection to The Board. If Raphael knows a bunch of good shit about Mygi, maybe it could be the break I need."

"Yeah, yeah," Paden growled. "Fine, but don't go dying on me, damn it. Without you, Sinclair would take over Phoenix within a week, and there would be no one able to stand up to him. You do realize, by living in this city, you've held him back from properly expanding his criminal enterprise, right?"

"Yeah, I know, which is why I have to win this now. If he comes into my city to do illegal business, what good am I as an Executioner if I can't even begin a proper investigation into what he's doing?"

"I don't know how many reminders you need, but *Investigators* investigate, Kaliya."

"You heard him. He knows I'm good at both. I know when I need to hand this off to Cassius, don't worry."

"Do you think he might have been baiting you?" Paden asked, and I had to admit it was a good question. I was under explicit orders not to toy around with Sinclair anymore, not after the run-ins we had in our past, which turned dangerous and destructive.

"Possibly, but it doesn't matter. I would have jumped

into this the moment I found out he was in the city, Paden. I don't need him to bait me."

"I know, and that's terrifying," he replied. "If it comes to the human or you, Kaliya, pick you. I don't care what sort of gold mine this guy might have when it comes to intel or your fucking board of paranoia; you aren't going to get yourself killed for it."

"Sure thing, but a quick question." My answer was a half-hearted lie.

"Shoot."

"When are you going to remember you are neither my boss nor my father?" I asked before tapping the hang-up button on my car's touch screen.

I drove in silence after that. Paden was rightfully worried, but I was a dog with a bone. There was nothing, including the idea of dying, that was going to pull me off this now. He knew it just as well as I did. I didn't much care for a friend I'd had for a few decades telling me to let go of something that happened long before I ever knew him. In the end, the choice would never be answers or my life because I put too much time and effort into my own survival. It would always be what *else* was I willing to lose for those answers, and that was an easy choice for me. It always had been and always would be.

Everything.

CHAPTER SIX

Getting home, I moved fast, reading through what I had copied from Sinclair's. I had to go quickly, or I could miss my only window. I ran through his aliases again and punched them into separate searches through local government databases. Mygi had reason to believe Raphael was in Phoenix, but they were wary of getting close due to his skittish nature. They nearly had him once in San Diego and once in Los Angeles. He once went home to New Mexico, but they had completely missed him there, only to find out about it afterwards. From there, he went to Houston and spent a stint in San Antonio as well. Now, he was in Phoenix, and they were damn near sure of it, which was why the bounty had originated in the area and brought everyone to my city.

Great. But now I need to figure out where he actually is in Phoenix. Can't they have something good on this?

I kept looking through the pictures, reading the small print. I narrowed the searches to southern Phoenix, near and in Tempe and Mesa, based on another report one of their agents had written. They found reasonable evidence in some security tapes that he was hiding in that region. They even had a few guesses on which alias he was using and a possible second, so I cut the rest of the searches off except those two.

Essentially, Mygi had enough information to find Raphael again, but they were afraid of scaring him off. They went to the bounty hunters, but they didn't feel comfortable giving out too much information. I wouldn't want most of the information out either if I were them. They talked about him as if he was an asset, but a dangerous one. It looked bad for one human to give a wealthy, highly trained team of supernaturals the slip, not just once but several times. They would have turned into laughing stocks, and that would kill their reputation.

I stopped on another letter and a cursory glance told me there wasn't anything important in it except for the fact that it shined a light on some internal politics at Mygi.

It was a board member, personally in contact with Sinclair. He was frustrated the board elected to go with the bounty hunter route, instead of just hiring Sinclair straight up. He was paying Sinclair ten million out-of-pocket to get started, and the vampire would be able to claim the bounty when it was over.

Yup, I was right on the money. Double. I knew they were paying him big money, and that explains why Sinclair has all this, and no one else does. He shouldn't have bragged about it, that overconfident piece of shit.

I scrolled past it, knowing Paden would like that kind of information. A board member going against the rest of them? That was easily good money on the blackmail market. I should have felt guilty, but there were shades of crimes for supernaturals. Blackmail wasn't even against the law, and really, most human laws weren't covered in supernatural law. Supernaturals were old and cunning, so to avoid major fights, sometimes blackmail had its purpose. People like Paden had to make money. Unsanctioned murder was against the law, but species dealt with that internally unless it was murder of another type of supernatural. Then things got ugly. Most of the laws, though? They covered ancient treaties to preserve a precarious peace between different species, or to help keep the supernatural secret from the world at large. While werewolves were very out and fae were kind of out, it was incredibly illegal for anyone to go public with a species that wasn't out unless it was decided by the leaders of that species.

Meaning, if I wanted to out the nagas to the human world, I could.

I wasn't enough of an idiot to do that.

Being the last nagini had its perks, as sour as they tasted when I had to use them. I was considered a leader of my species.

Easy to be when there's only one female and eight males left. Not many nagas to rule and no one else to rule.

I sighed, looking at The Board. While the searches ran, I needed to find something to do. I printed several of the photos, then recopied some of the most important information onto a small card and pinned it with Raphael's bounty. With a string, I connected Raphael to the brother of that one woman. Since that was all I could do, I fell back into my office chair and groaned.

"These can hurry up," I mumbled, moving my mouse around the screen. I had no one to call, no one to kill time with. Paden would be sleeping by now, and Carter was definitely locked away from the sun to get his own sleep. Cassius wouldn't take my call unless I promised it was work only, and I wasn't prepared to give this to him yet—should, but didn't want to—not while Raphael's face was on The Board, and I had no idea if it meant anything.

I used to have more friends—used to. None of them lasted very long. I was pretty sure Paden was the longest friend I had in my life, even though I'd known Cassius the longest. Cassius was a complicated mess. He was never my friend, nor was he ever really an ally. He was a colleague and a fuck buddy—the second part of that was thoroughly scratched out now.

I should have never slept with him to begin with. Tequila does bad things to people.

I need more friends.

I snorted. There was a time when everyone wanted to be my friend. Thank the gods, that time was long ago.

Checking the clock, I decided I would try to get some sleep. It was seven in the morning, and watching searches try to find anything in situations like this was like watching paint dry. They would be done by the time I woke up.

I locked up my office and went to my bedroom,

decorated in rich browns and reds, the way I liked it. There were flares of splash colors, and it reminded me of home. It was the only room where I let myself get sentimental and decorate it like any normal person would. Before getting into the bed, I went to my bathroom and brushed my teeth, letting my fangs drop to brush them as well. They were hidden behind my human canines, and they signaled I was just as venomous in human form as I was in snake form. Once I was satisfied with that, I washed my face, wondering if I always looked so damn tired.

Probably.

I opened the medicine cabinet and hit a button hidden in the back of the bottom shelf. A small hole opened up behind me and revealed my second safe room. I rarely forgot to check it before bed, and when I did, it was because I was exhausted. Tonight, after messing around with Sinclair and breaking into his place, I knew I wouldn't be able to sleep unless I knew it was ready for me. None of the food inside was expired, and the guns were properly loaded. Three vials of my venom waited to coat any weapon I could need, hanging from the walls inside.

Glad I checked, I hit the button again, and it closed. The button read my fingerprint, which was the best security I could have for it. If I had decked it out with a retinal scan like my office, I would have gotten killed a long time ago. This was the safe room I had to get to the moment I woke up, and I couldn't fight with finicky technology in those situations.

I fell into my bed and controlled my breathing. My room was fifteen degrees cooler than the rest of my house, and it wasn't because I hated the heat. It forced me to get tired, and eventually, sleep claimed me.

～

I was up at two in the afternoon with plenty of time before sunset. Jumping out of bed as the AC stopped in the room and let it heat up, I felt energized. Before going to the office, I made a pot of coffee and took a mug out to my back porch, standing in the sun with the hot drink. It had to be over a hundred and ten, and I loved it, soaking it in. I wasn't technically cold-blooded, but like my snake form, my human form enjoyed the heat much more than the cold. When I settled in Phoenix, that had been the only thing on my mind. Living somewhere it was hot most of the year.

"Mother would have loved it here," I said softly, sipping my coffee. Longing was a sharp pain I tried to avoid, but at that moment, I let it happen. Whatever the reason, my mind turned to thoughts of my family. Father would have been fine in Phoenix, but he liked humidity, a lot of it. So had my brothers. My mother and I loved dry heat. She and I were the only ones. Most nagas preferred places with a bit of humidity.

I can't do this reminiscing bullshit right now. I need to get to work.

I turned my back on the view and the sun, leaving thoughts of my family with them, and headed back indoors. When I sat down in my secondary office and checked the computer, I was glad to see both searches were done. It was always nice to be right about something.

I glanced over the monitor and hissed. That was the problem—The Board. Any time I dealt with The Board, I thought of my family more often. It was never a good time for me or anyone else foolish enough to get involved. Then again, The Board started because a group of people murdered my entire family in front of me, and I was still trying to figure out who. The why had been easy, but the who was an elusive bit of information I was still trying to find.

Looking back at the monitor, my mood soured. I clicked through the results. If Raphael was posing as an illegal immigrant, there was a slim chance I would find anything official or a real paper trail, but I could hope there was a minor arrest, a note in a file, or something small and innocuous somewhere. Raphael and his history of running didn't point to there being any bank accounts in his name. He would need to use his real name and identification, something he definitely couldn't do, or have enough falsified data.

I clicked through the results, wondering if I would find anything. His aliases were incredibly common combinations. He was smart, and I had a shred of respect for him as I realized none of the results were him. He was good at staying under the radar, which made me wonder how Mygi kept finding him. I went back to the print outs and noted how they used security cameras to find him in different areas. They must have been using some very illegal facial recognition programs. Not even supernaturals were okay with that little piece of technology coming out in recent years. We didn't want our faces tracked everywhere we went through the ages. I, personally, only had one photo of myself, and it was from when I was young. My parents decided we needed a family photo when photography was just really hitting its stride as new, capable, and affordable technology. It was so old, I was certain I was going to need to hire someone to restore it and make new copies.

So, a supernatural company probably using facial recognition software was a no-no. I tucked that thought away as I dug deep into what was given to Sinclair. Something here gave him enough information to think he could capture Raphael tonight.

I found it. I had taken nearly a hundred photos while I was there, so I tried not to kick myself for missing it the first time I went through them. They had four addresses of places where they caught him on security cameras. I cross-referenced the information with a map and discovered a few apartment complexes and a new subdivision being built. They said he frequently hid as a construction worker, which played up a lot of human stereotypes he was probably hoping made him ignorable.

I printed a piece of the map of the Phoenix area, focusing on the city of Goodyear and circled the four businesses they had caught him in. They were all still shots from traffic monitoring cameras, accidentally catching him coming out of businesses. It took some money to get a facial recognition program to constantly look through them since those cameras didn't take photos. The program had to monitor the footage twenty-four-seven and grab a screenshot once it found a possible match. The problem was it generally found thousands of matches, and someone had to go through and check each one.

No wonder they want him caught. They're probably sinking millions each year into this. It's amazing their company stays in the black.

I knew what I had to do. I needed to get on the ground and see if I could find him. All I had was a general area and a picture from ten years before. The photos they had weren't good enough for me to want to use, so I had to rely on recognizing him myself.

I checked the time. It was three. The sun was going to go down in only three hours, and I was going to have to hoof it to find him. I needed to move. My bag was still ready from the night before and on the passenger seat of my less audacious car.

This is the perfect time to back out, Kaliya. Paden would tell you that if you called him.

I jumped behind the wheel after locking up and pulled out the moment my garage door was open enough.

7
CHAPTER SEVEN

I found a place to park at the town's local ballpark at three thirty. Two-and-a-half hours until sundown. Grabbing my bag, I got out of my car and locked it, making sure by jiggling the handle. I used my phone to guide me to the locations where Raphael had been spotted, keeping my eyes open for either him or any supernaturals. I needed to know if a fae or witch was scoping the area before Sinclair woke up.

I chose to hit up the local construction first, hoping I could catch him at work. I didn't intend to approach him if I saw him, not immediately. If I called him out in public, the chance of him splitting was high, and I wouldn't be able to explain. In private, I could at least try to explain what was going on, and he might listen...if he didn't run the moment he saw me.

Walking fast, I entered the subdivision and headed down the roads. It wasn't a short walk, but it wasn't the worst, either. I saw the construction sites within thirty minutes of parking. Two hours until Sinclair was going to be awake and ready to get moving.

I didn't pause as I walked by the new houses going up, generously looking at the construction workers as if I was interested in the men building houses, getting sweaty. Some women are into that, so I shouldn't look too out of the ordinary. Maybe I should dye my hair though, which made me stand out, but none of them paid me any mind. I looked through the different groups, working on the six homes going up, but no one stood out and none of them resembled the young man in the photo. Frowning as I hit a cul-de-sac, I turned around, hoping to find him on the way back.

"Hey, miss! You lost?" someone finally called out. I stood and tried to look as doe-eyed as I could.

"Maybe?" I said, hoping to find the man who spoke. I caught him walking out of one of the sites onto the sidewalk about ten feet in front of me, wiping his hands off. I hurried toward him. "I'm looking for an old friend. I heard he might be working around here?" I twisted my hands uncomfortably. "All I have is an old picture of him."

"Yeah, let's see it." He gestured for me to give over the picture, and I pulled my bag to my front to dig Raphael's outdated photo from it. Handing it over to the guy, his eyes went wide.

"You're looking for Manuel? He's off today," the guy said, handing the photo back. "That's a really old picture, miss. He's a lot older now."

"I've been looking for him for a long time," I said softly.

"He's pretty closed lipped about his life, but man, he should have told me he knew a pretty woman like you." The guy smiled. "I'm Pedro. I'm in charge of everyone here." He extended a hand, and I took it. He did that weird thing where men won't give women a proper handshake, grabbing my fingers and lifting my hand up like he was about to kiss the top.

Immediate turn off, Pedro. I could kill you with that hand.

I pulled away and sighed heavily, trying to seem distressed. I was lucky they were even working on a Sunday, but it bummed me out he wasn't around. That much was honest.

"Do you know where I could find him today?"

"I have an address for him, but I'm not allowed to give that out, sorry, miss." Pedro shrugged indifferently. "You can always check back tomorrow. He doesn't come in for overtime over the weekends, but he's never late Monday morning."

He would be tomorrow. If Sinclair and Mygi have their way, he won't ever see you again.

"Oh, yeah, I could come back tomorrow," I mumbled, trying to pout. I had no idea if it worked or what it looked like. I licked my lips and bit my bottom one after, looking around. "Why couldn't you just be here today?" I whispered, obviously not talking to Pedro.

"Let me give him a call—"

"No!" When Pedro jumped at my suddenness, I bit

my lip harder. "I was hoping to surprise him. It's been a long time."

"Ahh..." Pedro nodded wisely and frowned, looking back at something. "You know, maybe I can bend the rules just this once. Manuel doesn't have much of a life. Comes to work and leaves. Well, he drinks. I don't think he'll be at home, but I have an idea as to where he could be. It's late, but he might still be there."

"Oh?"

"Yeah, he goes to church here..." He pulled out his phone and started typing. "Never remember the name of the place. Not the church my wife goes to with the kids. Here." He pointed to it. "That's it, Saint Thomas Catholic Church. He goes every Sunday. You might find him there, or someone can help you out."

"Thank you so much." I touched his arm and watched him blush before walking past him and leaving the subdivision. I didn't expect to find Raphael at the church since it was late, but I kept my hopes up. I had no other options unless I wanted to stake out random places in Goodyear, which wasn't a great plan with the time I had. Mind you, it *had* been my plan, but it seemed like I was getting lucky, so I was going to keep hoping it worked out in my favor.

I'm not lucky enough in life. Might as well ride this wave for as long as I can.

I found the church with only an hour and a half until sunset. Walking inside, I wanted to hiss in distaste at the décor. Catholic imagery wasn't my favorite. Nothing against the Christian god or anything, I just thought it got a bit much sometimes.

Bit hypocritical of me. I was raised Hindu, and there's nobody who beats the Hindus when it comes to religious decorating.

I was honestly a bit proud of Hindu architecture.

The Catholic look still isn't my thing. I don't much like Buddhism either. I'm not even sure why.

I only made it three steps when a priest stopped me.

"Ma'am, how can I help you this evening?"

"I was hoping to find someone." I shoved the photo at him. "I'm hoping to surprise him, and his coworkers told me to come here—"

"Manuel comes to late Mass, starts at five." The Father smiled. I wanted to curse. That was in another twenty minutes. "He normally comes in a little late and sits at the back."

"Thank you," I said politely. "I really appreciate it."

The Father smiled and spread his arms. "Have a wonderful day."

Luck is absolutely on my side today.

I left the church quickly, half afraid I was going to light up in flames at any moment. I was a supernatural from a different religion and really had no place in a Catholic church or really any church. Temples were more my place to go.

I found a bench outside and got comfortable. Watching the minutes tick by was excruciating as the Father's congregation slowly trickled in. It was like a madhouse in the last few minutes before Mass started, then suddenly quiet.

I crossed my arms, waiting, wondering if he would show up tonight. Would tonight be the night he decided to skip Mass? Would he run the moment I tried talking to him?

I could hear the Father begin talking inside the church, his voice friendly, charismatic, and energizing. I didn't believe a word he said, but then, that was just because I was a non-practicing Hindu and not a Catholic. I'd lived too long to take hopeful words at face value and long stopped caring about divine judgment on my immortal soul.

A small, beaten up, clunking car pulled up. I straightened up, narrowing my eyes on the heat signature I could see through the window. The man was running *hot*. It was like a beacon of warmth in an already warm evening, even after all those bodies had passed by me. He ran hotter than a werewolf.

I saw him get out of the car, and my mouth went dry as my fangs began to ache. Ten years down the line and Raphael had only grown into his looks. He sported a five o'clock shadow I wanted to touch, not caring if the stubble was itchy or ticklish. His eyes were bright medium brown, both warm and distant as he looked around the parking lot, too sad for his own good. His dark brown hair was thick but cut short. The only thing that even remotely marred his handsome face were two scars, one on his lip, the other on his cheek. And his body?

Women probably tried to plaster themselves onto that

man's body like wet towels. He might have been wearing a long sleeve black shirt in summer, which was wild, but it did nothing to cover up how well proportioned and built he was.

And my fangs ached, sending me past physically curious and attracted into blinding fear, then a deep-seated anger bubbled up in my chest. I had to force my fangs to keep from dropping and becoming visible if I tried to talk.

Of all the people, of all the times, it had to be now. It just had to be right now. I was wrong about my lucky streak. This is a fucking nightmare.

He walked closer and frowned at me.

"Ma'am, are you okay?" he asked softly. His voice was rugged and weary. He seemed so tired.

"Are you Raphael Dominic Alvarez?" I asked, finding my voice as I realized there was no turning back now.

He took a step back from me, looking around the parking lot and church, probably thinking others were hiding in the bushes. He was really paranoid.

"I'm alone," I said quickly. I tried to bury my feelings. There was no time for them. I had to act fast. "There's no one else. I'm not lying to you."

"Who are you, and how did you find me?" he demanded, fear and anger edging into his voice.

"My name is Kaliya Sahni, and I'm trying to save your life." A new objective, a new reason to be involved, and as much as I hated it, I had to care now. "Mygi is coming after you, and they're close. They hired a group who won't fail like the last ones did."

He was breathing harder now.

"How long do I have?" he asked, swallowing.

"They start hunting at sundown. Maybe we should go back to your place and talk. Better yet, come with me, and they won't be able to find you."

He shook his head slowly and backed away from me. I stood up quickly. He could *not* get away now. I couldn't let him walk away and leave me there.

"Raphael, please, you have to listen to me."

"I need to go pack. I never want to see you again. I never want to hear that name again. Do you understand me?" He was practically growling at the end. I licked my lips and tasted the air, but only picked up his scent, human and *vulnerable*.

Unacceptable.

"It's too late for that," I said quickly. "It's way too late for both of us. You need to come with me. At least give me a chance to explain. Take me back to your place, and I'll explain everything, okay? That's all I'm asking. You can leave with or without me after that. If you want to run on your own, you can, but let me explain some things before you make that call."

I was desperate. If he could give me just the trip back to his place, it didn't matter what his decision was in the end. I would get my way. I had to. There were no options, my fangs an aching reminder that I couldn't let him go now.

"Fuck you. I don't need to take you anywhere." Rage was the only thing I saw on his face now. I knew he was angry at being found again, probably because he couldn't escape his past, but the words were uncalled for.

I hissed, realizing the initial act he put on was just that, an act. This was an asshole who thought he knew what he was doing.

"Fine. If you want a fucking vampire killing you tonight—" I let my own anger get the best of me for a moment. I wasn't really angry at him. My problems weren't his fault, but the anger was there. So was the fear. So was the need.

"What?" he asked, fear overtaking his face again.

"Gods, you don't know anything, do you?" I hissed. "Look, Raphael, you need to listen to me. You need to let me explain. There's more out there trying to get you than you can possibly imagine."

He pulled his keys out of his pocket and looked at them.

"Vampire?" he asked softly. "I...I once thought they came after me with werewolves, but...Sometimes it's hard to believe they're real. Or the rumors about fae and witches and..."

"Fuck. Are you good to drive?" I demanded. They went after him with werewolves. Wasn't Mygi worried they could accidentally Change him? The moon curse wasn't something to toy around with.

"Yeah." He sounded stronger again. "I knew something was...off. I've always known, but..."

"You're about to find out everything you've ever had questions about. Let's go," I ordered.

His first step was tentative, but his next was faster,

more secure. By the time we made it to his car, he seemed concentrated and angry again. No, not angry—furious. His expression on any supernatural's face would worry me a little.

He hit the gas the same way I normally did, slamming the pedal to the floor and causing the tires to screech on the asphalt. The little beaten up and falling apart car took off like a rocket once we were on the street.

And while he drove, I had to quickly figure out how I was going to control myself.

My fangs continued to ache as I fought the need to sink them into his skin and pump my venom into his veins.

CHAPTER EIGHT

We pulled up to his dirty, small apartment complex and got out of his car in silence. We didn't talk for the entire drive, something I was grateful for since my fangs kept dropping. At one point, I was tempted to reach into my mouth and push them back into their normal folded position. I knew controlling the urge would be easier over time, but growing up, I had been warned, the initial greeting and confronting of the urge was a bitch to deal with. It took all my self-control not to strike and deal with the problem right then and there, but there were several more pressing matters to deal with, like keeping him alive.

And I barely know the man. I'm sure he would really love a strange woman sinking her fangs into him like a piece of meat.

Well, I can't be sure what he's into. His girlfriends did call him Dom.

"Well, this is a shithole," I commented lightly, trying not to open my mouth much as my fangs dropped again.

"Thanks," he snapped. "I'm on the top floor."

Of course you are, because if anyone shows up, getting out has to be as hard as possible.

I followed him up to the third floor and followed him into his apartment. Quickly taking in the environment, the first thing I was able to put together was that Raphael was a drinker. Empty beer bottles sat on every surface. They were the only mess, though. There was no laundry or dirty dishes anywhere, just empty beer and liquor bottles. He hit it pretty hard, but I couldn't smell alcohol on him nor vomit or anything in the apartment.

So, not a sloppy drunk. There are worse things he could be than a drinker.

"Start talking," he growled as we walked into the living room.

I picked up one of the beer bottles and decided to throw it in the trash. Why the urge struck me, I didn't know, but the need to clean up was strong. It wouldn't be hard to get a garbage bag and fix it up. I didn't say anything, but the very clear click of a gun going off safety made me turn to him slowly.

"Don't shoot me," I said carefully, looking at the gun in his hands, pointed at me. "If you think Mygi is a problem for you now, you can't even begin to comprehend the problems you'll have if you accidentally kill me."

"I don't know you, so I'm going to keep this on you. Sorry, it's nothing personal."

I nodded slowly, trying not to make sudden movements.

Smart humans are more dangerous than most supernaturals. His instincts are telling him that he and I are not the same, and that makes me a threat, no matter what promises I give him.

"You've been running from Mygi for five years. You have the right to be paranoid, but you really can't shoot me." I needed him to understand killing me was going to make his problems a lot worse, not a better.

"Damn right, I do, and I'll make the call whether I can shoot you," he growled. "Now, you said a fucking vampire? Why do I think you're telling the truth? Vampires aren't real."

"Because they are. The world knows about werewolves and fae, and they have some idea about witches now. There's more, there's so much more. Mygi Pharmaceuticals is a supernatural company, owned and operated by monsters that go bump in the night," I explained, wanting to strangle him. How dare he pull a gun on me? I was there to help.

"What are you?" he demanded.

"A naga. Well, nagini, a female naga. Um..." I tried to think of a good way to explain. His look of confusion told me everything. He had no idea what I was. "Indian species of supernaturals. I turn into a snake. Not Native American. I wasn't born on this continent kind of Indian." I hated having to clarify, but I lived in the United States long enough to know I had to, or the more ignorant would start asking what tribe I came from. Since

I liked most Native Americans I met, I didn't want to insult anyone by trying to joke around about being Navajo or something. Plus, no one in the supernatural world was stupid enough to insult the beings and people who inhabited the Americas before we arrived from all over the world.

"What else is there? What is Mygi going to send after me to catch me, and how do I kill them?"

Straight to the point. He's not going into shock like most humans do. He's either hard to shake, or he had already considered something supernatural was going on, more than what he knows possible.

"That sort of explanation would take too long for the limited time we have," I said gently, moving toward his beaten up and used couch. "We only have until sundown to get you moving and into a secure location. There are three definite people coming after you tonight. Only one of them I know for sure knows how to fight and kill. The other two are mixed bags. They could have tricks up their sleeve that could turn any situation in their favor."

And if they're working with Sinclair, there's an incredibly high chance they're really fucking good at what they do.

As I sat down on the couch, I had to admit I was scared. Raphael followed me every step, his gun pointed uncomfortably at my chest. He wasn't stupid enough to aim for the head. He would double tap me like a professional. I was immortal but not invulnerable. I hadn't thought to wear body armor. He could kill me, and there would be little I could do about it.

Talk about a confidence killer. One human could kill me when I'm trying to help him. I would become the laughingstock of the supernatural world. Years spent cultivating my reputation, wasted by one attractive, paranoid human male.

"One is a vampire, the leader. Easier to kill than the other two, but this one is pretty old and damn powerful. The chance either of us can kill him tonight is slim."

"What would it take?"

"The sun or fire. You can incapacitate vampires, but those two things finish the kill. Well, you can also behead him," I said, trying to get comfortable on the couch. It was probably the worst thing I had sat on in my entire life. Lumpy and awful, sitting down was almost as distracting as the gun in front of me. "Broken necks don't kill them. Heart injuries don't matter, they'll heal 'em. Cut off the head, throw them in the sun, or set them on fire. Those are your three options.

"The other two people I know for a fact are going to find you tonight are a fae and a witch. You can kill a witch like any human, but who knows what sort of spells you have to get through to do that. A fae, you can mortally wound with an iron weapon and hope it sticks. It'll stop their healing process, but someone else could save them if you don't stab them in the heart or cut their head off. They won't bleed to death, so don't rely on that. Like the witch, a fae can have a variety of annoying abilities you'll need to fight through."

"What else is out there?"

"Well, everyone knows werewolves, so I can tell you

about werecats. Be careful with them. If they get a good enough bite, you'll be turning fuzzy during the full moon. Just like werewolves, but a lot bigger, meaner in a lot of cases, and very antisocial."

"Werecats?" His hand was starting to shake. I didn't like that much, considering it was holding a firearm.

"Well, we can talk about my kind, the nagas. Or maybe the kitsune, they're always fun. What about banshees? They're cousins to the fae. We can try nymphs. What about ghosts or spirits?" I shouldn't have been egging him on, not with how nervous he already was. I hadn't even started on the real monsters, the ones that couldn't take human form. The sphinx, the manticore, the wendigo, and more—hidden away. Keeping those secret from the world was a lot harder, and they were going extinct at an alarming rate, but many of them were still around. There were so many supernatural or mythical creatures, there was almost no way for any single person to know what was out there. I was only giving him a taste of the terrible.

"You're...you're lying. There's no way..."

I opened my mouth and let my fangs drop again. I could taste the drop of venom falling from one of them. I spit it out before it got into my system. The last thing I had time for was that.

I'm going to need to milk them the moment I get the chance. I can't deal with all this right now.

"I'm a naga, just like I said. Snake people from India, going back to ancient times. I wouldn't lie to you about the rest. You need to come with me. Mygi put a ten-million-dollar bounty on your head, for all the public to see. I'm not planning on cashing you in for it. Money isn't much of a worry for me. I'm just trying to keep you alive." If anyone had asked me this time yesterday, my objective would have been different. Capture human, find out what human knows, then let him go on his merry way.

My physical reaction to him changed the rules. His life was the most important thing now. I reined in my anger over that frustrating fact and tried my hardest to keep calm. If I started getting pissy, his trigger finger was going to get twitchy.

"How do I kill werewolves?" he asked. "Some type of metal, right?"

"Silver bullets, obviously. A lot of them. They heal well, but once silver gets into their system, it's a toxin. It hampers all their abilities, and they can't Change when they have large amounts of it in their body. Just load them up or hit them in a fatal spot, head or heart. They won't come back from it. Good luck getting silver bullets, though. A silver sword or dagger is much easier." Silver bullets weren't easy to come by. Most were custom made by small supernatural companies, and those companies didn't stay open for long once a nearby werewolf pack found out someone was putting silver bullets on the market. Every few years, there was someone new I had to contact to make sure I had a good supply since I wasn't into making bullets for myself.

"Werecats? How do I kill those?"

"Exact same deal. They both Change on the full moon, without any control, but they can shift between their forms whenever they want to, full moon problem aside."

I checked the time while he watched me. Less than an hour until sunset, and he didn't seem like he wanted to come with me yet.

"Maybe you should pack," I said gently. "I won't move."

"I haven't decided whether I'm going with you," he growled. For just a second, I wondered if I caught a glimpse of red flashing in his eyes.

"Why don't you tell me your story?" I asked, crossing my legs and leaning back.

"You know my name, so you know what happened," he snapped. The gun was still shaking in his hand.

"I know very little. You were set up to do great things in the human world. One night changed everything, and you disappeared for ten years. I know for five of those years, you were with Mygi, though I'm assuming it was against your will. You've been running from supernaturals since you escaped." I licked my lips, and there was something else in his scent now. I had no idea what it was, and that scared me. What had the good people at Mygi done to him?

"I killed all my friends," he snarled. "You know that part."

"I do," I whispered. The gun rose up, and he took two fast, large steps across the room. The cold metal touched my forehead.

"Tell me why I shouldn't kill you right now just for knowing that and make my escape?"

"Because I might be able to make all this stop," I said softly. He could kill me, and I was just sitting there. This wasn't the first time I had a gun to my head. "I'm kind of important, and there's so much you still need to understand."

Keep cool. No sudden movements. The moment his guard goes down, disarm him. Can't kill him, but I can at least take away his advantage and gain control of this situation. Talking to him is obviously not working.

"I'm human," he said with a conviction I didn't really understand. It was almost like he was trying to convince himself. I could smell how human he was. There was no arguing that he was human. "I'm not a supernatural. Why is this happening to me?"

"I don't know, but you're in it now, Raphael. There's no turning back. Once you're in, you stay in. The only way to get out of the supernatural world is in a body bag."

Humans tried and failed before him and would continue to try and fail after him. Some dipped their toes in, going to witches to dabble in magics they didn't truly understand. When things got too hot for them, they tried to walk away, but by then, they knew a few real spells and knew magic was possible. They were always pulled back in, normally for misusing magic. Then there were people who accidentally got jobs with supernaturals. Even if they never knew the secret, they were in danger, a target to whoever their employer's enemies were.

"Why don't you tell me what happened?" I asked softly. We were running out of time, and I was getting more anxious by the moment, but I needed more of a rapport with him. He wasn't going to budge unless I really made him think I gave a shit.

Sadly, I did give a shit and really hated it. Of course, the one time I needed someone to think I cared about what happened to them was the one person who refused to get with the program.

"I was about to graduate, and my buddies finally convinced me to try something. I went through drug testing, so I stayed clear of all of it for a long time, but they promised this drug was a great high and completely natural, so it wouldn't show up on any drug tests. I was drunk." The gun lowered a little, which put it between my eyes, but he was relaxing, so I took it as a good sign. "I don't know...I woke up, and I was surrounded by them. They were all dead like something beat them to death one by one. I was covered in blood. Some people came and grabbed me before I could even get out of the house. Next thing I knew, I was spending my days strapped to a table."

I swallowed. That sounded worse than I had originally thought.

"Then you escaped, and Mygi has been after you ever since."

"That's right."

Great. Mega corporation into pharmaceuticals, doing illegal captures and experiments on humans. I mean, what else could this be?

"I said I can help you, and I will." I needed to make a call to Cassius and fast. He was going to want every piece of this to build a case, and the faster he could start, the faster I could get permission to take out anyone who tried to grab Raphael. There were still so many things I didn't know, like how Raphael escaped to begin with, but it didn't matter. Now, I had full confirmation this wasn't a standard 'capture the human to keep the secret' problem. This was a company trying desperately to cover up illegal activities, and hoping no one looked too closely at them. The Tribunal wouldn't unless they had reason to think this was part of something more. I now had that reason. I just needed to keep him away from everyone looking for him.

"How can you do that?" he asked, the gun lowering even more. It was pointing at my chest, but I could see how loose his finger was off the trigger and not primed to put two in me at any moment.

"I work for the supernatural government. It's called the Tribunal, and it's been in power for about eight hundred years. Its number one goal is to keep all supernaturals following the letter of the law. What Mygi has done is...well, I can't say it's officially illegal, but it's definitely cause for the Tribunal to step in and make a ruling, to give you some protection. You can never go back to a human life, but I can help you set up usable fake identities to use in the human world."

"What do you do for them?"

Smart fucking human.

"I'm designated a Tribunal Executioner—"

His hand tightened on the gun, but I was able to push it out of the way before his finger pulled the trigger. Two shots went into the couch next to me. I twisted his wrist until something started to pop, forcing him to drop the gun. Again, I could smell something strange on him, something that didn't match his totally normal human scent.

"I'm not here to *execute you*," I hissed. "I'm also a freelance bounty hunter and do my own investigations into illegal activities. A friend pointed your bounty out to me, and I decided to sniff around and discovered you needed my help."

Gods, he shot at me. He's completely okay with killing anyone he deems a threat.

In the beat of still silence in the apartment, I came to a quick conclusion about how I felt about what he had just done.

I can respect that. If someone came to me and called themselves an Executioner, and I didn't know what that meant, I would have tried putting bullets in them too. He has good instincts.

"How?" he asked, seeming shocked. I had moved so fast, I was pretty sure he didn't even see me.

"I'm a snake," I reminded him. "Lightning fast reflexes are kind of our thing." I couldn't move that fast all the time, but instinct really ramped up my reflexes when I was hunting or in danger. A snake had to know when it was time to strike. We conserved energy otherwise.

Slowly, I let his wrist and arm go, kicking the gun away before anyone thought to get a little too trigger happy again.

"Now, we definitely need to leave unless you want to

explain this to the human police," I said, glancing at the window. "Raphael, at least take a walk with me."

He didn't seem happy, but he nodded.

"Yeah. I can't get sent back to New Mexico. I know if I'm arrested for the deaths of my friends, I'm an easy target for those people chasing me."

"Exactly. Do you have a go bag?"

"Of course," he snapped, seeming insulted I would assume he didn't. He left the living room into one of the two inside doors. I figured one was the bedroom, and one was the bathroom. It was a tiny, shithole apartment. He came back out with a large duffel thrown over his shoulder. I picked up his gun and offered it back to him.

"Let's not try to kill me again?" I waited for his reply as he grabbed the gun. I didn't let go, though. I needed him to make me some assurances.

"I'll go with you for now," he agreed. "I won't try to shoot you unless you try to kill me."

I let go of the gun.

"Then let's get out of here. We have to hurry. Hide that. If the cops are already nearby, they'll be stopping people." I could have offered to hide it in my bag, but I figured he would be more comfortable with his weapon. I didn't need him defenseless.

We left the apartment together, and I was really starting to think I should have stayed out of this mess from the moment Paden brought it to my attention.

9

CHAPTER NINE

I could hear the sirens as we got into his car. He drove carefully this time as we pulled out, the cops too busy investigating the gunshots to realize the culprits were leaving. He was cool under pressure, I had to give him that.

"You've done this a lot," I commented lightly. "Avoiding the cops."

"Yeah. Whenever someone blows my cover, they show up, and I need to dodge everyone," he said, his voice tight, fraught with tension. "So, what is it you do? You said you were a Tribunal Executioner. You kill people?"

"I kill a lot of people. If a supernatural breaks the law, it's normally punishable by death, and I'm just the person who gets that done for the big guys at the top. There are investigators as well, your standard detectives who investigate potential criminals. They're also the prosecutors in the Trial. They gather evidence and present their case to the Tribunal. The Tribunal is both judge and jury, holding the court and passing a guilty or innocent conviction. I just come in at the end."

"Does it happen a lot? You needing to kill people for them?"

"Depends. I go to Trials when the potential guilty party is there, so I can act swiftly once the judgment is passed. Most of the time the Tribunal will call a trial, and the criminal has two choices. Either go speak in defense but die faster when found guilty, or use the Trial's distraction as a chance to cover their tracks and hide. If they're found guilty, my kill on sight list is updated, and I memorize the face and species. If they ever run into me by accident or vice versa, I am legally bound to act and end their life."

"Do you ever...go looking for them?" He was too curious, in my opinion, but since he was dragged into the supernatural world, it was only fair to tell him all of it.

"Sometimes. Depends on their crimes and how invested I am in their case. Some Executioners patrol their areas nonstop, looking for people. Since my area has so much open desert, it's a bit harder. If they go out there and want to starve to death or die of dehydration, I'm not going to stop them. It's not like they can get much done in the desert, where they probably won't have a connection to the internet or running water." I shrugged. "I'm on a long leash when it comes to how I perform my duties."

"So, killing is okay in your world."

"Not really."

"But—"

"I'm a sanctioned executioner through our ruling

government. Assassins and hitmen are murderers, and the people who pay them are as well. They are just as guilty in the supernatural world as they are in the human one. Bounty hunters aren't allowed to kill anyone, though it happens sometimes. Capture only. If it happens, they're brought in front of the Tribunal and have to plead their case. Self-defense normally works for bounty hunters. The people we go after can get dangerous."

"Okay. So, you're going to use your connections to help me. I can maybe live a normal life again one day."

"That's what I've been trying to say."

"And if I drop you off somewhere and reject your help?"

I'll knock you out, throw you in the trunk of this car, and keep you under fucking house arrest in my desert.

"You'll have to figure out how to survive on your own," was the answer I settled on. I couldn't tell him what I really thought because I was damn near positive he wouldn't appreciate it. "Let's get to my car. It's faster and humans tend to ignore it."

"Where are you parked?" he asked, keeping his eyes on the road. I glanced at his profile, and my fangs ached uncomfortably. He was frustrating—too many questions, too little trust—but damn, he was nice to look at.

I answered his question and started searching through my bag to grab my phone. I sent a quick text to another naga, asking a couple of questions. In the middle of everything else, I had to have some personal questions taken care of. Since we were relatively safe in the car for the moment, it seemed like the perfect time. As I put the phone away, the car rocked.

My head snapped up, and I looked out the windows. Beside me, Raphael cursed, turning down another street. I checked the back and hissed.

"We have a tail," I snapped without taking my eyes off the SUV behind us. "Do you know how to lose them?"

"I've done it once or twice."

I narrowed my eyes on the SUV as Raphael hit the gas and began to fly through traffic. It kept pace. I couldn't get any sort of thermal information through the SUV's windows and the heat of the vehicles on this warm evening. I knew it was useless to try to catch a smell.

"Get to my car," I ordered. "If we can't lose them for long, we can at least do a quick car change, and I can drive."

"Do you know who it might be?"

The sun was nearly down, so I had a fairly good guess. There were only three people in the city who had a rough idea of where to find Raphael, other than me. It was most likely the fae or witch, scoping it out before Sinclair woke up. How long they had been watching him, I didn't know, but they were obviously not okay with me driving off with him.

"Maybe." Reaching into the weapon section of my bag, I pulled out my Beretta and turned off the safety.

"You have weapons?" Raphael was looking at me and not the road. I hissed, showing my fangs—it was now pointless for me to try to keep them under control.

"Of course, I have weapons. I haven't left the house unarmed in nearly a century. Watch the fucking road."

His eyes went wide and he turned away. I went back to watching the SUV behind us. There was a chance whoever it was would just follow us, reporting on our location. I knew for a fact, Sinclair would know I was involved the moment he woke up, and that worried a large part of me. I was a little excited, too. A day when I could give him the proverbial middle finger was always a good one.

"We're here!" he declared, turning hard into a parking lot.

"Black BMW," I snapped. "It's my car. Get us to it."

He gave me a jerky nod and tore through the parking lot, slamming on the brakes as the SUV barreled after us.

Fuck. They aren't following us just to report. They're trying to stop me from hiding him out of Sinclair's reach.

I jumped out of his car, pulling my keys from my pocket as the SUV caught up.

"Get out of their way!" I yelled back at Raphael. I got my car unlocked and looked up, wondering where the damn human was.

He stood in the middle of the parking lot. I licked my lips as I tossed my bag into the car, catching his scent on the wind. It was even less human than it had been before. It was like he was constantly...changing. Every time I tasted his scent, it was a different amount of human, fluctuating back and forth.

"RAPHAEL!" I roared as the SUV drove for him instead of me.

As it slowed down next to him, he turned to me, and yes, his eyes were very red now. There was no missing the red eyes or the black, inky lines radiating out from them. He ran for the slowing SUV and slammed his shoulder into it.

I just stood there, feeling stupid.

The SUV's side crumbled with a Raphael-sized dent. He reached down as it completely stopped, grabbed the bottom, then lifted.

Now, I had seen people lift cars before, even big SUVs. Even for strong supernatural species, it was something they had to work to do. I definitely couldn't. I was fast, but I was only as strong as any human, deceptively fragile.

Raphael lifted the side of the SUV with ease and rolled it over with a simple toss. It slid away, upside down nearly twenty feet. The black, inky lines were spreading slowly over his face.

He's not human. He's not fucking human. What the fuck is he? What the hell is even going on anymore?

I didn't move as he jogged in my direction and jumped into the passenger seat. I kept staring at the SUV, my mouth gaping.

"Look, I'm deciding to trust you! Get in before they get out!" he growled across the front seats.

I hurriedly got into my car, turned it on, and raced out of the parking lot, my heart pounding. I couldn't bring myself to look at him. Nothing was making any sense. When he'd been talking inside his apartment, he'd sounded like he was trying to convince himself he was human. Maybe he used to be, but he certainly wasn't anymore. And that made even less sense to me because of the reaction my body was having to him, the need to bite him was generally reserved for two species—humans and other nagas. He was obviously neither. I licked the air and ended up more baffled.

His scent keeps changing. He's more human now than he just was. What's the other thing in his scent? What is he?

Driving in silence, hands tight on the wheel, I tried to consider everything I knew. No supernatural species could take human form and fool everyone. A fae's body temperature fluctuated when they did magic. Werewolves and werecats still smelled like animals when they were in human form. Nagas all had the same sort of scent, and our temperatures fluctuated a little.

Thinking back to when I first saw him, Raphael had run hot, much hotter than I had ever seen before, including werewolves and werecats, who were generally the warmest bunch in the room. I hadn't stopped to consider how warm he was to the touch when I had grabbed his wrist. I should have.

"Where are we going?" he asked after nearly fifteen minutes.

"My home. I have safe rooms, and only three living people know where it is, so it's as secure as we're going to find. We're going to keep talking about things when we get to my place, okay?"

"Yeah. Your phone is buzzing in your bag."

"It can wait," I said, swallowing. There weren't many

options about who it could be—Paden, Carter, maybe Cassius, or the naga I had texted. I wasn't looking forward to talking to any of them, so I decided, for the rest of the evening I was just going to focus on the human beside me.

The human, but not-human, rather.

I drove fast, turning hard to get onto my dirt road. I pulled into the garage and got out of the car before Raphael could say anything. I didn't grab my bag, going inside straight for my kitchen.

First things first—I had to milk my venom. Even through shock and fear, the painful ache of my fangs and my overly productive venom glands needed to be treated. The only thing that ever felt like it was a bad sinus infection, probably because my venom glands took up some of the space where I should have had sinus cavities. Raphael followed me in slowly, holding both of our bags, and dropped them on the table.

"Kaliya, right? Look, I know this is crazy—"

"Shut up and give me a minute," I snapped, grabbing a plastic cup from the back of my Tupperware shelf.

I wedged it under my fangs and flexed the muscles that pushed venom. Several drops began to fall, enough to kill probably fifty people. It felt endless, and the ache continued for a long time, but eventually, the pressure was gone, and the ache receded. I kept going, trying to force my reservoir of venom to empty. Once I was positive it was nearly dry and wouldn't give me anymore, I put the cup down, grabbed another glass, and filled it with water. I gargled for twenty seconds, then spit it into my sink. I couldn't accidentally ingest my venom right now.

"Sorry," I mumbled when I was done. "I don't use my venom enough, and sometimes I have to milk it." It was a convenient excuse but partly true. It was a lie because normally, I only had to milk them every three months if I didn't use them to kill anything, which was the proper way to regulate the venom. I had milked only a month ago. I was going to have to start doing it a lot more often if I had any hope of living comfortably anymore.

"Fuck," was the only reply he had for me.

"Yeah. Some species have normal human forms, no different from any other human. Nagas aren't like that. We're a bit snake no matter what. When you're in this world, you have to be prepared for anything because we all have tricks up our sleeves." I straightened up and looked at him. His eyes were back to a medium brown like coffee with a touch of milk. There was no evidence of the strange black inky lines that had been radiating out from them, and the whites of his eyes were once again white.

"Now, it's time to stop lying. Everyone thinks you're human, but you're not. What are you?"

He turned again, angry all of a sudden, maybe at my accusation, maybe at something deeper I couldn't see.

"I was hoping since you know so much, maybe you could tell me."

Fuck indeed.

10

CHAPTER TEN

"You have no idea what you are?" I asked, sagging against my counter. "None at all?"

"If I did, I damn sure would have told someone, but my best guess is that I'm a fucking freak!" he snarled at me. I watched the red flash in his eyes and hated the bolt of both attraction and fear that ran through me. I didn't know what he was, except he presented as completely human.

Until he wasn't.

"What can you do, and when did it start?" I needed all the information I could get.

"Since you don't have any idea of what I am, why should I tell you any of that?" he said, grabbing the back of one of my dining room chairs. I was beginning to hate his temper. It was a beast unto itself, and I needed him to keep it on a leash. Too bad I had a similar problem.

"Because I might know someone who can use it to find out what you are!" I yelled back, knowing my eyes were beginning to change in anger. My pupils would go vertical when I was angry. "Cut the fucking attitude with me, asshole! I've only been trying to help you since we met!"

"I'm here, aren't I?" he growled. This time, I got to see the change in his face as it happened. The whites of his eyes turned black around his black pupils. The lines bled out from there, looking like they followed his blood vessels. They didn't go very far.

My fangs were still down, and I knew I could maybe get half a drop of venom out of them. If push came to shove, I could kill one person with that venom before it replenished.

Too bad, I also knew it would be completely ineffectual on Raphael.

"We're...not doing this right," I decided. "I'm going to need you to calm down and explain things to me, Raphael. I need to know what I've gotten myself into."

He took several deep breaths, and I watched the signs of his less than human nature disappear. His scent changed from unknown back to his human scent.

"I'm sorry. I'm stressed out. This is...a lot," he conceded. "It started that night when I...killed my friends. While I was at that place, they kept pushing me further. I lose complete control if it goes too far." He rolled up a sleeve of his jacket, and I saw a scar that went all the way around his wrist.

"Is that from them binding you?" I asked, wondering how tight something would have to be to cause that sort of scar.

"No. It's from where they cut my hand off and let it heal back on," he explained softly. He covered it back up and lifted his shirt. There were at least seven gunshot scars on his abdomen, all healed and scarred. "They've shot at me a lot. Every time I get caught and have to run. But it's like I don't feel them when they happen, not while I'm like that. I feel them later, as they try to heal. It's not immediate, and I have to put pressure on them, but I can heal from a gunshot like these in twenty-four hours. Less if I'm…"

"How long did it take your hand?" I was breathing too hard, too mystified by the man in front of me and what he could apparently do.

"It was reattached within a few hours, but it took a few days for feeling to come back, an entire week for full mobility."

"And you spent five years there," I mumbled.

"Getting my blood drawn, getting cut open and looked at, getting drugged up and told to fight things. Yeah," he said, nodding.

Blood drawn.

"Shit," I muttered. "Hold on for me. I have to do something." I had left my venom sitting there on the counter like an idiot.

I grabbed a set of keys and unlocked a small cabinet in my kitchen and pulled out a blood draw set, tourniquet, needle, and tube. While he watched, I tied off the tourniquet and stabbed myself right in the vein and drew a vial of my own blood. Without pause, I poured the blood into the small cup of venom and watched them duke it out. I was immune to my own venom and acted as a natural neutralizing agent for it. A naga's venom was *only* stoppable by that naga's blood. There was no anti-venom, though some had tried, which didn't work because the venom composition for each naga was unique and the effects wildly differed. Someone would have to successfully synthesize anti-venom for each individual naga, which was damn near impossible.

"We're talking about how I was a science project, and you're going to do that?" he snapped, waving a hand at the cup of venom and blood.

I looked up at him then back down at the cup. When my eyes met his again, I shrugged. His pale face wasn't my problem. I couldn't blame him for being uncomfortable around needles and shit anymore, but it *really* wasn't my problem. Keeping him alive and catering to his delicate sensibilities were two very different things.

"I do what I got to do. Do you want a highly dangerous hemotoxin entering the water supply by accident and possibly killing hundreds? A drop of this will have you bleeding internally within thirty seconds, as well as from your gums, ears, nose, and eyes. Well, you would bleed out of every hole, but I don't think you want to hear about that." I smiled viciously. "My blood renders it useless and then I dispose of it all where humans won't be able to find it and run tests. Some of us are careful with our presence in a modern, scientific world so we *don't* become science projects."

"Bitch," he mumbled, shaking his head at me.

"And you've been an asshole since we met, so I guess we're fucking even," I snapped.

We glared at each other. Maybe I could have been nicer about what I just had to do. Maybe he could have not tried to put two bullets into me, which now that I thought back to it, was really a dick move. Every time I thought he and I were getting along, one of us got snappy, and I just didn't know how to rein in the situation.

"So, what are we going to do now?" he asked, shoving his hands into his pockets.

Sighing, I shrugged again, grabbing a lid for the cup. Once it was sealed, I went to sit down at my dining table, gesturing to the seat next to him to sit down as well, across the table from me. I didn't want him next to me. I needed to get used to the warring sensations I was going through.

"I'm going to try to figure out what you are. If I can do that, then I can find someone who can teach you, explain it better than I ever could. It's not going to be easy. It might take some outside help, but I'm going to start tonight. We're going to lie low. I need to make some phone calls to get backup. I can't protect you alone and have no idea how far this could go. Mygi might recall the bounty and the people they've hired and let it drop. They might keep coming and try to kill me for sticking my nose in this."

"You work for the...Tribunal or whatever. Would Mygi try to kill you?"

"At some point or another, Raphael, everyone tries to kill me," I whispered, giving him a sad smile. "If they're into something illegal, covering up my murder is the best option they have, but they would have to do it before I can testify at a Trial. Anything I say before that is considered inadmissible. It needs to be said directly to the Tribunal under their oath or it doesn't matter."

"This sounds like it's going to be harder than you let me believe," he accused.

"I sure as fuck never said it was going to be easy," I reminded him. "Do you really think this is as easy as making a phone call? After everything you've been through? First, I need to keep you alive. Now, I need to make some calls." I grabbed my bag off the table in a huff. "Let me show you the room you can use. Heads up, though, in the supernatural world, we're all pretty much night owls, and you might want to switch to that schedule as soon as you can."

"What about my job? Or really any of my life?"

"Did you have much of a life before I met you?" I demanded, wondering if he was serious. "And we both know you're overqualified for construction and getting paid under the table is probably garbage. Once we've secured your safety, I'm sure there's going to be some work you can find in the supernatural world."

"That's it? I'm in the supernatural world and have no say in it?"

"Yes," I answered with finality that, hopefully, didn't get any back-talk. *Because I need you to stay in the supernatural world, even if everyone else lets you walk away from it, damn it.*

He sighed, and I watched that red flash through his

eyes, but he didn't get angry, didn't make any attempt to argue.

Impressive.

"Come on," I ordered. He followed me toward the back of the house without complaint. "If you know how to use them and someone attacks, feel free to break into any of the display cases and take a weapon. I have something from everywhere and know how to use all of them."

"Are you showing off or warning me?" he asked with a low growl in the mix.

"Both," I answered, unperturbed by him. "And trying to help you. If you're interested in something, maybe I can show you some things."

"No, thanks. I'm not fond of killing things," he answered.

"That's...going to need to change," I muttered, keeping my pace. "Okay, so there's two bedrooms and two offices. One office you can use as you please. It will automatically log you in as a guest since you can't match my biometrics. The other office is and will remain off limits to you indefinitely. You can't get in it without me anyway, so don't try; it'll set off the alarm system. If there's an emergency, you'll come to my room."

"Excuse me?" That seemed to insult him.

"I have a safe room in my private bathroom," I explained.

"Why?" There was worry and curiosity in the question.

"Because people try to kill me," I answered blandly.

"Don't worry. There's only been one who's made it here, and he's been very, *very* dead since that night. Most attack me at my condo in the city. It's less secure."

"You have a dangerous job if people are trying to kill you so often that you need a safe room. Maybe you should get a new one."

"I have a dangerous life, and my job has nothing to do with it," I said, pointing to a door, hoping to get him off the topic. "That's your room." I pointed to the door next to it. "That's my room. Really easy. Just come into my room if the alarms start going off. Or if I tell you to. Don't argue, don't try to fight."

"You saw how strong I am—"

"I don't know if you can recover from a cut throat or a decapitation, so don't do anything stupid. This is a world of immortals. You've been really fucking lucky so far, but you lack training, knowledge, and experience."

"And how much experience could you possibly have? You look younger than me even if you do have white hair."

"I'm one hundred and seventeen years old," I said without inflection. I kept my face straight as he tried to work out what I had just said. I decided to throw a wrench into his process after a moment. "I'm immortal. I'll look like this until I die. My hair went white when I was a teenager. Unlucky, I guess."

"You..."

"I've been around." I shrugged. "Been an Executioner for eighty years, and a bounty hunter most of those. I've been killing people since I was fifteen. So, over a century on that. And my parents started my weapons training when I could walk. I was raised with a weapon in my hand."

He sagged against the wall, his eyes wide.

"Look, Raphael, you're in it now. For the most part, everyone you meet is going to be older than you by a long shot. We're talking people who aren't even trained killers being able to take you out just because they've gotten old enough to know how. Now, you have some neat abilities, and those will help you in the long run. From the looks of it, you're still aging. No one else is, and that's going to work against you. Vampires are locked at the physical ages of when they were turned. Werewolves and werecats hit their prime and practically stop. Same for many species, like mine." I was cold, brutally honest with him because he needed it. "If you lose your temper with the wrong person? Dead. If you get flippant with the wrong person? Dead. If you even so much as look at some people the wrong way, they'll try to kill you. Don't ever look at someone in this world and only see what lies on the surface. It can and will get you killed."

He slowly nodded, taking in my words. Good, he needed to stay flexible, able to adapt. Adaptation was the cornerstone of survival. Some species failed, while others thrived, and individuals had to stay on their toes.

"Get some rest. You look like you need it," I said, reaching to open the guest room door. It wasn't really the guest room. It was my room for Cassius when we were fucking. Before him, it had been pretty empty, a wasted space. I didn't want to tell Raphael that, though. For some reason, it seemed incredibly distasteful.

"Thank you," he mumbled, walking into the room. I watched him throw his bag on the bed as I closed the door. Right before I lost sight of him, I watched him sit down on the edge of the bed and lean over, covering his face.

Tonight, I effectively ended his human life once and for all. Some strange part of me felt guilty for that.

I walked away, heading for my unsecured office. As I walked, I pulled my phone out of my bag to check the text. It was from the naga I had texted earlier.

Adhar: A human is better than nothing. Bite him and get it over with. We don't have the numbers anymore to be choosey.

With a hiss, I shoved the phone into my pocket. One problem I wanted to leave for another day. A day hopefully in the *very* distant future.

11

CHAPTER ELEVEN

I turned on the computer and opened up my work messaging system. Every Executioner and Investigator could get ahold of each other using it. I clicked on Cassius, quickly typing out that I needed him to call me straight away. He, like most others, downloaded the program on his phone. I didn't because I didn't find that secure and also didn't want my coworkers to get ahold of me that easily. My phone rang within a minute. I picked up, steeling myself for his interrogation.

"What did you get into this time, Kaliya?" Cassius asked, his voice the same steely, cold, and impersonal thing I remembered it to be.

Why did I ever sleep with you?

"A bounty on a human came up—"

"If you did something illegal, I can't help you, and you know better than to ask," he snapped, cutting me off. "I know we have a history but—"

"I haven't done anything illegal. Let me fucking

explain, Cassius, or so help me, I will fly to where you are and kill you myself." When I was greeted with silence, I continued. "Mygi, the pharmaceutical company? They put out this bounty on a human, his name is Raphael Dominic Alvarez. At first, Paden was just curious and asked me to look into it. I didn't think it was that big of a deal since we see bounties on humans all the time even though they're illegal."

"We don't have time to go after the perpetrators of every illegal bounty. As long as no one dies, we Investigators turn a somewhat blind eye," he said, his obvious disagreement coloring every word. Cassius was a stick in the mud.

"Exactly. Well, I dug into this one a little because it seemed weird. Paden thought it was really strange and—"

"Let me guess because you aren't going to tell me. Paden wanted to see what sort of information this human might have since he's also part of the information business. His bar is just a convenient cover."

"I won't confirm or deny that," I answered calmly. "You know that."

"Sometimes, I wonder what our superiors saw in you. You live on the line. Some days, I'm convinced you're going to flip to the Lawless side, and we're going to be enemies."

"Aw, Cassius, you know I could never do that to you," I teased. "Now, can I continue, or are you going to continue with the judgmental ass act? How does your new fiancée like that kind of thing? Is she into the whole 'I'm holier than thou' routine?"

"We're getting married next month, and before you say anything, this is not a marriage of political convenience. I genuinely enjoy her company." He sounded like a wooden board that suddenly grew a mouth. I would know since I've seen talking trees. They're always bland, boring things.

"You don't love her?" I was curious. Cassius and I had worked well because love was never a part of the equation. Rather, we had always mostly hated each other and had great sex.

"Would it bother you if I said yes?" he asked softly. "Why don't you continue with what you've found, Kaliya. I don't think we should play this game anymore."

It did bother me, but not because he loved someone else. More power to him for it. The idea of Cassius finding love gave the rest of us hope for the future because he was by far the least likable person I had ever met—attractive but annoying.

"Good for you," I said kindly. "Really, Cassius. There are no hard feelings. I never really liked you all that much."

"You've never missed the opportunity to remind me of that. One day, I hope you meet a man who's willing to put up with being hated for breathing."

"I'm not a man hater," I snapped. "Dick."

"No, you hate everyone unless they're useful to you for whatever reason," he retorted.

"Back on topic," I declared, not wanting to touch that statement with a ten-foot pole. "Last night, I ran into Sinclair. Mygi hired him privately, along with two people who must work for him, a fae and witch, to go after Raphael as well."

"Gods, now we've got Sinclair in the mix," he mumbled. "You know what the Tribunal said—"

"Yes. No more tangling with Sinclair, but he's in *my* city, Cassius. He's *here*. I can't ignore that, and I had already started looking into it." I didn't mention The Board. Cassius knew about it. We had fought more than once over it, and I wasn't looking for another fight. Right now, I just needed his help because he had the job I couldn't take. "So, I broke into the place where he was staying to figure out why Mygi would put out a bounty, wait a week, then hire Sinclair. Something didn't add up with that."

"You found out what's going on?"

"The company had some disagreements. Sinclair was hired out-of-pocket by someone in power at the company, and if he's successful, he also gets the bounty. Would you like to know how much money we're talking about?"

"Please."

"Sinclair was paid ten million upfront for his time. The bounty is for ten million."

Cassius did something I almost never heard and whistled. It sounded like birds whenever he did it, probably because of his fae nature.

"That's a lot of money for one human," he said softly.

"Right? It gets more interesting. I stole the intel the Mygi guy gave Sinclair and was able to get to Raphael before Sinclair and his goons could. At least one of them tailed us for a little while, the witch or the fae, maybe both, because it wasn't quite sundown yet. That's when this got a whole lot weirder." I took a deep breath. "Raphael Dominic Alvarez isn't human."

"What is he?" Cassius demanded. "And why did the bounty say he was?"

"That's the problem and the ultimate question, isn't it? I've never seen or heard of something like it. I have no idea, and neither does he."

"You want me to take this case, don't you?" He sounded defeated as if I had just caught him in a trap.

"Yes. I need backup because I promise Sinclair isn't going to walk away from twenty million, and his ego demands he not fail this, not for a company like Mygi. His reputation is on the line. He's not going to let me hide Raphael away until everyone forgets about this, including Mygi, which could be a very long time."

"And protective custody would only last so long," Cassius added. "Mygi would probably just keep offering more until the Tribunal told them to stop what they're doing..."

"Exactly. So, I need an Investigator...investigating while I keep Raphael safe. Maybe you can help me figure out what he is."

"Why did they claim he was human?" Cassius went back to that, and I sighed.

"Because he used to be human. About ten years ago, he took some drug to get high with his friends. He woke up and realized he had killed them. Now, I don't know every supernatural species that exists, I'm pretty sure no one really does, but...that's not normal."

"It's not. How does Mygi factor in?"

"They captured him that morning before he could run for help or try to figure out what was happening. He spent five years being experimented on, then escaped. He's been on the run for the last five. Based on what Sinclair was told, they tried capturing him repeatedly and failed. They were hoping someone on the outside and the heat of so many people looking for him would finally lead to his recapture."

"You've got me. Keep him under lock and key, Kaliya. I need to push this up to the bosses and get their approval to investigate. Mygi is incredibly powerful politically and won't like an open investigation into their affairs. This is going to have to be played carefully."

"Yeah, but at least it would be something. I have to keep this guy safe, Cassius. I have to."

"Of course. What does Paden say? You're a dog with a bone when something catches your interest." The dry chuckle on the other end let me know Cassius was now one hundred percent on my team for this, letting me relax a little. "I'll let you know when they give me the...green light, as humans say."

"That's the one," I said, chuckling. Cassius had a problem with modern human sayings. He was catching up, mostly because *everyone* gave him shit for not figuring them out already.

"I do have one question that's not totally relevant," he admitted finally.

"What's up?" I was insanely curious now.

"How is it you have already stumbled on this when

you've only been home for...two days? You were just at the Jacky Leon Trial, and now you're in this."

"Oh, was that her name?" I frowned. "Yeah...The bounty came up while I was out of town, so I'm actually a week behind everyone else in the city who watches these things. Sinclair showing up really pushed up my time frame to figure out what was going on. Initially, I had no intention of getting involved and protecting Raphael. I just figured I would look into it for Paden, and he could decide what he wanted to do with it."

"You always did strike fast."

"I'm a snake, of course I do," I reminded him.

"Send me a report, and I'll look into it." Something about those words seemed final as if he was looking to get off the phone.

"Can do."

"Stay safe, Executioner."

"You too, Investigator."

We both hung up, and I stared at my cellphone for a moment. Cassius must have had company at the last moment if he said goodbye using my role. That was the sign someone was around who he didn't want to know that he spoke to me on a semi-regular basis. Maybe it was his soon-to-be wife, or maybe it was one of the Tribunal, who didn't like it when their Executioners and Investigators teamed up and caused trouble for them. Cassius lived with the male fae Tribunal member, so it would make sense he would have to be careful.

Before moving on with my list of tasks, I wrote a small report on Raphael's abilities and what he looked like when he used them—the red and black eyes, the black ink spreading from them in his veins, the unidentifiable smell, the super strength, and advanced healing. Maybe he would know someone similar or something about it. The more we knew, the better.

I didn't put anything about my reaction to the not-human, though. That wasn't Cassius's business. That was a problem only I could handle, but it meant keeping Raphael alive was extremely important.

I called Paden next, pushing aside thoughts of Cassius.

"Before you say fucking anything," Paden growled on the other end of the call, "just know that I know what you did. You have him, and Sinclair is furious. He's in the Underground right now, talking about you and how you're sticking your nose where it doesn't belong. His witch looks a little beat up too, and I'm guessing that was you?"

"No, that was Raphael," I answered. "Paden—"

"How does a human do that to a witch?"

"He's not entirely human, but I don't know what he is. He doesn't know what he is," I snapped quickly, tired of the berating tone in Paden's voice. "He's here at my fucking place, sleeping in my second bedroom, and it's been a fucking challenge, let me tell you, to fucking get him here." Taking a steadying breath, I realized I couldn't tell Paden much until I knew more. "Let me get back to you tomorrow night. I might have more, but the last couple of days have been crazy."

"I've noticed, and I only have myself to blame for it,"

he snapped back. "Should have never told you about this. Someone is going to get hurt."

"Someone already has," I muttered, thinking about the witch. Poor bastard had been in that SUV when Raphael flipped it. "Too late now. I've called Cassius, and he's getting the Tribunal's permission to investigate. This is going official, and hopefully we can keep Raphael alive and learn what he knows. I'm sure in the five years he was with Mygi, he heard some things that might not seem important to him that you would love."

"Something has gotten into you, but I haven't figured out what," Paden said thoughtfully. "I know there's an off chance he knows something you might care about, but the likelihood of that is tiny, Kaliya. What are you really fighting for?"

I don't know anymore. There are too many questions, not enough answers, and my fangs ache.

"It's nothing. You pointed out this all seemed fishy, and you were right. I'm in it now, and there's no turning back." I tried to brush him off, but his question stuck with me. Was I in this just for information, or was I desperate to keep Raphael alive thanks to my biology? I spent a hundred years avoiding the possibility I would find someone compatible with me, and here he was, and people were trying to capture and potentially kill him. He didn't know what he was, and I felt as if it was my responsibility to learn, not just for him but for the implication that information could have for me.

Everything was too complicated.

"I'm going to let you go. I just figured you should

know I have him in custody." I wanted to get off the phone now. I was tired of people, tired of the interaction. I needed some quiet music and a dark room.

"Sinclair has no intention of letting this go," Paden warned.

"I figured as much," I mumbled, then hung up.

Before heading to my bedroom, I did a security check around my home. The windows and doors were locked. The guest bedroom was secure. Raphael would only be able to go around the house and not leave it.

Unless he can rip a door off the hinges or crush the metal security covers on the windows. Seems like a real possibility.

I loaded every gun in the house, just in case, my paranoia getting the best of me. I didn't poison the blades. With him in the house, I had to be a lot more careful with my venom, and that meant doing without some of my weapons. If he accidentally cut himself, I would have a lot of uncomfortable questions to answer.

When I reached my bedroom, I locked the door. I had a stranger in my house. The lock was ineffective, but it gave me some comfort. He would try the handle first, which would wake me up, so I would have time to get moving if he tried to kill me in my sleep...if I even got to sleep.

I turned off the lights and turned on some soft music. I didn't lie down, though. Sitting in the middle of my bed, finding a comfortable position, I relaxed, closing my eyes as I steadied my breathing. An old friend taught me how to center myself. It heightened my senses, excluding sight, rested me, and kept me prepared for battle. When I was young, I realized I would never be truly safe. After my family was slaughtered, I got into a lot of trouble, trying to stay alive and get revenge. I was taken in by another assassin. He taught me the ropes, then pointed me in the direction of the Tribunal, saying working for them was dangerous but offered a high level of safety and respect. The best way to hide was in plain sight.

He also taught me to make it on my own. If I was ever caught on the run, I didn't need to sleep for a few days, thanks to the techniques he taught me. I just had to meditate.

With Raphael next door—a stranger and an unknown danger—sleep wasn't an easy option. With the possibility of Sinclair and his friends coming after me, if they found a way to my home, sleep was even further away. Tonight, I resigned myself to meditation. Trying to sleep would only make me restless.

12

CHAPTER TWELVE

It was a few hours later when I heard him walking around and opened my eyes. I decided to investigate before he got into something he shouldn't. Hopefully, he was just looking for a bathroom, which connected to the kitchen, but I needed to be sure. For my own peace of mind, I had to make sure before I went ballistic or got spooked and accidentally killed him.

If I even can, if push comes to shove...

I left my bedroom and walked silently to my living room. I could see the dining room, kitchen, and the door to the bathroom from my position. I watched him slip into the bathroom and relaxed a bit. When he came back out, I had the chance to see him when he didn't know I was looking, just like I had the moment I met him.

He still ran hot, much hotter than a werewolf or werecat. Even in my cool house, he was boiling but didn't seem sick or uncomfortable. I would guess his natural body temperature was closer to one hundred and six, maybe seven degrees, which should have been cooking his brain. His muscles were tight, ripped like he was at the gym eight hours a day. I couldn't see any unusual markings above the line of his shorts or on his legs. What I could see were his scars. They had really done a number on him over the years. The gunshot scars went out his back too. I watched him look around the kitchen, probably searching for a snack. He had evidence a werewolf had tried to do a number on him, long claw marks going over one shoulder. I watched him run a hand through his hair and wanted to chuckle. I hadn't noticed it earlier, but he had some grey coming in. At least I wasn't alone in prematurely losing my hair color.

"What are you looking for?" I asked softly, but it seemed loud in my silent house.

He jumped, spinning to see me. His eyes flashed red, but nothing more. He relaxed quickly, obviously holding back his instincts to fight or run.

"Something to eat. I can't sleep. It's been a crazy night."

"Hm." I nodded slowly and started walking forward. "Get used to it," I said without sympathy. "Sleep is a luxury we're not always afforded." When I got into the kitchen, I licked my lips, tasting the smells on the air. He was completely human right now, which meant I didn't have to worry too much. He could only do crazy things when he wasn't human.

"Is food a luxury too, or can I get some?" he asked, the annoyance in his voice clear.

I opened my pantry and began pulling down options

for him, sticking with snacks. If he wanted a full meal, he could wait until I decided to cook. Generally, I lived off snacks. I had the habit of eating one meal every few days, supplementing with tiny meals and snacks in between. Maybe it was my snakelike metabolism.

"Is this all you have?" he asked, frowning at my meager selection.

"No, but I'm not cooking right now. Probably won't until tomorrow night." With a shrug, I started to walk away, letting him know that was all he was getting out of me.

"I can cook. I need to eat a lot, or I start dropping weight and muscle. I get that you want to keep your girly figure, but..."

"Fine, you can cook. There's chicken in the freezer you have to thaw and a lot of pasta," I said, turning back to him, exasperated and pissed off by his comment. Of course, I had to house a man who needed to eat me out of house and home. I wasn't going to deny him his dietary needs, though. I just wasn't going to cook for him.

I'm not a housewife. And that girly figure shit is going to need to stop. Fucking total asshole. That's who I had to get, a prick who can't summon a good attitude to save his life.

"Thanks," he grunted. "I'll pay you back for the food."

"There's no beer here, just so you know," I said with a small bite. I wanted to cut him back for his comment, and that got him. He looked at me, his eyes bleeding into red now, the black beginning to take form, leaving him looking completely inhuman.

"You always this much of a bitch?"

"Yeah." I started walking away again, not sure what was wrong with me. I didn't need to say that to him, yet it came out.

"Want to tell me why?" he called out as I heard him rummage through my freezer.

"Not really," I answered loudly. "Why don't you just eat my food and be grateful I'm helping you stay alive?"

"I'll eat your food, but I'm not sure about the grateful part," he growled. "Considering it was monsters like you who got me into this entire fucking mess, to begin with, and tortured me for five years. Maybe I consider this is what you supernaturals fucking owe me after everything you all did to my life."

"I promise you, if you think I'm a monster, you are in for some *nasty* surprises." Gods, I wanted to kill him right then. "And you're the one who showed a moment of weakness and decided to try drugs. No one forced them down your throat. You know what they say, it only takes one time."

"Fuck you," he snarled.

"Asshole," I snapped back before storming out of the room. I went out the back door, heading straight for the gym I kept. I wanted to murder him. I wanted to get a sword and see if he could heal through a decapitation the same way he could apparently put his hand back on.

Going to the weights, I started loading up. I wasn't physically the strongest supernatural and had to work for what muscle I had. Being angry seemed like a good time to work out and push myself. Maybe that would stop me from killing him.

I was in there for two hours, working up a sweat when he walked in.

"Nice. Food is ready. I saved you some if you want any."

Wow, now he has a change of heart. This guy is fucking ridiculous.

"No, thanks. I don't need to eat that often." I didn't look at him as I did my bicep curls in front of the large mirror I had installed. He stood behind me, but I didn't want to look at him so I watched my muscle flex and relax with each rep.

"Really?"

"What about being a naga, a snake person, didn't you get?"

"Excuse me, but I only learned you existed earlier tonight, so maybe you should cut the fucking attitude."

"Look who's talking," I hissed. "I didn't do shit to you, Raphael. I've only tried to help you since we met, but you've got an attitude bigger than this fucking desert. Tell me, if a human decided to shoot a werewolf, should werewolves hate every single human?"

"No," he answered, his voice tight. "But the human didn't irrevocably change the werewolf and ruin his life."

I laughed bitterly. "You should talk to some werewolves. Or vampires. They used to be human. They had those mortal lives taken from them, sometimes against their will. You know what they don't do? They don't get pissy and mad. They get over it. They adapt. They *survive*." I dropped the weight and stood up to look him in the eye. "What happened to you is terrible, and we're going to fix it. What was done to you is wrong, and I'm trying my damnedest to figure out how to get you through it. I'm not the person who cut you apart for five years. Not every monster is the same. Just like every human isn't. Hell, half of the monsters used to be human, just like you."

"You? Did you lose a human life?"

"No, I was born a naga with all the baggage that comes with it. There was never a human life for me. I knew I would grow up, hit my thirties or so, and stop aging. I knew about the monsters from the very beginning. What do you think is better, Raphael? Living in ignorance then losing the blinders, or knowing someone wants to kill you for being born because you live in a world of monsters?"

"Both suck," he said, sitting down on a workout bench. "I'm sorry. Since this happened to me, my temper has been...uncontrollable. Like it's a thing of its own, and I have to hold its leash. I don't understand it. When I do that thing, I have to make sure I don't lose control and lose my place in my own...brain like I did the night it all started. And yeah, I'm fucking pissed. I'll be pissed for a long time. That's something we're both going to have to live with. I don't care what other supernaturals have done to adapt and survive bullshit. I had a good life, and it was stolen from me. I don't see any reason to let that go."

"Fine, but when push comes to shove, no one else is

going to care about the life you used to have. They're only going to care about what you are now, whatever that fucking is," I said, shaking my head. I grabbed a towel off the rack and pointed at the equipment. "Feel free to use any of it, just don't break anything."

"Actually, I thought I would concede a little defeat and ask you to teach me some of these weapons," he admitted. "The food was supposed to be a peace offering."

I sighed heavily. "I'm not a good teacher."

"I'm a good student, though. Maybe I can make up for it."

I wanted to roll my eyes. I wanted to leave him there to figure out his own shit.

Instead, I went to my training weapons cabinet and pulled out two simple wooden swords.

"We'll start easy. Nearly every supernatural knows how to use a sword except for the modern ones. They like guns too much. Don't get me wrong, a gun is a good thing to have, but a sword? It's personal, and a lot of supernaturals like to get up close and personal. It's how they'll kill you. Werewolves and werecats will rip your head off or eviscerate you. Sometimes, they'll eat you alive once they're done. Vampires want to break your neck and bleed you dry. Fae and witches are more ranged combatants, but I promise you, they know how to fight. I'm a close fighter. I don't have many skills that make me effective at a distance. Based on your abilities, you would do well to learn some simple sword techniques. You could easily cut off limbs and heads."

"Do you always talk about fighting and killing with such indifference?" he asked, taking one of the wooden swords from me. "It's starting to worry me."

"Yes." I flipped the sword a few times, loosening up my wrist. I was tired from working out, but I figured I would still be faster. "If I got hung up on it, I would already be dead." I had been desensitized to death for a long time. Kill or be killed. That was the world I lived in. "Should I feel guilty for surviving as long as I have?"

"You make it sound like you're fighting for your life every single day."

"I don't see a problem with that," I said softly. "Now, let's get started. The sooner you get some of this down, the better."

I started off with an easy spar, watching him wildly try to block me as I sent in attacks, seeing how he tried to defend himself. When I gave him a chance to attack, he missed it, and I knew I was dealing with a modern man. He wasn't hiding some hidden immortality I didn't know about. He was doing this for the very first time, and it showed.

"Okay, now I know where you stand. Let me show you a basic stance." I went behind him and kicked his legs apart. "Shoulder-width apart is always a good idea. It will keep you balanced." I moved his shoulders, putting his sword arm closer to an invisible opponent in front of him. "Keep your vulnerable side away from the attacker and make yourself a smaller target. Don't give anyone the chance to go after you from a place you can't defend."

He nodded, and I corrected how he held the sword,

moving his fingers. This was the first time I touched his skin and took a moment to consider it. It was blazing hot, like a heat rock with a sunlamp on it. I stomped on thoughts of curling up next to that kind of heat and enjoying it. Being so close made me come to terms with how much taller he was, probably six five.

"Were you always this big?"

"No. I went through a growth spurt while I was…there."

"Have you completely adjusted to it? Growing up makes us clumsy."

"Yeah, I have. It's been six or seven years since I stopped getting taller."

"Good," I said, stepping away. "Now, just follow my movements. If you're motivated, do these in your free time until you've memorized them. This should be muscle memory by the time you get into a real fight. We don't have time for that, but maybe one day, you'll be able to hold your own against someone with a blade."

We worked for an hour, and I corrected him as we went, remembering how my father taught me. Hopefully, it would be enough.

You're not allowed to die on me, asshole. Do you understand? More than just you and me are counting on you sticking around for a long time.

Even as I thought those words, I hated myself for them.

"We'll continue practicing this while we wait for my people to get back to me," I said, grabbing two fresh towels and tossing him one. "You have no talent for it, but oh well. As long as you have some idea what to do, with your strength, you should manage."

"Thanks," he snorted. "I really appreciate that vote of confidence."

"Dawn is coming soon," I said, looking out the small window in the door. "Try to get some sleep. Now's the safest time."

"What are we going to do tonight?"

"This. And I want to see more of what you can do. It might help me and my friends figure out what you are," I said, wiping off my face. "Good night." Leaving him standing in the gym, I headed for the house. I checked the security cameras with my phone, waiting for him to get inside, then locked the building down. Once he was in the guest room, I turned off the app and laid in bed, finally forcing myself to sleep.

13

CHAPTER THIRTEEN

When I woke up, I was disappointed to see no one had contacted me, not even Cassius, who was normally on my ass when we were working together on something. When my stomach growled, I knew it was time for me to eat a full meal and sighed.

Maybe I can ask Raphael to cook something...

I shook my head vigorously, trying to banish the idea. He wasn't a roommate. He was here because I needed to keep him alive and out of the hands of less than desirable people. If he wanted to cook, he could, but I damn sure wasn't going to ask him—absolutely not. Plus, I hadn't even known the guy for twenty-four hours. That seemed a little too much for such a short acquaintance.

For a second, I missed my family. My mother had a system. Every three days, she and my father made a feast. We all ate our fill, then we were responsible for any smaller meals we might need if we got a little peckish. It had been nice, the consistency, the rhythm. I could never get into the same flow, but then, I hated to cook. She had been great at it. I had wanted to run around with my brothers, even though they were both adults.

Grinding my teeth, I reminded myself why I got into the mess that surrounded Raphael. He could know something that could help me. Tonight, if things stayed calm, I was going to grill his ass like a steak.

I showered, brushed my teeth, and finally did something with my hair, braiding a few sections back to keep it out of my face. It was a slow rise for me, but the sun was still up, and the world was still relatively safe, so I could take my time. I didn't hear Raphael moving around, so it seemed like I was on my own for a moment.

Once I was dressed—standard black pants and black top, simple but effective—I went to the kitchen and started pulling out chicken and pasta, my go-to meal to cook.

I heard him rustling as I thawed the chicken, annoyed I hadn't thought to put any out in the morning before going to sleep when I knew I was going to need to eat tonight. Looking over my shoulder, I narrowed my eyes on him as he went into the bathroom without a damn shirt again.

He's in someone else's house. Can't he put some clothing on?

When he came out, he saw me.

"How long have you been there?" he asked, his eyes going wide. "You always walk around so quietly?"

"Yeah. It's a habit. You always go around half naked?"

He looked down and shrugged. "Sorry. I get really warm sometimes, and it gets uncomfortable."

"Sometimes? You're like eight degrees hotter than most humans," I said, frowning. "Did you know that?"

"I don't go to doctors, and I don't get sick, so no, I didn't know. How...how do you?"

"I have a bit of...thermal imaging." I didn't really know how to explain it. "Like some snakes can use thermal information to hunt for prey. Pit vipers are the most common example."

"You are so weird," he mumbled. "Should I go get a thermometer and make sure I'm not running a fever?"

"No," I said, shaking my head. "I'm not weird, I'm just not-human. Don't start off the day being an ass, please?"

"You know what? Why don't I cook and shut my mouth?" he said, reaching for the knife I was holding, without any fear. I handed it to him and lifted my now empty hands up harmlessly.

"We might survive this," I muttered as I walked away, only stopping as I remembered what I had been thinking about before he showed up. "Tonight, we're going to sit down and talk about everything, about your time at Mygi, okay? I need to know every little detail."

"Yeah, that's fine. You need to build some sort of case to get them shut down, I'm guessing. Would you be okay talking about it after I'm done cooking?"

"Yeah," I answered, nodding as I walked out of the kitchen. "We can talk over food."

I went into my open office so he could get me when

he was done. I sent Cassius a message, hoping he would get back to me quickly, though he may still be asleep. For the first time in a very long time, he didn't immediately call me, and something about that worried me.

I started looking through the database the Tribunal kept on different supernatural species. It was a digitized version of the official Tribunal Archives, a pocket dimension. I thought I had it memorized, but I wasn't stupid enough to actually believe I did. There were plenty of supernatural species who didn't want much to do with the Tribunal. There was a search function, so I started by looking for red eyes. They were common in vampires, but he was definitely not one of those. I went through the list, but nothing matched his physical features or reported scents.

Nothing smells human. Everything has a scent. Vampires are the only exception, but...he's not one of those. He can't be.

I was beginning to think Mygi had decided to make something new. Maybe they had done something to him that changed him into something new.

Cassius didn't call back by the time Raphael was done making the food. He brought in a plate for me, placing it on the corner of my desk, then left again. When he returned a moment later, he had a plate for himself with three times the food.

"There's more, too. I didn't know how much you wanted," he said, sitting down on the other side of her desk. "Nice office. What's in there?" He nodded toward the habitat behind me.

"Oh, I'm helping someone with one of their snakes. Naksha is an Indian cobra. Be careful, and don't stick your hand in there. She's pretty aggressive and very territorial," I explained, looking over my shoulder. My app for her systems hadn't alerted me, so I hadn't been thinking about her. I looked back and saw her curled up under a rock, avoiding the heat lamp above. Before I started eating, I checked the temperature of her enclosure and was satisfied she was fine. Nothing seemed out of the ordinary.

"I'm going to take a wild guess and assume you like snakes." He shoved a forkful of pasta into his mouth.

"How insightful," I replied, spinning my fork in the pasta on my own plate. "So, let's talk. Then we're going to see what you can do."

"Mmm." He held up a hand and finished what was in his mouth, covering his face. I was grateful because it looked like he ate like a pig. "Sorry, I'm always starving," he said, almost sheepishly. "So yeah...It's like I'm something else. When I get angry or need to fight, it turns on, and I see things differently. I know I look crazy when it happens."

"Yeah, and you can flip SUVs."

"Yeah, I'm really strong when it happens. Fast too, but not like you. Things hurt less as if I become kind of invulnerable. I can still bleed. If that SUV hit me wrong, it could have crumpled and cut me, but my bones don't break easily."

"Lucky you. Now, about Mygi."

He sighed. "I don't know if you're looking for

something specific. I only know what they did to me. They didn't really talk about anything but me whenever I saw them. Sometimes they gossiped about who was stealing lunches from the fridge and shit. It was so normal, it stood out."

"Funny." Not really. It was actually disturbing, and it was unusual for me to be genuinely disturbed about something. Office gossip while essentially torturing a man. Did they have any self respect? Torture was serious business.

"They talked about my healing factor a lot. I told you they cut off my hand once." He lifted his left arm again to show me the scar. "It was a lot of stuff like that."

"Damn. So, you wouldn't know if they're practicing illegal experiments on any other supernaturals?"

"Nope. I didn't even know they weren't human. That all started becoming apparent after I escaped." He looked down at his food, his eyes flashing red. I figured he was angry at what had been done to him, and that I understood. "I don't think I can do this yet," he admitted.

"That's fine. There's going to be plenty of opportunities going forward for you to talk it all out. We don't need to do it right now," I promised, letting him drop it.

I resigned myself that Raphael wouldn't be able to tell me anything. I would remove him from The Board later—it was pointless to keep him on there.

We ate in silence after that. He must have realized I was disappointed by what he had to say. It was nothing new, and I didn't blame him for not wanting to dive into the disgusting details yet. He would have to repeat them later for Cassius, who would need him to relive all the horrors to really build the case.

He finished before me; how, I didn't know. I kept looking for Cassius to get back to me, but he never did. I was hoping it was because he was dealing with our bosses to open a case against Mygi and nothing more serious, like the possibility I wasn't going to get help at all. The moment I was finished and tried to put my plate down on my desk, Raphael snatched it and carried the dishes out. I sighed again, staring out the open door. It was time to get some real idea of what he could do, but part of me just wanted to drop the whole thing.

He has no connection to The Board, and he doesn't know anything beyond what they did to him. He needs witness protection or something, not me.

My fangs ached, pulsing as I thought about sending him to someone else. It was like they vehemently protested the idea of sending him away.

Never mind. I'll keep him around until I'm willing to deal with that. Fuck, that could be decades. He's an asshole, and I'm a bitch. That's a can of worms I really don't want to open.

As if the gods were laughing at me, my phone started to ring before I could leave it on the desk and get away. I checked the caller ID and hissed in annoyance before answering.

"Yes, Adhar?" I asked. "To what do I owe the pleasure?"

"I've been alive for three thousand years. In that time,

I have never met someone as good at avoiding things as you are." His thick Indian accent reminded me too much of home. I preferred the other nagas never called. I liked to keep as much distance as possible.

"I should have never texted you," I mumbled. "What do you want?"

"Should I begin preparing a ritual?"

"Absolutely not," I snapped. "Are you fucking mad? Do you think I'm *excited*?"

"He's compatible," Adhar reminded me.

"Like I don't fucking know that." Realizing I didn't need Raphael hearing, I closed my office door, then locked it. "There's a reason I didn't get back to you. I'm in the middle of a shit show with Sinclair. I've got Cassius coming into town to hopefully start a full investigation into a company that could very well hire someone good enough to kill me and my charge. On top of it all, they're trying to capture him. I don't have time for rituals and biting and shit, Adhar; I don't want to do it."

"You're the last female of the nagas, Kaliya. We need—"

"Don't fucking say that to me like I don't know it. I was there the night my mother died, along with the rest of my damn family. I remember running for a *year* before you found me and told me how your sister was murdered only a few weeks later. We lost all three breeding females within four months. I was a child with a whole lot of fucked-up burdens on my shoulders afterward. You *never* need to remind me what I am."

"I know you understand—"

"Breeding compatibility doesn't mean I'm required to breed with him," I snarled into the phone. "My mother was compatible with two people and was able to choose which one she wanted to mate with for life. I think I can reserve the right to say this one might not be right for me. On top of that? I don't *want* kids. Four nagas have human mates, and one of them is pregnant. They can save the fucking species by breeding. I'm going to do it by killing the bastards who are determined to see us wiped out. I'm not going to hide and fuck like the rest of you have been trying and failing to do. First, I need to survive my fucking job and don't need you riding my ass." I hung up and slammed my phone down. Stomping out of the office, I stormed past Raphael in the living room.

"Let's go," I ordered. "We're going to find out what you can do."

"Okay..." He followed behind me, trying to keep up.

I walked off my back porch into the desert, not bothering with shoes. I heard the distinct rattle of a perturbed snake and hissed at it.

"Watch out. We don't know if venom, poisons, or toxins can kill you."

"They can't," he said. "They hurt and work, but my body heals faster than they can do damage."

That made me stumble and misstep on a rock, nearly meeting the dirty sand in a massively ungraceful moment. He reached out and grabbed my arm, and I used it to help regain my balance.

"Really?" I asked softly.

"Yeah, they tried a lot of stuff on me," he answered,

frowning. "I should have mentioned that earlier. None of it works. They would say something like 'performing cyanide injection,' and I would hate everything for about a day, then it would pass, and I would be okay."

I stared at him with wide eyes, wondering how the hell that was possible. It also made me insanely curious if that was why he was compatible with me. He was naturally immune to everything, which made him a possibility, but maybe that wasn't right. Maybe I just knew he was immune, and my body was confused.

I have to tell Adhar about him, eventually. Whether he likes it or not, I don't know, but I'm going to have to tell him. Once we're done with everything, I'll call him back. Maybe.

I don't know. Maybe it's best I don't tell any of the other nagas about this.

Fuck me sideways, why is this so complicated?

"Okay. Well, since you're immune, never mind the rattlesnake literally a foot away from us. Or really any of the deadly creatures out here. I mean, sure, they'll hurt you, but you don't die, so whatever." I tried to shrug it off, but I knew I had shown my surprise for a little too long.

"Are there no other supernatural species like me? Who can heal the way I do?" He almost seemed freaked out. He was an oddity in a world of weird, so I really couldn't blame him.

"I'm immune to snakes. All of them, but scorpions can give me a real nasty hit if I'm not careful. I'm not immune to poisons, but I have some tolerance for them. I *might* not die. To give you an idea of the weirdness surrounding you, there are no supernatural species that consistently survives cyanide. You've survived fatal doses, and that's weird. It's one poison I know would kill me and everyone else I've ever met. Even humans can have a limb put back on if they get to it fast enough. I would assume most supernaturals could have it done, but the way you described yours? That's something I've only seen..."

Vampires do.

He's not a vampire, though.

"Seen?" He tried to pry.

"Vampires, since their bodies aren't alive, need blood, and can heal through nearly anything except decapitation or burning in the sun." I started walking again, trying to get us where I needed us to be. "Or being set on fire, but they can put themselves out or run to the shade before they die of those last two. Decapitation is the fastest, most effective way to kill them. If you rip an arm off, they can take it back, run home, hold it on and drink some blood. I don't know the specifics, but I do know they can put limbs back on."

"But I don't drink blood..."

"And you can walk in the sunlight," I said, nodding as I gestured up at the low evening sun. "So, there's the problem. You have similarities but not enough to be the same species. Don't worry, there's plenty of supernaturals with abilities that cross over. Lots of us can turn into different animals, for example. I, obviously, can shift into a snake."

"See...that I wouldn't mind," he said with a bitter

laugh. "Instead, I just turn into the fucking monster from under some kid's bed."

"Yeah, and we're going to test how much you can do, monster boy," I said, trying for some semblance of lightness and humor to drag myself off the conflicting and intrusive thoughts bouncing around my brain. I stopped walking as we passed a small ridge, and I saw what I needed. There were tons of rocky outcroppings in the North American desert, of all sizes, which suited my purpose.

"What else should I know about supernatural... people out there."

I noticed how he stumbled over 'people' and let it slide. He was adjusting fast, but there may be hang ups like that for a few years as he tried to come to terms with everything. Every human had a hard time when it was dropped on their head.

"There's too much to just sit down and talk about," I answered, crossing my arms and taking in the view. "Dozens of species, all with human intelligence or higher. Real monsters, beasts from legend and lore, though those are quickly disappearing or being hidden. Politics between different species that could take a lifetime for you to really understand." I sighed. "Let's just figure out where you stand first. The rest can come over time, naturally, as you're exposed." I wondered if I needed to find a werewolf or werecat who was once human to help. Or Carter. Carter would be perfect at this discussion. He used to be human before he was turned into a vampire without his permission. He and Raphael could have a great chit chat about the whole thing. I couldn't relate. This was my world, had always been my world.

"What are we doing out here?" he asked, looking over the same view as me.

"See those rocks?" I asked, pointing toward a little outcropping. "We're going to test your strength and see how much you can do. Any information at this point is good information."

"Yeah, sure," he mumbled, walking past me toward the rocks.

I stayed where I was because if there was one thing that could kill me, it was being crushed under four thousand pounds of stone. Hopefully, he wouldn't be able to throw it very far.

"Aren't you coming down?" he called out.

"Nope. Come on, monster boy. Go all scary for me, pick up some rocks, and try to throw them."

14

CHAPTER FOURTEEN

His eyes shifted from warm brown to blazing red.
"I'm not liking the nickname," he growled. "Old lady."

I hissed in return. "Just get started. I don't mean anything by it. I'm just trying to lighten the damn mood."

I watched as the whites of his eyes turned black, and the lines began to spread from his face. His muscles bulged as he went for the biggest rock in the stack and began to lift. His fingers dug into the stone like it was clay.

My heart raced. There was no one that strong.

The rock began to lift as he got a solid grip on it, since he hade his own handholds. The black ink spreading through his veins from his eyes grew as he lifted it higher. Once he had it about three feet off the ground, I got to witness him toss it ten feet. When it hit the ground, everything shook and the stone split into several large chunks. He walked up to the large piece remaining and put his hand on top of it. I watched him shove down, and the stone began to crumble and sink into the dirt. Once it was nearly half buried again, he stopped and looked at me.

I sat down, my mouth gaping. Apparently, seeing it the second time didn't make it any more believable.

"How was that?" he asked, walking back to me. "I don't think I need to do the smaller rocks."

"Nope, you really don't," I agreed, looking at the massive rock pieces in their new home. "We can work with this. Let's get back to training with the sword and getting you prepared for any real fights."

"Kaliya...why are you helping me?" he asked suddenly, as I stood up and brushed the dirt off my ass.

"Why did you accept my help?" I answered back, looking up at his face. He still had red eyes, but the black was leaving. I knew if I caught his scent, it would be turning back to human as we spoke.

"I..." He looked away.

"Yeah. Same." I couldn't tell him too much. There were things I wasn't comfortable with—like how I looked at him, and my fangs ached. How could I begin to tell him about my species and the problems with it when we didn't even know what he was? It seemed unfair, to both of us.

He frowned, and I wondered what was going through his mind.

"I knew I was going to need help one day. Eventually, my luck would run out," he said softly. "And there you were, trying to talk to me like no one else had. I took a chance. Running is tiring, and you started giving me answers, something I'd wanted for years."

"I wish I could give you more," I said, crossing my arms. "But in a lot of ways, I'm more blind than you are."

"Yeah, but even if you can't stop them from getting me, you're giving me a heads up on this thing I've been in for a decade but didn't know about. All this supernatural shit. That's something. If I have to keep running, at least I'll know more now than I did."

I blinked several times, letting what he said sink in.

"Well, I'm glad I could help in some way," I finally said, swallowing. "But I'm going to make sure you don't have to run anymore. I'm not going to let them whisk you away. That's not fair to you or to anyone else, really."

"What do you mean?" He walked beside me, heading back for my house.

"Mygi shouldn't be allowed to detain and experiment on whoever they want," I said, crossing my arms. "The problem is, only certain species are protected. There's no murder allowed, but there's a lot supernaturals can get away with. If a werewolf kidnaps another werewolf, it's handled by werewolves, internally without the Tribunal involved. Same for most species, which means if it's kept quiet and no one makes a fuss..."

"It happens anyway," he finished.

"Exactly. The point of the Tribunal isn't to make us human, because we aren't. It's to stop wars that would expose us. To stop us from exposing ourselves. To keep us from driving each other to extinction. They don't care much for petty things unless someone dies from it."

"So, they wouldn't notice if one human gets captured, and if they did, they might not care."

"As long as it doesn't expose us in the end." I shrugged sadly, wishing I could help him more. "I've got someone trying to open a formal investigation. If we can prove they're kidnapping humans off the streets, we might get a chance to take them down. If we can prove this is a multi-species conspiracy to potentially threaten and expose supernaturals who haven't agreed to go public, we have a bigger case against them."

"And it still might not work."

"Yeah...Mygi is powerful. Not your run-of-the-mill criminal organization who was caught doing bad shit."

"About your job," he said, shoving his hands in his pockets. "You are a Tribunal Executioner, but...do you only kill people?"

"No. I send them to prison too. Killing people is just more common. If they try to evade their sentence, which we know they're doing, and they don't surrender when we find them, we kill them. End of story. No debate, no oversight. If they go on the list, they either surrender to us, or we kill them on sight. Supernaturals who go to prison are generally caught beforehand, and depending on the species, different crimes have different punishments."

"What? That doesn't seem fair," he said, his frown so severe I wondered if he was going to wrinkle right in front of me.

"It's not, but every supernatural has their own rules to play by. That's what makes the laws so damn complicated. On top of that, they really aren't about protecting the weak or keeping a functional society. The supernatural world is like the wild west. There're rules... good luck getting anyone to follow them unless you're willing to back it up with brute force. Therefore, Executioners."

"Jesus," he mumbled. "Where's the prison you barely use?"

"Why? You want to make a visit?" I raised an eyebrow at him in confusion.

"No, just curious. I feel like I've been dumped into a movie, and there's a lot I don't know and should."

"In my region, actually. We tucked it out in the middle of the desert about two hundred years ago. I'm the first line of defense against escapees."

"Let me guess...if they escape from prison, it's punishable by death," he mumbled.

"Yup. You have a lot of hang ups about the killing thing I do," I commented, seeing my house as we went over a hill.

"I think killing others is wrong," he replied.

"I can't say you're wrong, but I think it's naïve, and that's not a bad thing. Everyone in my world is jaded. It's refreshing to see someone who believes in right and wrong and not the grey in the middle. And there is grey, Raphael. Lots of it. Most of the time, there's more grey in a situation than black and white."

The sun was going down, and I picked up my walking pace. I wanted us inside when the rest of the world came out to play.

When we got inside my gym, I grabbed the wooden swords and we got to work, the conversation put aside for the moment. Thankfully, because I wasn't really looking to discuss morality and shit.

We sparred, clashing as I pushed him to remember what we went over earlier. I wanted him to learn quickly. It would only help us both in the long run. After twenty minutes of pure sparring, letting him figure it out, we went into forms and patterns as I corrected his form and showed him what each movement could do for him in a fight.

It was near eleven in the evening when my phone started going off. He nearly hit me on the side of my head as I pulled it out of my pocket and saw it was Paden.

"Stop," I snapped, answering and pulling it up to my ear, wondering what Paden needed tonight.

"Kaliya, you have to hide," he said, coughing.

My blood ran cold.

"Paden, are you hurt?" I asked softly. "What happened?"

"Before opening, that witch and fae working for Sinclair came by. They promised my wife would be okay if I did as they asked, but you know, torture is sometimes an irresistible urge. Warning, the fucking witch has a hard-on for pain."

"I'm sorry," I said, slowly moving toward the side of the gym and leaning on the wall. "Oh, Paden, I'm sorry."

"It's fine. We all know the risks. They didn't kill me, so you can't kill them, yeah?"

"Yeah..." But I wanted to, those motherfuckers. "Why you?"

"They know you have him, and after getting over their pissy shit, they came back with a plan. I had to give them something, Kaliya. I had to protect my wife."

"I know," I whispered. "What did you give them, old friend?"

"Your condo. It's closer to me, and I figured it would buy you time," he explained, coughing. "Can they find your desert place using it?"

"Yes, but it's fine. It'll take them a little time to connect the two places." Or it should. I was already plotting how to get what Raphael and I needed and get out before we were caught in the middle of nowhere with no backup. "How long ago did they leave?"

"Two-and-a-half hours ago, roughly," he answered, groaning. "Wife had to heal my vocal cords and my hands once Henley got me to her. He's pissed. We're going to hide out until this all blows over."

"I'm sorry, Paden. I really am." I felt terrible. Guilt shredded my resolve about Raphael, about all of it. I slid down, letting my legs spread out as I let it sink in. Sinclair and his people were torturing now to get him. The escalation was fast, which meant I had been right: the vampire wasn't going to let this go—not now, not ever.

"I got you started on this," he reminded me. "I started this. It's a lesson learned, not to toy around with these things so brazenly."

"We didn't know..." I tried to find something to say. I knew Sinclair was dangerous. I had seen his work more times than I could count, but this was open. This was stupidly in the open. The only thing was, I couldn't get Sinclair on the torture. His minions did it for him, and Paden didn't mention him being there. I had nothing on the vampire himself, which was the way he always got away with things. Paden also brought up a good point. They didn't kill Paden, so I couldn't kill them.

Not yet, anyway. The moment they moved against me personally, they were fair game.

"No, we didn't. Kaliya, you have to get somewhere else to hide."

"I know," I said, forcing myself onto my feet. Raphael stood close, frowning, the picture of concern. My fangs ached terribly, trying to tell me I should bite him, keep him, and use him for my own comfort. I shoved that feeling down so far, I was certain my face went blank because he got very confused.

"Paden, I'll call you when we're on the move," I said coolly, knowing I needed to keep my head clear if I wanted to steer clear of Sinclair and the gang.

"Good luck," he said, then hung up. I hated how raspy his voice had been, but that was a problem for another time. I could pay for him to have a repair done. I owed him for that.

"A good friend of mine, one who knows where my homes are, was attacked and tortured to try to find us," I explained quickly, shoving my phone back into my pocket. "They left him two-and-a-half hours ago, which is plenty of time for them to have found my condo in the city and maybe even deduce where we are out here."

"How?"

"No supernatural worth its power only owns one home. A smarter one has fake names and shell companies to keep fortunes and properties secret. The smartest supernaturals know how to work through all that and figure out where others are hiding, or hiding their money," I said, beginning to jog out of the gym, letting him keep up. "Sinclair is one of the smartest supernaturals I know. He's not going to take too long to find us here. We need to leave, and we need to leave right now. You have ten minutes to grab everything you own and two weapons."

"Even guns?"

"I have all the ammo you could need in my car," I said before darting away. He followed, but I made it to the house faster and started grabbing weapons from their cases. I found my bag and shoved them into the weapon case. I had a thigh holster and slid a handgun in it. I grabbed a thigh sheath for the left and put a simple hunting knife in it. My talwar was sheathed in its case, and I threw the belt around my waist, securing it. Finally, I went into my back safe room and pulled out one of the vials of my venom. I couldn't take any chances. If this was going to be a fight, I was going to kill every fucking one of them.

They really think they're going to come to my house and cause a problem? I don't fucking think so.

"Raphael, you ready?" I called, heading toward the garage.

"Yeah!" he called from inside. I found him next to my BMW. "I didn't see it last night, but nice Aston Martin."

"Thanks. We're not taking it. Get in." I grabbed the keys for the BMW and unlocked it. He threw his bag in the backseat, and I saw the gun tucked in the waist of his pants. I had to bite my tongue to keep from getting onto him for it. I hadn't told him where to find a holster, so that was my fault.

I hit the garage door opener as I got behind the wheel and cursed as I saw headlights coming up the drive.

"Fuck. We're in for it now," I mumbled, revving the engine and pulling out at an alarming speed. Glancing to my right, I saw him grab the safety handle, his eyes going red.

"Who are they?"

"One of them is the witch who was in the SUV. They're our biggest nightmare right now," I answered, still flying backward. The vehicle coming up the drive quickly slammed on the brakes and turned, blocking the entire dirt drive. A gunshot shattered the back window.

"Raphael, neither car I have can go out into the desert. We're going to need to move them." I grabbed the gun from my thigh holster and looked back through my destroyed back window. "And we might need to get the Aston."

"Might?"

"Yeah, let's see how the BMW holds up first. The Aston is my personal drive, not my work car," I answered, opening my door. Luckily, the BMW wasn't in the way at all since the dirt parking area in front of my house was large, but I needed Sinclair off my road.

I watched as the vampire in question stepped out of the SUV.

"Leaving so soon?" he asked. I saw his arrogant smile, that cold, cocky thing I wanted to rip from his face and felt my temper growing. "A good host should never leave guests without at least a refreshment or hearing why they stopped by."

"Nice ride," I said, ignoring his attempt at an insult. "Looks familiar. Have I seen it around before?"

His arrogance turned angry, but the smile never left.

"Yes, I got the strangest report from one of my team. They say Mr. Alvarez...flipped the other. You wouldn't happen to know anything about that, would you?"

"I do, but I'm not entirely sure it's your business. You can afford a replacement, obviously. Or you can just bill me. I'll replace it. No worries." I grinned. "Nice visit, Sinclair. Now, Raphael and I are off to meet some friends."

"You do realize because he showed off his abilities in public, he can no longer hide behind the shield of humanity, correct?" Sinclair leaned on the hood of his car. "Meaning the ten-million-dollar bounty on his head is completely legal."

Yeah, I was really hoping that wouldn't come up.

"And? Maybe I want the ten million. It's not like you can kill me and take him. We both know that won't turn out well."

Raphael coughed from inside the car, leaning to look

out my window. He was glaring, but then, I had just said I might want the bounty on his head.

"I don't need to kill you, Kaliya," Sinclair reminded me. "I just need to take him."

"You can't even attack me," I snapped. "Don't pretend you can beat and torture me like you did Paden and walk away from it. I'm an employee of the Tribunal, and I'm allowed to use deadly force to protect myself. If any of you step to me, expect to fight to the death."

Sinclair's eyes flashed in rage.

"So be it."

"Raph, get out of the car," I yelled. "Now."

There was a fireball growing in the SUV as the doors opened.

CHAPTER FIFTEEN

I jumped away from the car as the witch threw the fire across my lot. I saw Raphael rolling out the side as a blaze erupted on contact where the fireball landed on the trunk, pieces flying inside the car and igniting the seats. Jumping back toward it, a gunshot went off over my head. I reached into the backseat and grabbed my bag, throwing it to the side before rolling to avoid more gunfire. Glancing up, I saw Sinclair waiting at the hood of the SUV, still smiling. The fae and witch were walking toward Raphael and me, another fireball growing in the witch's hand.

I needed a plan. Raphael needed to get that SUV out of our way. It would leave the assholes stranded if he did enough damage, which would give us time to get the fuck far away from them.

"Sinclair, don't be fucking stupid!" I called out. "You don't want to have this fight with me."

"Why not? You die here, I take the prize, and I never

have to deal with you ever again. No one will be able to prove I killed you."

He was right. If there were no witnesses and if the witch disposed of me with no evidence, then there was nothing anyone could do to stop him.

"And how do you know I won't kill you?" I asked, eyeing the two walking closer. Raphael was backing up toward the house, not the stupidest idea. I started walking backward, as well. If we baited them inside, it would be easy for me to kill at least one of them and get around behind them and get out.

"Because I don't think you're that skilled," he taunted. "Light them up."

The witch threw the second fireball, and I jumped out of the way, letting it scorch the dirt where I had been standing. Running for it, I looked back only to see the fae lift his assault rifle again and begin firing, this time in bursts.

"Go, Raph! Inside!" I roared. He turned and started at full speed as well, picking different entrances. He crashed through one of my windows, for which I couldn't blame him, and I went through the garage. Glass shattered, and I hissed.

"NOT THE ASTON MARTIN!" I roared. Someone laughed, and I really couldn't blame them. Every supernatural had their favorite toys and appreciated pretty things. The Aston Martin was mine.

"Apologies!" a man who I didn't recognize yelled out. I could hear the laughter in his voice. "It's a nice car!" More bullets rained into it, destroying the inside.

Shaking my head in disgust as I ducked inside, I didn't bother finding a weapon. In a magical second, I shifted into my snake form and went looking for Raphael. He was going to need me. Hopefully, he didn't try to kill me on sight like some people did.

I heard his breathing and could see his thermal readout under the door of the guest bedroom. Carefully, I reached up for the door handle and twisted around it until I heard the click of it opening. I had done this on numerous occasions, and it wasn't too difficult. I was also certain it could give Raphael a fright, so as it swung open slowly, I fell to the ground to dodge any gunshots. I heard other doors opening; the fae and the witch must have followed us in. Sinclair was probably going to wait outside. That didn't fit my plan, but I was certain once one of the assholes died, he would come running.

"Holy shit...Kaliya?" Raphael whispered, so quietly, I almost didn't hear him. I bobbed my head and made my way to him, wrapping myself around his leg and moving upward. "What the fuck are you doing?" he asked, hissing it at me in a way that damn impressed me. I thought I was the only good hisser on this side of the Mississippi.

I continued up, ignoring the ache in my fangs as I flicked my tongue, picking up his scent. Still too human. He needed to get angry and fast if he wanted a chance to win. Carefully, I moved around his chest and perched my head on his shoulder. He was tall, very tall. I was guessing he had to be six foot six. He gave me a high vantage point.

Since I couldn't speak, there was no way to tell him what I had planned.

Get moving, you damn whatever—you—are. We need to fight and get the hell out of here.

He didn't move, looking at me with wide eyes as if he was still trying to comprehend it was me. I moved to duck my head into the back of his shirt, hoping in the darkness, I would be hidden for as long as I needed to be.

"There you are!" someone said. I heard the footsteps of someone approaching. "Come quietly. Kaliya can't protect you, and she obviously isn't going to try. She's probably snaked off somewhere into a dark hole and won't come out until we're gone. She's notoriously scared of witches."

True and not true. This motherfucker knows way too much about me. Sinclair must have made sure they knew who they were dealing with because I've never seen them before.

"I'm not going anywhere. Mygi can't have me back."

"Mygi owns you," the witch sneered.

Bad choice of words, stupid.

Beneath me, Raphael's body heated up, and it felt comforting. I wanted to curl around him like a damn rock like Naksha did all the time.

"No one owns me," he snarled.

Ah yeah, dumbass pissed him off. Good.

"You're a piece of property with no more worth than any other human. They just made you a little special, but it doesn't change what you are. They made you, they own you. Like any other animal in a lab."

Raphael's snarl made me shake. I felt him move, and there was a lot of banging. I moved around him as he connected with the witch. Gunshots caught my attention. They must have caught Raphael's because he jumped back. Before he could get too far away from my target, I struck, coming out from his sleeve and nailing the witch on the arm.

"FUCK!" the man screamed, trying to bat me away as I pushed every bit of venom I had. Just enough to kill one man. It was all I needed.

He whacked me on the head, and I released, knowing my duty was done. Before the fae could retaliate, I shifted back into my human form and reached for his weapon. He and I glared at each other as he pulled the trigger, firing shots past my ribs. One grazed, and I hissed in pain and annoyance. Fighting dirty, I sent my right knee up and got him in the sweet spot. His grip loosened, but something knocked into me before I could pull the weapon away. Looking over my shoulder, I saw the witch stumbling around, his eyes wide as they started to bleed from their tear ducts.

"Yeah, it sucks, doesn't it?" I hissed softly. I yanked the assault rifle hard from the fae, not caring to see what kind it was. It didn't honestly matter. When I pulled the trigger, though, I cursed as I realized it was empty.

The fae recovered and jumped into action, tackling me to the ground. Something began to glow, and I felt what should have been a rope grab one of my ankles and yank it to the ground.

Shit, light binding. Of course. I don't have any fucking iron on me.

"Sinclair! She got Jeremy!"

"Damn it!"

Sinclair sounded much closer than I expected.

"Raphael! The plan!" I roared, trying to hold off the fae from hitting me in the face. He got a binding on one of my wrists, and it was pulled away, but my free hand managed to work at keeping his blows from hitting me.

I didn't know where the idiot had gone.

"Don't worry about Raphael," Sinclair said. I paused for just a moment too long, and the fae was able to land a solid hit to the left side of my jaw. He pulled back, wrapped a hand around my neck, and twisted my face to see something. Bindings grabbed my other wrist and ankle, yanking all my limbs down to the floor. Sinclair held a gun to the back of Raphael's head. "While you were having fun, I just followed him. It wasn't hard. Seriously, Kaliya. You know I like to take the most direct route to what I want."

I did. The broken fucking window that Raphael had used would have been easy for Sinclair to get in. Why hadn't I thought of it?

Raphael's eyes were blood red, and the black on his face was spreading, growing past what I had seen before, but he didn't move. I was tentatively certain he knew he couldn't move before Sinclair fired one into the back of his skull. Whether that would be fatal, I didn't know.

"Ok. You've got him," I said, trying to sound defeated. "You can go now."

"No, Kaliya, I think this is the last time I'm going to deal with you. I'm quite tired of this." He nodded at his fae, who pulled a handgun from a holster at his waist. As he pulled it up, I took a deep breath.

Right as he pulled the trigger, aimed at my forehead, I shifted out of the bindings and moved to dry bite him. I had nothing to inject, but going into a strike was the easiest way for me to get those lightning fast reflexes.

I shifted back into my human form and kicked the fae away from me. It felt like everyone else was going in slow motion as I darted into the room. Sinclair moved back from Raphael, looking down at me. I tackled the vampire, and we rolled painfully across the wood floor.

"GO!" I screamed.

The sound of crunching glass as I struggled with Sinclair was all I heard as he tried to get his hands around my neck.

"GO GET HIM!" Sinclair roared at his fae before looking back down at me. "I can sell your body for a pretty fucking price, nagini," he growled. "That can make up for the shit you've caused me this time."

I hissed, my fangs down. I reached up and ran my nails across his face, making him scream. Outside, there was gunfire and creaking metal. I was certain Raphael was lifting something.

Sinclair didn't let go, and I was beginning to have a hard time breathing. I didn't shift because I would be vulnerable. Sinclair knew that trick and would have an answer for it. Probably keep his hands around me and beat me against a wall. The fae would have realized the bite was dry by now because he wasn't dying. Sinclair would probably know it too.

I reached up to claw at Sinclair's face again and realized I had learned this nice piece of self-defense when I was eight. With both hands, I slammed Sinclair on both sides of his head, right over his ears. He screamed and pulled away now, trying to cover his head. Something crashed outside. I didn't bother trying to kill Sinclair—we couldn't win this fight. As more guns went off, the thought resounded that I needed to find Raphael. One hit me in the shoulder, making me stagger. Looking over my shoulder as I ran down my hall, I saw Sinclair there, holding up the fae's handgun.

I shifted this time, knowing my snake form was harder to hit, and made it to the garage before he could catch up. Shifting back, I grabbed the Aston Martin's keys from their hook and jumped in, trying to ignore the damage. The key was still able to turn it on, even though the sound was garbled from the speakers, and none of the electronics on the dash worked.

I went into reverse and pulled out as Sinclair staggered into the garage, the gun up. I ducked below the dash with my foot on the gas as he fired.

"RAPHAEL!" I screamed, twisting the wheel as I forced the car into drive. My BMW, I noticed, was not where I had left it, now twenty feet away, crushing the fae's leg.

Raphael was near the SUV, the black veins going down his neck for the first time since I met him. With ease, I watched him shove the SUV off the road. Sinclair wasn't firing anymore, but I wasn't sure if it was because he was shocked or had run out of bullets.

I didn't come to a complete stop, forcing Raphael to practically jump into the car. The moment he was seated, I slammed on the gas, the momentum slamming the door shut.

"Hold on," I ordered, not bothering with headlights. I knew my road well enough, and adrenaline pumped through my veins. Unlike some people, I was so used to the feeling that it didn't make me shaky. It gave me clarity, a sharpness that many couldn't achieve. I was probably able to drive this road blindfolded. There was a time when I used to do timed runs of it, making sure I knew it in case I needed to make an escape.

Of course, if I needed to make an escape, and I didn't have Raphael, it wouldn't have been the madhouse it was. I would have gone into my snake form and let them search for me until I could sneak into my car and drive off.

Headlights blinded me near the end. I squinted and hit the gas harder.

"I knew I should have flipped it," Raphael snarled. "Of course, it could handle the terrain."

"Too late to worry about it now," I hissed, turning hard onto the main road. "We can lose them."

"Where are we going?" he asked as our speed climbed, and the headlights became more distant.

"I have an idea," I answered. "Did you grab any of our things?" I asked.

"No, it all got left," he answered. "Sorry."

"It's fine. If they're following and trying to find us, they might not go back to steal everything I own." I sighed. "It's going to be a pain in the ass getting a new phone set up."

"That's what you're fucking worried about? A new goddamn phone?"

I gave him a level look.

"Yes." I thought about it for a second. "And Naksha. She doesn't deserve to get hurt, but she's safer where she is than getting dragged around by us."

"A phone and a snake," he muttered. "Your priorities…"

"Are just fine, fuck you very much," I retorted, turning off my street and hitting a main road. We had left the SUV lights behind, but I kept up the speed. I knew where to go, even though I was pretty sure the owner of the place was going to hate me for it.

Cassius will understand. He has to.

16

CHAPTER SIXTEEN

I pulled into one of the nicest neighborhoods in Phoenix, La Place Du Sommet.

"Where the hell..." Raphael's voice was an exact match for mine the first time I had driven through.

"Yeah, I have a friend who lives here. His house is as secure as mine, if not more, because he has a bit of magic on his side. We should be safe here."

"How..."

"We live a long time and amass a lot of wealth," I said softly, looking out my window to see the insane, mountain vista homes worth millions, built directly into the cliffs. I turned back to him, trying to keep things casual. "I love living out of the city, but I could afford a house here."

His head whipped around to me so fast, I was certain my neck would have broken if I had done it.

"You have this kind of money?"

"Yeah. A lot of it's inherited, but a solid portion is

from my own work. I don't need a house like these, though. Not worth it, too much to clean. My friend has a three-person staff. They'll be able to get ahold of him when we show up."

"Will they let us in?" He looked me over, then himself. When I narrowed my eyes on him, he gestured to the destroyed car we were in.

"Good point," I conceded with a sigh. "Yeah, they'll let us in and be nice about it. You'll confuse the fuck out of them, but they know me really well."

"That's good," he said softly. "You have a lot of friends?"

"Very few," I answered. "Three off the top of my head, and one of them is more complicated than a friendship really has the right to be."

My fault for fucking him, but Cassius is gorgeous. He doesn't have Raphael's realness, though. Or the big, killer body.

What the fuck is wrong with me?

I wanted to hit my head on a wall to knock the thoughts out. Now wasn't the time or place to be comparing an ex-lover with...Raphael, who wasn't a lover at all, and if I had my way, never would be.

I barely fucking know the man. Gods, if Adhar knew I was even remotely attracted to him, I would never hear the end of it.

I pulled into Cassius' driveway and sighed as I waited for a gate halfway up to open.

"I hate this," I mumbled as it opened. "Hate being

here. Hate this fucking mess. Hate Sinclair. Hate being the last nagini."

I wasn't paying attention, just talking to myself, so when Raphael coughed in surprise, I wanted to curse.

"The last?" he asked.

"Yeah. Story for another time," I said softly. "Sorry. I'm not used to people being in the car with me and I talk to myself sometimes."

"Okay." He dropped it quickly and looked away from me.

I eased through the gate when it was open enough. The magic of the gate had to recognize me, which always took a moment for anyone except Cassius. If he was in the car, it started to open before he was even close to it. He was the one who had made the fae spell, though.

I didn't pull into his garage, parking my car in the drive at the front door. His Phoenix area butler, Leith, was already there, looking at my car in barely disguised shock.

"Madam Sahni," he said, not quite covering up the shock in his voice as I got out of the car and waved at him. I was pretty certain there was glass and shit in my hair, but I hadn't had time to worry about that an hour and a half ago when I raced away from my own house. "We weren't expecting you."

"Are you expecting anyone?" I asked, genuinely curious to see if Cassius was about to arrive, or if it was just me they were shocked by.

"No, madam. Lord Cassius hasn't contacted us—"

"Lord?" Raphael sputtered as he got out of the car as

well. "You don't have many friends, but one of them is a Lord?" He was looking at me, not the butler, thank the gods. His eyes were still red, which would scare the poor man at the top of the stairs, waiting at the door.

"His parents were a lot more important than him, and his uncle is very important. He's a Tribunal Investigator with a little more money than the rest of us. Calm down. You're showing." I motioned to my own eyes, hoping he understood. He took a deep breath, closing his eyes. It was like he was trying to meditate. When his eyes opened again, they were warm brown again. Looking above him at the butler, I gestured at my car. "As you can see, Leith, there's been a bit of trouble."

"Why don't both of you come inside?" Leith's face twitched a little, and I wasn't sure if it was because of the state of us or my using his name. He preferred just being called Butler, but I was never going to do that. It felt strangely degrading and impersonal. Leith made him a living thing, a normal thing, a guy who just worked in the household—him and one maid, little miss Annie-Lyn. The cook, a cranky werewolf named Terry, only came in when Cassius was in residence.

I nodded, jumping up the steps in silence, letting Raphael decide whether he wanted to come in or not. The smart man decided he would and followed once I was at the top of the stairs. Leith held the door until we were both in, and I didn't miss that he locked it the moment Raphael passed the threshold.

"You didn't call ahead," he said immediately. "Madam Sahni—"

"Sinclair and a couple of his friends attacked my house looking for this one," I explained, gesturing to Raphael. "Wasn't able to grab any of my shit before leaving. We weren't in the best position and had to get out."

Something flashed in Leith's eyes.

"The vampire, Sinclair, is in Arizona?" he asked softly. "Does Lord Cassius know?"

"I called him...yesterday morning before daybreak and explained everything to him. I think. The timeline is a little fuzzy right now, but he definitely knows. Hasn't been twenty-four hours since I told him."

"Good. I take it by not having your 'shit,' you don't have a cellphone on you. No worry, I can have a line set up, and you can call Lord Cassius from the kitchen while I make you something. Tea...yes, tea is good."

There was a reason I called Leith by his name. He had his own history with Sinclair. He, Annie-Lyn, and Terry were all once Las Vegas residents. Thirty years ago, Cassius and I had tangled with Sinclair, and Cassius had ended up taking both fae and the werewolf with him and brought them here. They were still in an environment they liked, the desert, but they were far away from Sinclair—until now.

"I'm sorry," I whispered, reaching for Leith. "I'm positive he won't come here—"

"Vampires aren't allowed on the premises," Leith said, anger in his voice. "If he's foolish enough to try to attack here, he will burn the moment he tries to cross the property line."

"Good," I said, patting the butler's shoulder.

"Tea," he snapped, then marched away. I grabbed Raphael's shirt and shuffled after the man, knowing if I told him no thanks, Leith would just try to pour it down my throat.

"Are you okay with me leaving my car out there?" I asked.

"Yes. Lord Cassius will want to see it, and there's no space in the garage currently. His...new fiancée likes nice things, especially cars, and we're running out of space between his properties to put them all." Leith sighed. "I always hated you and him, but she's a spoiled fae Lady. I don't know what he sees in her."

"Everything that isn't me, probably," I answered, chuckling. "And you know it."

Raphael stiffened behind me, a confusing reaction.

"This guy used to be a boyfriend?"

I turned slowly and tilted my head back. I wasn't short, five ten, but Raphael was a giant.

"Is that a problem?" I asked in disbelief.

"Just a little weird that you would run to an ex-boyfriend's place with everything going on."

"Well, he was never my boyfriend," I said carefully. "We worked together, didn't like each other, and had great sex. There's a difference."

"Madam Sahni doesn't have relationships the way most people do," Leith said as he put the kettle on the stove. "She's an acquired taste, and it takes a strong personality to put up with her. Lord Cassius can only tolerate her so much, which is why this is not his permanent residence."

"Wow," I whispered, looking back at the butler. "Let's just...not ever say any of that ever again, please."

Leith had the balls to chuckle.

"I'm beginning to come to the same conclusion," Raphael muttered behind me. He made the smart decision of stepping away from me as I whirled back on him. He continued moving away to sit on a stool at the breakfast counter. I dropped my fangs and hissed at him.

"Here you go," Leith said suddenly. A phone appeared on the counter. Grabbing it, I called Cassius. I didn't have time for the verbal foreplay. I just needed Cassius to pick up the damn phone and get his ass to Phoenix. Then I could reengage in battle with the cunning ass butler and the idiot not-human.

"Leith—"

"Not Leith," I snapped. "You fucking prick, you should have called me back fucking hours ago. What the hell?"

"Oh, dear gods, you're at my house," he muttered. "What happened?"

"Sinclair and his lackeys showed up at my fucking house, that's what fucking happened. They're playing fucking hardball. Sinclair is now on the kill list."

"Kaliya—"

"He tried to fucking kill me, Cassius. He said, and I fucking quote, 'I think this is the last time I'm going to deal with you,' then had one of his fucking goons try to shoot me in the fucking head. I have a witness."

"Okay, okay, calm down, please," he said gently. I knew the tone. It was the tone he used when we fought. It only pissed me off more.

"Why didn't you call me back?" I demanded.

"I was kind of busy, explaining to our bosses why I needed to open a case against one of the biggest supernatural companies in the world. You do realize that Mygi is considered one of the more respectable supernatural businesses—"

"They put a bounty out on a human! How respectable can they fucking be?"

"He's not human, though," Cassius reminded me. "They called in the CEO of Mygi about it. He's not human, wasn't human when they initially captured him after he killed a bunch of humans, and he wasn't human when he escaped. They consider him a danger to the public, and the Tribunal is inclined to agree. It's not looking good for him or you, Kaliya."

I was speechless for a moment, looking up at Raphael, my heart pounding. What Cassius was saying... was the perfect fucking spin Mygi had needed. They had known they could get caught. They had a backup plan.

"He's...he's not..." I tried to form something. "Cassius..."

"There was a small vote," he said quietly. "And your case barely won."

"Who was the swing?" I asked.

"Hasan," he said with a sigh. "The werecat is back for good, it seems, and it looks like we're going to see him a lot. It's thrown the entire Tribunal out of whack. They had gotten used to life without him."

"He was gone for a hundred years," I said, licking my lips. "Did the Mygi CEO have an explanation why they marked Raphael as human on the bounty?"

"They noticed the same thing you did. He presents as human in smell until he's...not human anymore and has his abilities, then he goes back to human. They figured it would be the easiest way for people to track him down since they don't know what he is either."

"They experimented on him for five years, and they don't know?" I didn't believe that for a damn second.

"We couldn't put him under oath, so there's a chance he was lying. It was all done via video conference, so who knows?"

"The Tribunal really trusts this guy that much?"

"Kaliya, he's a half-brother to the fae King and a Tribunal member," Cassius said in a hushed, angry whisper. "It's not about trust, it's about implicating the most powerful fae's family in something devious. None of them were going to press the issue of an oath and risk offending—"

"Either of your uncles," I finished. It wasn't what Cassius intended to say, but it was the truth. "You're also related to the Mygi CEO. He's also a fae Clan founder if he's a half-brother to the King and has like two dozen fucking half siblings. Does this one really matter more than the others?" Fae families were fucking complicated.

"I've never met him before," he snapped. "I'm on

your side, but I have to stick my neck out on this. They know you're uncontrollable, but I have a reputation."

"Are you flying in or not?" I asked, tired suddenly. "Why do you keep your house so damn cold?"

"I'm used to the north," he answered softly. "And it makes you relax, which I don't think you do often enough."

Something about that was very sweet. It annoyed the hell out of me, but it was very sweet.

"And here I thought we hated each other," I mumbled.

"Oh, I do hate you most of the time, but there's a certain charm to you as well," he said with a chuckle I despised—husky and romantic. Fae could be pretty things, perfect things, depending on the type of fae. Cassius knew what he was doing. He was trying to sweeten me up, so there wasn't any more bitchiness over the phone. He was playing me, and I was allowing it. "I also bet you're coming down from adrenaline."

"Most likely," I said softly, leaning onto the counter. "Get here, Cassius. I'll talk to one of the bosses about tonight's developments and get Sinclair officially on the kill list. Who's the best choice?"

"The obvious choices would be Callahan or Corissa. Being werewolves, they both hate him. Alvina, the current fae Queen, is an easy choice as well because she's never much cared for any of her half siblings. Don't go to my uncle. He doesn't want to hear from you since you're trying to go after a half-brother he likes. I wouldn't recommend the vampires either. Mygi is making progress on the synthetic blood project, and the vampires don't want to see the company under any sort of fire until it's done. You know the politics. If you didn't hate them so much, you could also try the witches, who could probably be swayed in your favor." Cassius gave a thoughtful hum. "You can also get Hasan. Have you ever spoken to him before?"

"No, he went on his sabbatical before I got the job," I answered, yawning. "Fuck. Leith, turn up the heat. Please."

"Of course, Madam Sahni," the butler replied as he put a cup of tea in front of me.

"Well, Hasan is...well, he's enigmatic. He's the oldest member of the Tribunal by far, so don't toy with him."

"He's a werecat. I'm not stupid enough to consider toying with him," I snapped. "What do you take me for?"

"Do you really want to know?" he asked dryly.

"Ah, the sweetness has ended already."

"Yeah, it's hard to keep up that act with you sometimes," he said. "Kaliya, why don't you just write a report and send it to all of them? That way, it goes live, and they can all bicker about it."

"That's an amazing idea...and it would keep me from having to call any of them."

"Exactly, which means you won't, as the humans say, shove your foot in your mouth."

"Yes. I'll do that while you're flying here. *Right?*"

"I'm standing over my suitcase." He didn't sound excited. "I'll talk to you when I get off the plane. Stay with your charge in my home until I arrive. Don't go out looking for trouble."

"I won't," I promised. I had no intention of going anywhere until I had some real backup. "Before you go... Sinclair had his people torture Paden. That's how he found out where I lived. Just thought you should know. I'll have Leith call in the rest of your staff here for safety. Once Sinclair knows you're coming into town, he'll target them if he thinks he can get his way."

"Thank you for letting me know." Cassius sounded genuinely grateful. "Talk to you soon."

"Yup." I hung up and sighed, exhaustion and relief threatening to pull me into sleep right there, standing up at the counter. "He's on his way. Leith, did you hear what I said?"

"Madam Sahni, I had already contacted both of them to come in and be ready to stay awhile. Don't worry. They'll be here and safe shortly." Leith patted her shoulder. "Drink your tea and rest. I'm going to make something for Mister Alvarez to eat."

"How..." I looked between the fae and the not-human.

"We had an entire conversation while you were on the phone with Cassius," Raphael said.

Should have figured.

"Well, I'm going up to my room. I still have a room, right? It's not been taken over by whatever her name is?"

"Cassius has made it very clear, you are to always have a safe room in this house," Leith explained. "Don't worry, it's just as you left it, except cleaner. There's also a spare laptop in there because one never knows what you might need when you visit."

"Thank you." I ignored every slight jab. That was normal with Leith, Cassius too. It was normal for the entire household.

Tired, I left them there. When I got into my room, I opened the laptop and wrote a short but sweet report about the evening, then sent it. I went into the private bathroom, showered, and removed all the foreign bodies from my hair. I ignored the bruises blossoming all over my body and only checked if there were any injuries that needed medical attention.

Then I promptly fell onto the bed and passed out, unable to make it much further.

17

CHAPTER SEVENTEEN

I woke up to someone opening my door. It took me more than a few uncomfortable moments to remember where I was as I hissed at the intruder, who stopped moving.

"I'm not foolish enough to wake you up," Cassius said softly. "I wanted to let you know I was here."

Blinking several times, I cleared my vision, and he came into focus. The lights were on. Had I left them on when I fell onto the bed?

"Hey," I said softly. The last time he and I had seen each other in person had been the last time we were together. "So...sorry about crashing at your place. I know I promised it wouldn't happen again."

"My door is always open to a colleague needing shelter," he said professionally.

"Is that the story you tell her?" I asked, raising an eyebrow.

"Considering I have no intention of sleeping with you, it's the truth," he fired back. "She knows you and I used to..."

"Yeah, this is just incredibly weird," I mumbled, swinging my legs off the bed. "Did I leave any spare clothes here?"

"Yes." He pointed at the dresser. My naked body wasn't what made this awkward. It was everything he and I had left unsaid. He must have realized it because he sighed. "Kaliya, there's no reason for this to be strange—"

"Yeah, you left in the middle of the night and never came back, only leaving a note explaining how you thought it was time to end the toxic relationship we had," I said, pulling open a dresser drawer to find none of the clothes were actually mine. He had made sure there were things in his house for me, for situations like this. "No reason to be strange at all," I said as I pulled out a t-shirt, then opened the second drawer—pants, all black leather, all supple and well made. I knew they would fit me like a second skin and still be flexible enough for me to move in. Cassius did nothing if he couldn't do it perfectly.

"You know I was right. Tell me, if I had stayed, would we have fought, then proceeded to get back into bed?"

Probably. But then you refused to come to Phoenix for three years until this.

"That's not the point. Let's just forget it, okay? We're working." With a sigh, I opened the last drawer and found the intimates. I grabbed a sports bra and the most comfortable looking underwear I could find. Thankfully, Cassius hadn't made things awkward by putting in a bunch of lingerie. "I knew it would never last, but it stung," I admitted as I started pulling on the clothing. "The way you did it."

"I know," he whispered. "I just didn't know how else to do it."

"Me neither," I said, my fingers rubbing a soft black shirt. "So, friends now, huh?"

"I would like to attempt a friendship, yes," he said, nodding. "I miss coming to this city. I miss Leith and the rest of the staff here. I want you to meet my fiancée. I think you might like her company."

"That's the stupidest idea I've ever heard." I snorted, shaking my head.

"She already knows. She knew before she and I got together. She was the first person I told when you called me the first time, and she was the first person I told I was leaving to come here to help you."

"She trusts you like that?"

Cassius laughed softly. "She trusts me. As she said, I gave her the ring. My commitment is clear."

"Thank God you gave it to her," I said with a laugh. "I know you're right, Cassius. I've known for three years it wouldn't work, and when you aren't around, it doesn't sting. I think it's just strange, being here, seeing you again, and having Raphael..." I trailed off. I didn't know whether I should tell Cassius about him yet. At the thought of the not-human, my fangs ached. I worked my jaw, trying to ease it, trying to get everything to stop hurting for just a moment.

"Have you milked recently?" he asked. Normally,

when I had fang pain, it was because I needed to milk the venom.

"Two nights ago," I answered. "Right after I got Raphael back to my house. Thirty-six hours ago? Something like that? Used the rest of my supply to kill Sinclair's witch."

Cassius paled. "You killed one of them?"

"He was under orders to invade my home and take something that belonged to me," I explained. "Damn right, I killed him. I'm a naga. Anyone who comes on my property against my wishes can and will be met with deadly force. It's the law."

"I mean...you killed one of them with your venom? That must have been gruesome."

"It was the first time Raphael got to see it in action. By the way, have you met him yet?"

"No. I just got in and decided to come see you to make sure you were okay," he said, leaning on the door frame. "Everyone is asleep except us and Leith."

"When you meet him, I want to know how you feel about him. His powers seem to be emotionally driven. He gets angry, and they present themselves. I don't know if other strong emotions can bring them on, but I think fear can as well." Frowning, I finished putting on my clothes. "Thanks for these."

"It's no problem."

"Why did you leave all this here?"

"Because I figured one day, you would need a place to hide," he said softly. "Because it's you, and you can't stay out of trouble."

"You realize it's not just me, right? I don't ask for some of the shit I get involved in."

"Yes, but if I said I left this here to give the last nagini a place to hide from poachers, you would be insulted I only think of you as the last breeding female of your kind."

He has a point.

"Well, thanks. You hungry? I need a snack."

"Leith is already making something," he said, still leaning on the doorway.

"Why am I cornered here, then?" I gestured at him. He hadn't moved. He was blocking the path, and he knew it. He knew that I knew it.

"I wanted to make sure you knew what's at stake with this. Kaliya, if this goes the wrong way, we could both lose our jobs."

"You can back out any time." I didn't much care about that. I was an Executioner because I needed more legal leeway to kill people, but being the last nagini, I had a large berth to do as I pleased, anyway. Losing my job was just losing an income and political power. I was still protected by several Laws that other supernatural species didn't have the right to. It meant I couldn't be an aggressor anymore, though. Any work I did to catch and punish the criminals I was after would be illegal. I would no longer be a sanctioned killer for the Tribunal. Dishing out justice would no longer be my right.

"So can you," he pointed out.

"No, I can't," I retorted. "This is more than Sinclair. Hell, it might be more than Mygi."

That caught his attention, and his ethereal light blue eyes narrowed. His perfectly styled hair bled to its original color, red. He normally used a glamor to make it more natural—the red he had wasn't natural at all. It was like someone had tried to dye his hair with red ink. His glamor normally only slipped when he was spooked or angry.

"If you say this has anything to do with that fucking board of yours, so help me—"

"I thought it might, but it's not. That's what got me dragged in. Some small connection I just had to check out. Then Sinclair showed up, and it's all spiraled out of control. The problem is, I...I feel for the guy. His situation sucks, and if there's anyone who knows how bad things can get in our world, it's me and my kind."

"I see," he whispered. "Well. At least I'm the nephew to a king. If I lose my job, I'll have the resources to continue my lifestyle for my fiancée."

"Does she have money?" I asked. "Not normal money but *money*."

"No," he said, looking away from me. "No, she doesn't have old family money. Everything she has, she's worked for."

"Oh, so she's..."

"Her title was bought and paid for, something my uncle hates, but it's not his life."

"Your father would have loved it," I said gently, seeing the pain in Cassius' eyes right after I said the word 'father.'

"My father isn't around, so his opinion doesn't matter." Cassius backed out of the door, freeing me from the little cage of a bedroom. "Let's find you something to eat."

I felt bad. I knew better than to mention his father. I was there, along with every Executioner and Investigator, every guard, and every Tribunal member, the day it was announced by Cassius' uncle that the Fae King had walked away from his family, his throne, and his spot on the Tribunal. Cassius was expected to rule, to lead, but he turned his back on the duties his father had unfairly and suddenly left for him. It led to Cassius' uncle, a fae named Oisin, to take the position. It was still a fresh, open wound as well. Not even a century had passed, and no one knew where the previous Fae King had run off to.

I wondered for a moment if Cassius ever tried to contact Oberon, his grandfather. If anyone could find the wayward one, it would be the Old Fae, the first King and his Queen.

Not my business and he would kick me out for asking. I need his help, so I'll put my curiosity in a box and pretend I wasn't thinking about it.

Walking into the kitchen together, Cassius took his seat at the breakfast counter. I checked the time on the fancy clock above the door and saw it was only noon.

"What's the plan?" he asked as Leith quietly put a plate in front of him. The butler placed a plate in front of me next. I started nibbling on the chips, considering Cassius' question.

"I need to get back to my house tonight. Before you say that's a terrible idea, because I know it is, just know I have an Indian cobra under my care right now. I don't have my cell phone or any of my things. I need to see the damage and if they've stolen anything."

"I can agree that it's vital, even though it is a terrible idea," Cassius conceded. "We can make the trip tonight, but I want to bring this Raphael along. I'm not leaving him alone with people in my care."

"Of course. We're taking one of your rides, though. Did you see my poor Aston Martin?"

"I saw. Do you need help replacing it? I'm certain the Tribunal will shell out to replace a cellphone."

"They'll owe me two cars, too, once I finish my report and send in my expenses. I don't need their help with that. I just want to be petty. Sinclair wouldn't be a problem if they had let me kill him twenty-five years ago when I literally had him in my hands."

"Oh, joy. I have to be friends with the only Executioner who likes sticking the middle finger up to our bosses," he mumbled, taking a bite of his sandwich.

"Not the only one, just the best at it," I retorted. Most of the Executioners had something wrong with them. The Tribunal was smart. Their Executioners were mean, deadly, and pissed off most of the time. Morally grey at the best of times unless being a good guy suited our self interests. I didn't know a single Executioner who didn't take the job for more than one reason. It allowed us to kill in a world where kill or be killed was the Law we lived by. Being sanctioned saved a lot of trouble.

"Point made," he said when his mouth wasn't full. "Narumi is much more cunning and underhanded about it."

"Narumi is cold," I said with a chuckle. "Damn kitsune. We were at the Jacky Leon trial together, you know. She pretended to be a guard to keep an eye on the werecat. The little fox was ready to stab that cat in the back at a moment's notice."

"I heard. When do you want to leave for your home?"

"The moment Raphael wakes up and eats. He's a black hole, that one. Apparently, his abilities burn up a lot of calories, and he constantly needs to replenish them."

Cassius gave a very undignified grunt and continued to eat. I nibbled on the chips, knowing the sandwich was probably too much food. I got sluggish when I ate too much too often. The curse of my human-looking body also trying to be a snake.

Not ten minutes later, Raphael wandered into the kitchen, wearing only a pair of sweatpants. Cassius jerked upright and stared at him. I knew Cassius well enough to know my once lover was surprised and maybe even a little insulted by Raphael. He turned slowly to me as Leith put two sandwiches and the entire bag of chips in front of the not-human. His eyebrows furrowed as he stared at me, his eyes telling me everything he wanted to say.

"Do you think we can stop somewhere and get him more clothes?" I asked lightly. "We had to leave his place in a rush after he tried to shoot me, then the rest of his things were left in my driveway."

Cassius took a noticeably deep breath, stood up slowly, and grabbed my arm as he walked past. I let him pull me out of the kitchen, Raphael giving us a confused look.

Once we were out of earshot, Cassius let me go.

"You didn't tell me..." He was glaring, but I hadn't really figured out what his problem was yet. "He's..."

"Huge? Six and a half feet tall and all muscle? Not wearing nearly enough clothing as he should be? Yeah, that's Raphael. Why don't you go back in there and meet him?"

"The scars?" Cassius asked softly.

"He heals amazingly. The one around his wrist is where Mygi had cut his hand off then bandaged it back to him, and it healed back on by itself. The gunshots are from the several times Mygi had already tried to recapture him. They say he's a danger to society? He's been living out there on his own for five years without any incident that clued the rest of us to his existence."

"He couldn't wear a dirty shirt to cover himself up?" Cassius asked, exasperated. "I have traumatized employees."

"Sorry. I'm sure he'll agree if you let him know."

I stepped around him to head back into the kitchen. Raphael was holding one of his sandwiches up but put it down the moment he saw Cassius hovering behind me.

"Have I done something?" He jumped up from the stool, extending a hand toward us. I moved out of the way for Cassius to do the 'man' thing. "I should have introduced myself, but Leith put down food, and my mind went straight to that. I'm Raphael."

"Cassius," my friend said softly. "I don't want to give you a hard time, Raphael, but I want to bring something up. First, I needed to ask Kaliya some questions about you, so I knew if I was stepping on toes. All my staff here are victims of abusive employers and relationships. While I'm sure you mean nothing by it, I would prefer if you covered up, so none of them are...intimidated or scared by you."

"Yeah, I can do that. My bad." I noticed the red flash in Raphael's eyes but wasn't sure what the catalyst was, Cassius or the idea the household staff were all traumatized people who Cassius provided a safe, relaxed workspace for. Raphael turned to Leith and frowned. "I hope I didn't cause any trouble for you, Leith."

Leith waved a rag, dismissing the idea before leaving the room, probably to find Raphael a shirt that would fit. I knew Leith was strong enough, but Cassius wasn't worried about Leith. He was worried about his cook and the maid, both of whom were much less fit for the public eye. Both of whom had once been in the care of men who looked like Raphael in a sense, big scarred men known for fights and being brutal and cruel. Raphael could trigger them, could very easily terrify them if he got pissed off. Thinking about it, I hadn't even seen Annie-Lyn or Terry yet. He would have told them to let him meet Raphael before they had to.

"Now, Kaliya would like to go check out her home

during the day while it's safe from Sinclair. I agree with her. Obviously, you both will use this home as the base of operations for your safety until we feel the situation is resolved."

Leith walked back in while he was talking and handed a black tank top to the giant. It was a little too small, but it would work. I tried not to stare at the broad planes of his chest in the incredibly tight tank top. He dwarfed Cassius, which was impressive. I never thought the six-foot-tall fae was short, but standing near Raphael, he was.

"And I must agree with her, you can't wear this all the time. I know where we can get clothing that will fit you before nightfall. Kaliya, are there any other stops you want to make?" Cassius turned back to me, crossing his arms, waiting on my answer.

"The Market," I answered. "If anything I need was stolen or destroyed at my place."

Cassius groaned.

"What's the market?" Raphael asked, looking between them.

"The fae black market," Cassius explained. "Kaliya, you know I can't be caught there. You can get away with it, but..."

"I'm not asking you to come in. You'll stay with Raphael in the car. It's just in case."

"Fine." Cassius straightened his jacket. "I'm ready to leave when you are. We'll get Raphael what he needs first, so he doesn't stick out, then we'll go to your home. If it's needed, I'll drop you off and wait near The Market."

BOUNTY

"Thank you," I said graciously.

I left them in the kitchen to work things out so I could finish getting ready. I had to find some shoes.

18

CHAPTER EIGHTEEN

I groaned as Cassius stopped in front of probably my least favorite place in Phoenix. He didn't say anything as he cut the engine, twisting to look at Raphael in the back seat.

"This place is run by fae. They come from all over the world. They will do magic on you, so if you have a problem with that, say so now."

"Why will they do magic on me?" Raphael sounded concerned and confused. The concern, I understood. This was a terrible place.

"They have a large variety of premade garments, but those garments need to be spelled to fit you perfectly. Ask Kaliya how good they are. The pants she's wearing were done by them."

"Oh fuck," I muttered. I turned and looked back at the massive man, somehow crammed into the backseat. "They're fine. The magic is whatever, but they can be pushy about what looks good on you and shit. Don't let them rope you into any crazy ass suits or anything. They'll try. Get what you need to last a week and get out."

"And the magic doesn't...track me or anything?"

"No, it's a one-and-done spell. It just ensures it always fits the intended wearer," I explained. "You being the intended wearer. If you lend out a shirt you get from them, it'll match your size at all times, not someone else's. But they have to make a spell with you keyed into it."

Cassius nodded, then gave me a look as Raphael got out of the car.

"He might want a suit, Kaliya."

"I don't want him in a suit," I said, annoyed. Gods, he would look fucking amazing in one. My fangs pulsed painfully at the idea. "And I was right. The last time I was here, about six years ago, they were trying to get me into a sari. Me. A sari."

"India is your native country, and I know for a fact you look stunning in one," Cassius pointed out plainly as if he hadn't just complimented me and said I was pretty in a dress.

"I don't like them."

"You don't like anything," he pointed out. "Ah, hold on." He got out of the car and met the owner of the boutique at the door, nodding as he pointed at Raphael, standing just behind the owner. The owner nodded a lot, a smile growing. Her devious look toward me in the front seat of Cassius' car scared me.

When Cassius sat back down, he smiled evilly.

"What did you do?" I demanded.

"Nothing. I'm allowed to spend my money as I please."

"Oh, I fucking hate you," I hissed across the car.

"I know." He drummed his fingers on the steering wheel. "I asked them to get Raphael a suit. If he's going to be in the supernatural world, he needs to be more presentable than...well, you."

"I'm completely presentable," I snapped. "I know how to dress myself."

"And yet, all you own is leather pants and black tops," he pointed out. "And let's not talk about those steel toed, hideous combat boots you wear."

"You used to fuck me," I reminded him. "So, something must be working."

"Tequila."

"Wow." I slumped in my seat. Deciding the topic needed to change, I watched the dark windows of the boutique and thought of the man we had just sent inside. "What do you think of Raphael so far?"

"He hasn't spoken much, but he seems like a good man. I could feel how real his apology was in my kitchen. He felt bad."

"His eyes, did you catch those?"

"It was hard to miss when I was staring right at them," he said with a touch of annoyance. "It wasn't unexpected; you already warned me about some things, Kaliya."

"Yeah..."

"You seem intrigued. I don't think I've ever heard you talk so much about anyone unless you were planning to kill them," he pointed out, leaning on his door. "Are you?"

"Am I what?"

"Planning on killing him," Cassius asked as if it was an everyday question that bore no more thought than asking if someone was enjoying the weather or if they had gone grocery shopping recently.

I sputtered before I was able to answer. "No! If anything, Raphael *can't* die," I said passionately. "You know, I don't try to kill everyone, Cassius. If that were the case, you would have been dead years ago."

"I'm just saying, I normally don't see you so curious about someone."

"He...he doesn't talk much. We've trained a bit, but mostly, he asks questions and grieves over his own shit. He's not secretive per se, but he's not...he's not chatty. He's like a weird puzzle box of information he probably doesn't even find important. I don't know how to crack him. I just keep answering all his questions, trying to catch him up because he *is* supernatural, and he knows nothing."

"Do you think he might be mythical?" Cassius asked softly.

"I...I don't know." Mythical was a special designation for certain supernatural species. Werecats and werewolves were cursed. Vampires were just supernatural. Fae were mythical, so were nagas. The difference was in the nuance. Fae were once regarded as gods, but only certain fae, so only certain fae were considered mythical. Nagas were born of the gods and, therefore, mythical. Werewolves and werecats were humans under a very old, very powerful curse, but apart from that, they were just human. Whatever cursed them was probably mythical. Vampires were once human but were now undead and needed to feed on the power of a human's life force. Just supernatural by their official designation.

Raphael was still human, and that was the hang up I kept getting stuck on. He smelled human, he looked human, he was raised human. No one introduced him into the supernatural world, and no one really knew what he was.

"I checked everything," he explained. "There's nothing else like him out there, not by any knowledge the Tribunal has, and they have species in the database we don't govern."

"Yeah, I was stumped, trying to find something like him," I said, crossing my arms. "See what I mean, though? He's...like nothing I've ever come across. He's in a situation we've never seen before." *And he's got to stay alive because he might be the only person I'll ever be able to breed with. I don't want kids, but I'm not stupid enough to let him die either.*

My fangs pulsed suddenly. It was like a bug bite. If I didn't think about it, I could manage. The moment I considered what he really was or thought about how attractive he was, the ache began, unrelenting and aggravating.

"Okay. I was just making sure there was nothing else you were thinking. It would be a bad move to lead him to trust us only for you to kill him at the eleventh hour."

"Yeah, I'm not that much of an asshole," I snapped in exasperation. "When I want to kill someone, they damn well know it the moment they meet me."

We sat in silence until finally, Raphael walked out of the boutique.

My throat and mouth went dry. My fangs dropped into my mouth. My heart rate accelerated. A bolt of want and need raced through me.

Since I met Raphael, he had been in very casual clothing—sweatpants, shorts, t-shirts, and tank tops. He looked good in all of them, but something about this new outfit fit him, not just physically but in other ways I couldn't put into words.

He walked out in black jeans that hugged the muscles of his thighs. He still wore the black tank top, stretched over his pectorals like the damn things were going to rip the fabric. A black leather jacket and black boots finished the look. He dripped with a bad boy energy I should have stopped being attracted to when I was sixteen, but there he was, a grown-up version of my every teenage fantasy.

It was too hot for the leather jacket, but when the fae who worked in the boutique got something in their head, it didn't matter. They probably spelled it to keep him comfortable while he wore it, keeping him warm or cooling him down. The pants I got from them on occasion had similar spells.

I let out a slow breath, trying to rein in the attraction.

I had been attracted to men with the same intensity before. Sometimes a man was just the gods' gift to anyone with eyes. Raphael was like that. The aching fangs were a new addition to my reaction.

Well, at least biology picked a looker.

I wanted to laugh until I cried as Raphael walked to the car and folded himself into the backseat.

"They said they would send the rest to your place," he said, looking at Cassius. He didn't say anything to me. I wanted him to. I wanted him to ask me if I liked it or something. I don't know why, but not being talked to by the immensely attractive man in the back seat really fucking bothered me.

Here I go. The regression into being a fourteen-year-old girl because a pretty boy is around. Just what I needed this week.

"Looks good," I said nonchalantly, trying to make it sound as casual as I could.

"Thanks," he replied, but it didn't really sound like he cared about what I thought.

Cassius pulled out of the parking lot and started the long drive to my house. Crossing my arms, I tried not to think about Raphael in the backseat, completely uninterested in me. In the time since I met him, he had given exactly zero signs he cared about any of my opinions at all.

He tried to shoot me. He barely talks to me about anything except to learn what the hell is going on around him. He didn't care if I thought he looked good.

Oh yeah, Adhar, you think this is going to be easy? Just bite him? Funny.

I sure as hell would never bite a guy who was completely uninterested, and I barely knew. And that was *if* I even intended on ever biting anyone. Nagas mated for *life*. Once the choice of mate was made, if there was more than one option, that mate had to *die* before a naga could mate with another. If I did it without thinking, I could easily end up with a guy who fucking hated me, and there would be nothing either of us could do about it except kill each other.

Hmm. No thanks.

I stayed lost in thought, not looking up from the dashboard until we were pulling onto my dirt drive. Cassius mumbled a curse.

"What?" I demanded.

"Why can't you live near civilization? Or at least get the driveway paved?"

"Ah. Yeah, I thought you were just bitching," I said, nodding sagely. "You always bitch when you don't have the creature comforts of a long, paved drive and might get a rock kicked up and scratch the paint."

"You love your cars," he said with a bite. "You don't worry about this?"

"I can easily get the little shit fixed. I don't like when someone shoots at my car. Big difference," I said, trying to sound like I was the reasonable one.

Cassius snorted, shaking his head.

When my house came into view, I wanted to cry.

"Holy shit," Raphael said from the back. I felt the car

shift as he moved to get a better look through the front seats. "Sorry about the BMW."

"Yeah, the witch had already set it on fire, so..." I shrugged.

Cassius coughed, hopefully out of shock. I thumped his shoulder a few times, sighing.

"Yeah, Sinclair had a witch and fae with him. I told you that. The witch set the BMW on fire. The fae put a lot of bullets into the Aston Martin."

"Did the BMW roll down the damn mountain?" he asked, pointing as he pulled to a stop.

"No, I threw it at the fae when he came after me," Raphael explained.

"Well..." Cassius cut the engine and gestured at my poor house. "Let's go see what kind of damage they did."

As I got out of the car, I started taking it in. I could see the broken window Raphael had jumped through, trying to find cover. I didn't blame him. If it got him inside to safety faster than a door, so be it. I could see the front door had been kicked open, and there were scorch marks on the frame. The witch probably had a bit of fun with the fire. The BMW Raphael was sorry about? It was a heap of burned metal, ruined electronics, and mechanical parts, much too close to my house. I could see where pieces of it had fallen off after he threw it.

"Kaliya..." Cassius whispered, looking at me. "I'm so sorry."

"It happens," I said sadly, staring at the devastation. Before either man could say any more, I went in through the front door, knowing the garage was going to be a hazard of broken glass from the Aston Martin.

My display cases were shattered, my weapons tossed everywhere. That was the first thing I noticed, realizing I was going to have to do a full inventory to make sure I had everything. I didn't know if they decided to look for something or just wanted to ruin my home. Either was possible.

I picked up a katana I was given by a friend, testing it. It seemed they hadn't done any damage to the weapons if the katana was a fair judge of the rest.

"Nice," Raphael said, stepping next to me.

"I've had it for about ninety years," I said softly. "I got it when I completed my training." I was immensely glad to see it, to be able to hold it. If Sinclair had wanted to hurt me, he could have stolen and sold it off, forcing me to find it.

"Hisao gave you one of his weapons?" Cassius asked, frowning. "Why didn't I ever know that?"

"Because it wasn't a big deal. It stayed in its case." I grabbed the sheath from the floor and found a belt. Once the blade was secured to my waist, I felt more comfortable. Just a reminder I was trained, that I had earned the sword, made me feel more secure. I could survive this as I had survived so much else. "Raphael? Can you go outside and see if you can find our bags? I need my cellphone."

"Sure."

I walked deeper into the house when he turned and

left. Cassius stayed by me, and I was glad for the familiar comfort of his presence.

"He did a number on your place," Cassius said, toeing a piece of furniture out of the way. It was my coffee table, and it was flipped over. I could see where the wood was cracking. Another thing to replace.

"Yeah..."

"Why did you send him outside?"

"Naksha is here, and I don't want him to see me upset if they killed her," I admitted, swallowing.

"The snake you're taking care of? You know, it might not be perfect, but I'm certain I can get something set up today at my house for her. Something small and temporary. If she's..."

"That would be nice. Make the call," I said softly, walking through my back hallway. I checked the handle of my secure office, sagging with relief to feel it was still locked. Neither fae nor vampire would have been able to get in. One room, the most important room, didn't need to be checked, not yet.

I went into my unsecure office next and sagged against the door frame.

"They tore apart my computer, Cassius," I said, looking at the mangled remains of the tower. "Probably stole the hard drive."

"I'll text the others and let them know our communication channels have probably been compromised. Give me a moment. I still need to tell Leith about the snake so he can prepare something." He backed away and left me there to stare at the wreckage. I couldn't take all day, planning the renovation to keep this from happening again.

I walked quickly around the table and started looking over the habitat. I would have known already if Naksha was out. I would have smelled her through the house, but her scent was still confined to this office. The habitat was secure.

I guess not even Sinclair and that blasted fae were willing to upset a very dangerous cobra.

That's good. Okay. I know how to do this.

I hadn't done it since I was a child. It was one of the more private, beautiful naga gifts, and my parents had made sure I could do it just like them. I never did it because unlike my other skills, it evoked too many memories of a childhood that died and took my peace and sanity with it.

I opened the side door of the habitat and started to sing.

19

CHAPTER NINETEEN

Snake charming, from a human perspective, was seen as a parlor trick or just dangerous and stupid. I couldn't blame humans for that perspective, either. It was stupidly dangerous for most humans to attempt, and those who did it well didn't charm the way snake charming was meant to be. In ancient times, they had seen nagas doing it and imitated them, but didn't have the magic to back it up.

Lifting a hand, I began to rock my body back and forth while my hand moved in the opposite direction. The tune I sang was melodic and simple, calming and patient. Snake charming was magical, but it still relied on the snake to budge, to give a little in return before the magic could grab hold.

Naksha slithered off her rock and came toward me. She rose up, and her hood opened, but I wasn't worried about her spitting. She began to follow my hand, not my face, which was the reason I was taught to do it differently. Naksha could now spit at the hand if she so desired, but my face and eyes were safe. She couldn't kill or blind me, but it would sting quite a bit, and I would have to wait to try again.

"What..." Raphael was behind me, but I didn't stop singing.

"Don't move," Cassius whispered urgently.

"What is she doing?"

"Charming the snake," my ex-lover answered. "Consider yourself blessed. Outsiders don't usually get to see this."

"Have you ever?"

"No."

I wanted to chuckle. Cassius was right. This was something nagas normally did privately or with others of our own kind. We didn't do it for show or to show off. To charm a snake was to make a bond with it, to bend its will, and be something more than another predator. Nothing crazy or permanent, but if I succeeded, Naksha would do anything I wished for a time. I needed that if I was going to move her without proper equipment.

I continued to sing gently and lowered my hand, keeping my palm up. Naksha lowered her head, resting it in my palm. Still singing, I lifted, and she began to wind around my arm, climbing up to my shoulder, then wrapped twice around my neck. Since she wasn't a constrictor, there was no worry. I kept singing as I stood and continued the side to side, smooth motion, rolling my shoulders. She played on my arms and shoulders, keeping one coil around my neck at all times. She was mine.

"Good girl," I whispered as the song ended. Naksha moved up and laid her face in my hair. "There are no threats here," I promised, reaching up to run a finger over the top of her head. There was a sense of awareness nagas had with snakes, and charming a snake only heightened it. I would be able to read her mood until I released her from the charm.

"That was..."

"Beautiful," Cassius finished for Raphael. "Is she okay to travel?"

"Yeah, she'll be fine on me if I stay calm," I said. "Raphael, did you find anything?"

"The stuff in our bags was tossed around, and I looked through everything as best I could, but your phone is gone."

"They tore up this computer. It would only make sense that they stole your phone, Kaliya."

"Yeah, they're looking for information. They'll want to know every place I own, where I hide when things get tough. If they've already broken in, there's a chance the fae could be watching us on the security feed—"

"You hooked your security cameras with your phone?" Cassius asked, his eyes bugging out a bit.

"Just the habitat cameras," I answered. "I can't leave Naksha unattended for too long, but if there's nothing wrong, I can leave her undisturbed for a couple of weeks and having a state-of-the-art, internet-enabled system allowed me to go do my job."

"Any fae could have used magic—"

"No, not any fae could have," I snapped at him.

"Don't make your kind more powerful than they are. You could, but excuse me, we weren't talking about you. Paden couldn't do everything I needed for Naksha, and I didn't want him having to drive out here every day I was gone to check on her. So yes, my phone is hooked into part of my security system."

I left the office with the cobra and went into my bedroom, gritting my teeth at the devastation. They'd thrown my clothes around and dug through drawers and boxes in the closet. Thankfully, anything really important was hidden somewhere safer than my bedroom closet.

I looked through everything, careful of Naksha as she moved around on me. I picked up weapons and clothing, finding a bag I could toss everything into. Raphael followed me in and started to help. When I snatched a thong out of his hand, he lifted his hands in defeat. I realized the thong had been tangled up with a shirt. He hadn't been looking for my underwear.

"I wanted to help. This is...this is because of me. Cassius went to check some things and disconnected the power to shut everything down."

I sighed and patted his chest—his big, kind of considerate chest. Touching him caused the dull ache in my fangs to become insistent, and they dropped again.

Okay, hormones. Let's hit the brakes. I don't have time to deal with you and don't really want to.

"Thanks," I said, quickly pulling my hand away when he looked down at it. "Just...leave my intimate belongings, please. I can always buy more..."

"Okay." He reached down and picked up three shirts and tossed them on the ruined bed. "So...uh..."

"Yes?"

"You have a nice singing voice," he finally spit out. "And that song..."

"That song is the naga...spell that helps us charm snakes. No, I won't translate it for you. It's...a bit like a personal prayer." I felt my cheeks heat. This was just one of the reasons nagas didn't snake charm in front of people. It drew a lot of attention.

"Your eyes changed while you were doing it. Like a fiery orange."

"My snake form eyes," I explained. "Things were moving fast, so you didn't get the chance to really see me in the light when Sinclair visited." I blinked and pulled my ability to shift my eyes. Looking up from sorting my clothing, I caught him watching me. His eyes flashed red in return, and my pulse jumped at how he really took in my face, stepping closer.

"They look good on you. A lot better than my freakshow face," he said, leaning in. I knew he was studying something new, trying to understand and form an opinion, but my fangs ached so hard, I had to pull away—the need to bite him and claim him was too strong.

"You don't look like a freakshow," I said carefully. "You're supernatural, and in our world, the more interesting you are, the more people want to know you. You've never been seen before. Everyone is going to want to know you."

"I'm really never getting my human life back, am I?"

There was despair and heartbreak in the question. "I keep hoping..."

"No. You can pretend, but it'll never be the same. You can't get back the humanity you've lost."

His eyes flashed red again, and black began to form this time.

"I haven't lost my humanity," he growled.

Fuck.

"That's not what I meant—"

"I get that everyone here last night and in your world might be okay with killing, but I'm not a monster. I'm still going to try my best to be a decent person."

"Raphael—"

He stormed out, and I tossed my hands up in defeat.

Fuck.

I hissed in annoyance and continued to stuff clothing into my bag. Cassius had some good stuff at his place, but I liked *my* clothes. I tried to shove Raphael out of my thoughts, so I could consider the problems at hand.

Sinclair had everything. If he had his hands on my tech, then he had his hands on my communications with the other Executioners and Investigators like Cassius. He had my database and would be able to look through my personal search histories. My bank accounts were no longer safe since even I needed a hub to manage the different shell companies and aliases that managed my money. Was there anything I needed to worry about right now, though?

I thought back on the days since I came home, and Carter picked me up.

Carter.

I froze, unable to keep my forward momentum for a moment as I remembered Carter had helped me find where Sinclair was staying. Those texts would still be there, and Sinclair wasn't a fool. He would already have someone working to break into my phone for intel. It sucked, being a supernatural in the modern world. Chained to the conveniences of technology, but everyone worth paying attention to was smart enough to break through. That was why Cassius was cranky about my security being hooked up to my phone. His security was completely magical, so he didn't care if people knew where he lived.

Everything had its pros and cons.

The power went out, lights shutting off around me. Well, now the phone couldn't be used against the house. That was something.

I randomly shoved a few more pieces of clothing into the bag and tossed it over my shoulder.

"Cassius!" I called. "Cassius, we have a problem!"

"What?" He walked in from the garage as I walked into the hallway.

"My phone. Carter, you know Carter, right? Well, he helped me the night Sinclair showed up in Phoenix. They had gone to Midnight Reverie and—"

"Kaliya," Cassius said with that stern, 'what the fuck were you thinking' tone. "What—"

"He was able to get an address, in case the fae in Sinclair's group wanted to hook up before they left town." I refused to let guilt stop me from getting this out there. We needed to make a plan, and Cassius had to understand what kind of danger Carter was in. Not that I had any doubt that Cassius knew the importance of the problem we now faced. "I broke into Sinclair's place to get the intel some board member at Mygi had given him. It led me to find Raphael before they were able to."

"Kaliya...Carter is part of the Phoenix vampire nest, correct?"

"Yes."

"I'll make the call to the nest Mistress. She's the granddaughter of Isaiah. She'll listen to us and try to keep him safe. She's going to be furious with you."

"She's always angry at me for something," I said, shrugging. Her connection to Isaiah was important, though. Anyone related to the male vampire on the Tribunal was worth trying to work with. "As long as Carter stays out of Sinclair's hands, I'll manage."

"Okay. You ready to go? You can drive while I call her." He looked around, frowning. "Where did Raphael go?"

"I said he'd lost his humanity, but I didn't mean it in the way he thought I did." I shook my head. "He's...he's going through that stage every human turned supernatural goes through. You know, they freak out. They don't want to be a monster. They think we're terrible and shouldn't live the way we do. All that."

"Ah..." Cassius nodded sagely, staring out of a window in my living room, probably looking out for the not-human in question. "Sadly, he's with two supernaturals who can't relate."

"Yeah. We just have to manage. Let's get going."

I strolled to the busted front door. I saw Raphael sitting on one of my big yard rocks, meaning a rock in the desert, staring at the sun as it slowly went down.

"We have to get moving," I called out. "We need to get back to Cassius' place before sundown."

"Okay," he said, jumping off.

"Do you want to talk about—"

"No," he snapped before getting into the car's backseat and slamming the door shut. I got in more carefully, thanks to the cobra I had hanging on me. She would stay there until I let her know she could go somewhere else. Once I got her into a temporary enclosure, I would release the charm, giving her back the independence she deserved. I didn't want to haul her across a major city in a pillowcase. She was more comfortable with me, and I was more comfortable as well, knowing she was safe with me instead of sliding around the trunk, wild and afraid. Plus, she could escape, and that would be incredibly bad for everyone in the car.

Cassius got in last, handing me the keys.

"Can you drive with her?"

"Yup." I turned the car on, driving away from my home. "It's going to take at least two months of renovations to get that place back to where it was."

"Let me upgrade it while it's getting fixed," he said, dialing Imani on his phone. "Please. I know I... disappeared on you after leaving, but if Sinclair or that fae get away at the end of this, they will always know where you live. While I think it's paranoid of you to be this secretive, I also understand why. You make enemies like the rest of us meet people at parties to hand out business cards."

"Fine. When the physical renovations are done, you can come by and add an extra layer of security."

"I don't know why I never did to begin with," he mumbled.

"Because I told you no. I didn't want someone else's magic stinking up my property," I reminded him. "Well, specifically yours, but..." I gave a one shoulder shrug and was greeted by a glare when I glanced his way. I watched him hit the call button.

For the rest of the drive home, Raphael and I had to listen to him argue with several humans who worked for the Phoenix vampire nest. All I could hope for was that come sunset, Carter would be in a secure location.

20

CHAPTER TWENTY

Night was nearly upon us when I pulled into Cassius's garage, and Leith came running in to meet us.

"Madam Sahni, the terrarium awaits. I contacted someone at the Phoenix zoo and a local snake expert for advice. Between the two of them, I was able to round up what you needed..." He stopped as I rose out of the car, and he could see the snake winding around me, searching for the most comfortable spot. She picked under my shirt at my back, absorbing the warmth that had built there while I was sitting in the car.

"It's fine. Don't freak out, Leith. She's completely calm, and she's going to stay with me until I can look at the tank."

"Leith, you help her," Cassius ordered. "Raphael, you and I will talk in the dining room while they work this out. We should stay out of the way."

"Lord, I put the snake's terrarium on the dining table..."

"We'll go to the kitchens, then." Cassius started walking away, and Raphael followed him, giving me a look I couldn't discern as he left.

"Let's go," I said to Leith, and he led me to the dining room, not that I needed him to. I knew Cassius's mansion like the back of my hand. Once in the dining room, I saw the enclosure Leith had put together on the fly.

"It'll work, but I wouldn't want to keep her here permanently," I said, sighing. It was smaller than I liked, but it was appropriate. "You found good people to help you put this together."

"Thank you. It cost a small fortune."

"Bill me," I said, knowing that's what he intended to ask. Naksha wasn't my snake, but Leith knew never to spend any of Cassius's money on me without giving me the option to pay them back. I didn't want to be financially beholden to anyone. "Speaking of, bill me for the clothing Cassius stocked my room with. I know I didn't purchase any of it. It's not stuff I accidentally left here."

"Ah..."

"Leith..."

"Well, Lord Cassius is fine with you paying my household accounts back when it's an emergency, but he bought those with his personal accounts. I don't have access to those..."

"He's getting married. He can't be spending money on me," I muttered, shaking my head.

"He cares about you. You have a long history, and his fiancée is fine with it. She knows he keeps a room for you here."

"Just as long as neither of them gets the idea I'm some mistress he intends to tuck away."

"Madam Sahni!" Leith gasped. "You know Lord Cassius would never."

I gritted my teeth and looked at the butler.

"But most fae do, and I'm not willing to get that reputation, which would be easy, especially since he and I used to sleep together. Please let him know that all the money he's spent on me needs to be billed to me. I don't want to fight with him about it, but I'm not going to budge on this either."

"What about expenses for Mister Alvarez?"

"Those too," I mumbled. "All right, I need to focus."

He didn't respond, standing back from me and the cobra hanging on me. Singing a song of goodbye, telling Naksha her time with me was over, that she could go, I guided her gently into the temporary home. She found a fake log to hide under as I sang. Once she was completely inside the terrarium, I pulled my arm out and closed the door at the back.

"She doesn't need to be fed. Just keep her here and check on her every so often to make sure she hasn't squeezed out. I'll replace her water dish nightly. Do not, under any circumstances, open her enclosure. Tell Annie-Lyn and Terry as well."

"I shall. Is it okay if they come in and see her? She's beautiful."

"Yeah, they can come look at her but no tapping the glass like a child at the zoo." I ran a finger over the glass, her head following the movement. "You are beautiful, aren't you?" I whispered before stepping back. "She should be willing to stay in there and find a good place to sleep most of the time. She ate a few days ago, so there's no reason she needs to be fed. Just...check on her."

"Does she spit?"

"She does, another reason you need to keep the glass between you and her." I looked around. "They went to the kitchen, right?"

"Yes. Should I tell him now or later that you expect a bill for the clothing?"

"Later, when I'm not here." I didn't want to be around if he put up a fight when he realized I was trying to pay him back. Leith would make my opinions clear, and that would be the end of it. Cassius wasn't willing to fight with Leith about things. The butler could commit murder, and if he had a decent reason, Cassius would just shrug and ask for it be cleaned up. He was incredibly lenient with his staff, something I always respected...and exploited.

Both men looked up when I walked into the kitchen. I hadn't heard them talking, which had me worried. Had they been sitting there in silence the entire time?

"Any word from the nest about Carter?" I asked, heading for the fridge before Leith could jump into action and start making anything.

"Not yet," Cassius said with a heavy sigh. "I can't believe you used Carter to get at Sinclair."

Yes, you can. You're just trying to avoid being angry at me. Eventually, you won't be able to hide it, and we'll fight.

"It was supposed to be completely safe. The Mistress of Phoenix hates Sinclair, anyway, so I promise you, she had her own spies, trying to figure out what the hell he thought he was doing in her city and her club. She would never turn him away because her club is the safest place for vampires to feed here, but she doesn't like him."

"She doesn't like you, either," Cassius pointed out once again.

"Why does it seem no one likes you?" Raphael asked, giving me another strange look.

With a sigh, I pulled out a bottle of water. Looking at the two men, I didn't think I could imagine a less likely audience. Cassius, uptight, perfect suit, flaming red hair, and those nearly cold blue eyes. Raphael, dark, warm, massive in leather, the typical bad boy look. They didn't fit together.

"I'm confrontational and politically outrank most people in the city. I can say 'fuck you' and almost always get away with it."

"She's rude and has no sense of decorum," Cassius translated.

"Okay." Raphael practically rolled his eyes. "Of course, I get saved by the one person everyone in the state hates."

"Yes, your luck has run out," Cassius said with a heaping helping of pity. "But, like most Executioners, she's very good at defeating an enemy. There are better killers out there, but the best killers don't want to fight against each other. They want to keep a wide berth. If you need a weapons expert in your corner, you have one right now."

"Is there anything..." Raphael narrowed his eyes on me. "Is there anything you're good at besides killing things?"

"Possibly, but I haven't had a hobby in a few decades. You should be grateful. I could have just...not saved you." My fangs ached in protest. "You weren't my business. You should be glad I stuck my nose where it didn't belong. Sinclair would have had you if I hadn't convinced you to come with me. If you couldn't tell, Sinclair is the bad guy."

"I could tell," he bit out.

"Maybe we should get the werewolves involved," Cassius considered, sipping on something Leith put in front of him the moment the butler walked into the kitchen.

"Absolutely not. And we can't get a werecat on Duty, either," I said, frustrated even with just the idea of involving more parties into the mess. As it stood, it was me, Raphael, and Cassius; Sinclair, and his friends(I was certain the witch was already being replaced);the city's vampire nest, and Paden with the crew at The Jackalope. Mygi the mega pharmaceutical company, and the Tribunal were on the outskirts, watching everything happen. There didn't need to be any more.

"Duty?" Raphael once again was lost by where the conversation went.

I gave Cassius an exasperated look he recognized. I had told him Raphael knew nothing and asked a lot of questions, and part of me was starting to get incredibly annoyed.

"Werecats are duty-bound by parts of the law pertaining to them. They can't interfere in the affairs of other supernatural races, mostly werewolves, but they can be called to Duty," Cassius explained.

"They used to make it their personal business to protect humans from the supernatural world," I continued. "It caused...problems. If a supernatural mistreated a human, the werecats took it as a personal offense and stepped in to fix it, mostly when the human was somehow connected to the werecat, even if it was just living in their territory or growing up nearby. Where they got that mentality, I don't know, but it caused *a lot* of problems."

"A war," Cassius cut in. "It caused a war with the werewolves. Nearly wiped out the werecats and exposed the supernatural world at large to the humans. It was probably the biggest supernatural conflict that's ever happened. The only thing that comes close is the vampire and fae situation, but it's never boiled over into open conflict."

"And..." Raphael looked between them.

"Essentially, a human, if they know how, can find and beseech a werecat for protection from a supernatural problem. The werecat can and will fight to the death to protect said human. It gives the werecats a sense of purpose." I lifted my hands in a shrug. "The problem?

You might smell human most of the time, but the moment a werecat knows you aren't human, and it will happen, they aren't bound to protect you. If anything, they will want to get the fuck away from you. They don't like trouble being brought to their doorstep and do their best to handle everything internally concerning their species, without involving anyone else. They self-govern better than most of the supernaturals."

"I'm going to need all this written down," the not-human mumbled, rubbing his temples. The concentrated, pained look on his face made me want to smooth the worry lines on his forehead and calm him down.

"I have a copy of the law as it currently stands," Cassius said. "You can read through it."

"Oh, gods, Cassius. Don't torture the man," I said, shaking my head. "That thing is awful."

"He needs to know," Cassius replied, walking out of the kitchen.

"How bad is it?" Raphael asked me once Cassius was gone.

"There are several supernatural species. You've heard of many already. Werecats, werewolves, fae, vampires, nagas, witches. There's also kitsune, nymphs of different types, demigods, mermaids, and so many more who never left the land of their birth, keeping small communities. Nearly every legend exists, hidden under the surface of the human world, carefully crafted to keep us safe." With a deep breath, I continued.

"For nearly every supernatural species, there's a

portion of the Laws dedicated to them, specific to that species' needs and their abilities. No two species are covered by the exact same Laws. Some pay more attention to the Tribunal than others. Some aren't covered by the Laws because the leaders of their species don't want to bow down to other supernaturals, and that's okay too, as long as those out of the governing of the Tribunal don't mess with those who are. It started out with...four species." I couldn't quite remember, but I hadn't been alive at the time. As humanity exploded globally, so did the Tribunal and the Laws. Now there were dozens.

"Five," Cassius corrected as he walked in. "The problem children, werewolves and werecats, and those of us most impacted by their war in present day Eastern and Western Europe and Northern Africa; the fae, witches, and vampires. The Big Five."

"Werewolves, fae, and vampires hold the strongest numbers," I said, sighing sadly as we were caught explaining even more for the new guy. This was why I was glad I wasn't one of those species who did this on a regular basis. It was tiring to have to explain everything. "Werecats are considered one of the most powerful, even if they have low numbers. Witches are...nosy and important at the same time."

"They bridge the world between human and supernatural in a way no one else can because they have a foot in each world," Cassius said, smiling at Raphael. He dropped a small book on the table. I wanted to snort. That was a dirty little trick.

"That's it?" Raphael frowned at the book. "This won't be so—"

Cassius snapped his fingers, and the book began to grow...and grow...and grow some more. After a few seconds, it was a foot wide, two feet long, and nearly a foot deep. Thousands and thousands of pages. Some supernaturals invested in becoming experts on the Law, but I knew even they had to reference the book on many occasions.

"Bad..." Raphael finished. "This...this is worse than every college textbook I had."

"You're college educated?" Cassius asked quickly. "Human college?"

"I was just about to graduate when everything happened. Unless the school expelled me for the incident, there's no reason to think my records aren't there, and I could get my diploma," Raphael answered. "Why?"

I groaned. "Cassius has always wanted to go to a modern human college but work and his family keep stopping him."

"A place of higher learning beyond my fae education? Of course I want to go."

"It's not all that great," Raphael said with a chuckle. "A lot of studying, a lot of hard work."

"What did you go to college for?" I didn't check when I looked into him. I only knew he was going to be going into the military as an officer when he was done.

"Law," he answered with some chagrin. "I was going to be a lawyer."

"You were almost done with law school at twenty-two?" I asked, frowning. "I don't know much about human education, but that seems young."

"No, I was leaving for Harvard in the fall. I was fast tracking my way through school, but I had to keep my grades up to keep the Navy's promise to pay for college when I was done," he said, looking at me, his eyebrows coming together.

"Fuck, how did I miss that?" I asked, looking at Cassius. "He's smart."

"Miss...did you look into me?" he asked.

"How do you think I knew your real name the night we met? I knew you had some sort of deal to join the military when you were done with school. I just assumed you were going to ship off to boot camp, or whatever they call it, the moment you graduated." Shrugging, I dismissed my mistake. "Not like it matters. I don't ever plan on going to a human college."

"Neither of you have ever been to a school?"

"You're the only person on this property who has gone to a traditional school the way you think of schools," Cassius answered. "Except maybe Terry. He was once human, but that was seventy-five years ago." Cassius sat down next to Raphael and checked his watch. "Since we're still waiting on Imani, we can keep talking."

"Oh, joy," I muttered.

"Most supernaturals are homeschooled in the basics—reading, writing, arithmetic, and supernatural history. We're taught survival knowledge, magical knowledge, and how to blend in, which is very important."

"We're taught what to know and to know when we need it," I said, rolling my eyes. "Like don't move to a country before understanding the country and its people. Know its landmarks and its politics if you're interested. Anything that can help you blend in."

"We receive less formal education as we get older, but we're expected to educate ourselves. Some supernaturals choose to look at human schooling, but most of us do private research and teach ourselves skills as time goes along."

"Can we find something less boring to—"

Cassius's phone rang before I could finish my complaint. He looked down and nodded.

"It's her," he informed us.

CHAPTER TWENTY-ONE

I found a seat as Cassius picked up and greeted Imani, chuckling softly. I knew she must have hit on him the moment the conversation started.

"I'm engaged, Imani. You've missed your chance," he said with enough grace to make him seem irresistible without being conceited. "Has anyone told you why I've been trying to reach you? I'm worried about the safety of one of the vampires in your nest, Carter."

He frowned as Imani spoke. I wished I could hear what she was saying, but my hearing wasn't sensitive enough.

"I believe Sinclair is currently a threat to him, yes," Cassius said, looking up at me. "Does it matter...Yes, Kaliya is involved. So am I. This is a matter of importance..."

I sighed, leaning over to let my head hit the counter. *Fuck me sideways, she was giving Cassius an attitude. This was my fault.*

"Let me remind you of something very important," Cassius whispered dangerously. I knew the tone. Something Imani had said upset him and Cassius was hard to upset like this. "Carter was only part of your nest because Kaliya led him there, even though you had failed in your duty to keep rogue vampires in check in Phoenix. It was your mistake that led him to be turned. We entrusted his safety to you, but you know as well as I do, Kaliya and I both like to check in on him. If he voluntarily agreed to help Kaliya, that was his rightful decision, regardless of being in your nest. Find him and protect him like you promised *me* you would."

I watched as he hung up on her and put the phone down in silence.

"Cassius—" I tried to ask him what she had said, but I didn't get the chance to finish.

"I should go to the Tribunal and ask them to revoke your Executioner privileges," he snapped.

I winced. *Yup, this is it. This is when he loses his ability to hold back the anger I knew he had about Carter being in the line of fire.*

"You wouldn't—"

"Carter is a younger vampire, and you abused your friendship with him," he growled. "And he could get hurt for it. Since she woke up, no one has been able to find him. Mind you, they couldn't get into his lightproof room. You better hope he's in there, Kaliya. First, Paden gets tortured and has to close down The Jackalope until this blows over, and now, Carter might be..." Cassius took a deep breath. "Paden, I could ignore. He asks for trouble and lives in a dangerous world, even for supernaturals. He deals in information, knowing the risks. Carter is a different story."

I closed my eyes, looking away from Cassius.

"I didn't think they would get my phone. It's normally glued to me. I'm sorry, Cassius." It was stupid. It was an excuse. It was a mistake I had never made before. It was unforgivable.

He sighed, shaking his head. "We'll talk about this later in private," he said, picking up his phone again. He walked out of the room, leaving me with a confused Raphael and Leith, who shuffled after Cassius a moment later.

"You're in trouble," Raphael said softly, "because you wanted to find me."

"And I sent a friend to get the intel I needed. It...it was supposed to be innocent and easy. Carter knows how to defend himself. I just have to hope he doesn't need to," I said, refusing to look at the not-human.

"What would Sinclair do to him?"

"Torture him for information. Ask to trade him for you. Kill him just to prove a point. Sinclair is capable of anything," I answered, clenching my hands in fists so hard my nails threatened to break the skin on my palms. Carter knew what had been at risk. He wasn't a fool, even if he was young, but that didn't ease my worry. They hadn't been able to find him yet. He was part of the nest. There's no way he should have been able to hide from all of them.

I got up, unwilling to stew any longer, and went to

find Cassius. Raphael didn't need any more information to know how serious this was, and I couldn't stand sitting there with his scent making my fangs ache constantly. I found Cassius in his office, leaning over and looking severe. He glared at me as I entered the room.

"Sinclair went to Midnight Reverie. Carter was already there because it was a Saturday night, and he's *always* there on a Saturday night. I asked him to just keep an eye on them, maybe listen in. He couldn't hear anything, so I suggested maybe asking one of Sinclair's friends to dance. He hit it off with the fae and got an address. That was all. He joked around about why he was doing it, but he knew the score. He even let me know when they were leaving, so I could get out. I didn't coerce him. If he hadn't wanted to help, I could have tailed Sinclair. I promise you, Carter knows me well enough to know I could have. I had options," I explained, feeling less upset and more angry. "Carter knows me just as well as you do. Just as well as Paden does. He's not a fool or an idiot, and I didn't take advantage of him or manipulate him."

"I know," Cassius said softly. "You just didn't think about how it could fall back on him."

"It's Sinclair! No, I didn't think because it was a tiny margin. There were a thousand ways I could have gotten that intel from Sinclair and grabbed Raphael before he could. The likelihood he would have gotten my phone at my house after going after Paden? You really think that was a likely scenario?"

"If he hadn't gone after Paden, no," Cassius said,

raising an eyebrow. "But once he went after Paden, you should have known Carter was at risk."

"You're right, but I was too busy running for my life."

"I know."

"It doesn't count for anything, but I am sorry."

Cassius shook his head a little, looking down at his desk.

"You...you get obsessed and have blind spots when you're like that. Tell me, does Raphael have any intel you or Paden would have cared about when this started?"

"No," I said sadly. "No, he doesn't, but at least we're saving him from being experimented on, right? That has to count for something."

"If Sinclair wants a trade, Carter for Raphael, what do you think we should do? It's the most likely scenario, and if we plan for it now, we won't be surprised later in the evening. We don't know what kind of deadline he'll give us."

"He's playing this very...dangerously," I said softly. "It's not like him, is it? He's normally done everything he can to stay out of real trouble, using others to do his bidding and keeping his hands clean. He tried to kill me last night. That's not toeing the line like he usually does. That's blowing right past it."

"Yes, which means we need to take into account he's not going with his regular MO," Cassius agreed. "Do we fake a trade, then go in for the kill?"

"No," I snapped quickly. "We can't put Raphael at risk like that."

"It's an easy way of getting it done without raising suspicion."

"No," I repeated, my every instinct against the idea. A naga doesn't send someone who might be a potential mate into the line of fire. It wasn't done. I couldn't allow Cassius to do it—not under any circumstance.

"He would know what's going on. We wouldn't be betraying him. Let's hope he can act and—"

"Absolutely not," I hissed across the office, closing the door before walking closer to the desk. "Find another option."

"Since we don't know the location yet or who he might have with him..."

"Find. Another. Way." I couldn't budge on this. Cassius would be handing Raphael to Sinclair over my dead body.

"Paden was attacked. Knowing them, he probably needed extensive and fast healing before he could warn you they were coming," Cassius said, glaring at her. "Carter is probably already in their hands; we're just waiting on Imani to confirm it. Hopefully, Sinclair will get word to us sooner rather than later. This is off the rails, as the humans say. The train has left the tracks. We don't have many options. Raphael is powerful, and from your description of his powers, he's damn near unkillable. He will be fine. We'll move fast enough, they won't be able to get him into a car."

"No," I repeated.

"Why were you willing to risk everyone else but not him?" Cassius asked softly. "What aren't you telling me?"

"A lot," I answered honestly. "Too much and none of it to do with you."

"Kaliya..." he warned. I bit my tongue. Did I tell Cassius? Did I trust him to understand what was at stake?

He keeps a room here for me, so I can hide if things get too hot. He does it even though we both know his uncle hates me, even though he's moved on from us and is getting married to someone else.

"He's...I could mate with him," I said softly, watching Cassius's face change from the glare to surprise before landing on concern.

"Kaliya, are you...?"

"I don't want to. I barely know him, but I can't...I can't take the risk of him dying, either. Cassius, he has to live, and he has to stay close because..."

"He might be the only person you ever meet," he finished. "Oh, this is bad," he mumbled, falling into his chair. "When did you know?"

"The moment I saw him. I was professionally curious, then I became personally invested, like that." I snapped my fingers. "The connection he might have to anything that I've been looking into is so obscure, it's... irrelevant. The moment I saw him, I knew."

"One in several billion," Cassius said. "And he somehow ended up in your city, running from a supernatural problem. Kaliya, you could stop all this right now. You can give him protection under supernatural Law."

"I...I need time to think about that," I replied, finding

a seat. "You think I don't know? I could go to the Tribunal right now and say, 'Hey, this guy can have kids with me, so he's off limits.'"

"Why haven't you? Why didn't you do it the first night and declare it to the world, so he had another layer of protection?"

"Because it gives him more enemies. He would no longer be a strange oddity one company wants for whatever reason. He would be...a naga mate. I'm lucky in my world, Cassius. I know how to kill. I made a name for myself and placed myself around powerful people. But there are four male nagas with human mates, and they just want to be normal families. Their defenses are tested nearly on a weekly basis. Someone is always trying to get to them. Most are low-time poachers, human and supernatural alike. Disgusting, awful people, but sometimes..."

"Sometimes, it's something more," he finished.

"Exactly. And now, I have this...guy." I gestured at the door, indicating Raphael. "And he's running from his own demons, people who have done terrible things to him. If I declare him a mate to the naga, I do two terrible things to him."

Cassius had no response, gesturing for me to continue.

"I give him all my enemies for starters. Then I take away his freedom. I don't want forever with anyone. It's a burden I have run from for a century. I don't want to pop out kids for my kind. The others can breed. I'm more than my womb. But if I declare him a naga mate, he'll be expected to stay by my side for the rest of his life. Does that seem fair to you? To be bound to a woman who might never want you? Might never think it's safe? Hell, he might not even find me attractive. I don't know what's going on in his mind. It's happened before. A naga can make the wrong choice when it comes to these things and create a mate bond with someone who is totally wrong for them." When I was done, I sagged into the chair. "It's not as simple as you think it is."

"You're right. We'll work on finding a way to protect him without going to the last resort, but Kaliya, you need to be ready to make that call because something is going to force you to one day."

"I know," I whispered.

There was silence as we stared at each other until Cassius relaxed and looked over my head toward the door.

"He's not a bad guy," the fae said finally. "You could have found worse."

"Wow," I huffed, shaking my head. "Really? Are you going to invite us to a dinner party with your fiancée next?"

"I was considering it. Are you really thinking about ignoring the breeding compatibility between you and him?"

"For as long as I'm able. If I'm forced to acknowledge it, so be it, but I'm never going to force a mate bond with him. Adhar told me to do that, and I wanted to reach through the phone and strangle the old bastard. He's..."

"It's always scared you, the mate bond," Cassius

pointed out. "Was he really so tactless to tell you to just do it and get it over with?"

"Yeah," I spat out. "Which is funny because when I was fifteen, he saw how much I hated the parade I had to endure. Did I ever tell you about that?"

"No, I don't remember hearing about a parade."

"Long story short, when a naga is entering adulthood, he or she is taken in front of all the other eligible nagas to see who they might be able to mate bond with. We're required to open our mouths so others can see if our fangs drop. It's pretty humiliating."

"Sounds like it. Also sounds like a fae coming out party."

"Coming out? Are you all gay now?"

"No...coming out into society party. Being presented to the royalty of the court, meeting your peers as eligible to marry another member of society."

"Ahhhh. That. Yeah. A bit like that. Old, weird, humiliating traditions that refuse to die."

"Yes."

Leith came in twenty minutes later, and I was almost sad to end the peaceful silence that Cassius and I had found. It was relaxing.

"Terry is here and...him and Raphael..."

"We're coming," Cassius said, sighing heavily. I was the first out the door, walking fast. As I drew closer to the kitchen, I heard the growling and stomped in.

"Raphael, leave the werewolf alone. Terry, this is Raphael. He's a friend of mine. Kind of. Can I call you a friend?" I asked the last question to Raphael.

"He smells off," Terry muttered, glaring as he walked around the counter to his side of the kitchen. "A touch of something in his human scent. I don't like it."

"Really? I didn't catch that. Tell me more." I sat down innocently and was happy to see everything calming down as Cassius walked in with Leith. "Everything is fine. Terry was just going to tell me about something he caught in Raphael's scent."

"Ah..." Cassius looked between both men, down at Leith, to me, then shook his head slowly. "I know too many ruffians, Leith."

"You do know many, Lord Cassius."

"It's not good," Terry grumbled. "I don't like his scent here."

"I'm sorry," Cassius whispered. "But we're going to have to live with it for a time. Now, let's settle down and have something to eat. Terry, you're the best cook I employ, and I've missed your cooking."

"Thank you, but you'll all go eat in the living room." He pointed at the door, and no one argued, leaving as quickly as possible. As we sat down, Cassius's phone started ringing again. He answered quickly and looked at me, giving a hard nod.

"We're going to get him back, Imani. Don't worry." He waved a hand at Leith and motioned for a pen.

Leith started shuffling around in a drawer of a side table. The moment Cassius had both, he started writing, scribbling down everything Imani was saying. He tore off the top sheet, and it floated across the table toward me. I snatched it out of the air and read it while he continued to write notes before he hung up.

It's a trade.

I sighed. Just as we had discussed. This was probably the most predictable thing that happened since I got back to Phoenix.

22

CHAPTER TWENTY-TWO

When Cassius hung up the phone, everyone tried to talk at once. Cassius, Leith, and Raphael were trying to get a word in, though I wasn't sure why.

"Quiet!" I snapped, bringing silence to the table. "Cassius, you go."

All the men looked at me with various levels of annoyance.

"He's willing to give back Carter for something—"

"Me. I'm the one with the bounty," Raphael cut in. "Let's do it. I've escaped Mygi before. I can do it again. Carter is important to you two, and he shouldn't have to—"

"No," I said evenly. "We're not trading anyone. We're not even going to fake a trade. Cassius, tell us the rest."

Raphael glared at me, his eyes flashing red. Such an angry, passionate man. He wanted to play hero, which astounded me. Heroes got killed. Did he really want to go the way of the dodo?

"He contacted Imani and let her know that he also considered her hostile since her vampire felt so comfortable helping you," Cassius said, looking straight at me. "You and I already had this discussion."

"We did, and I'm not having it a second time." I would eat the guilt in private from here on out. I didn't need another public shaming to feel any worse. *Right now, I just need to focus on getting Carter back. If I get him back, he can never help me again, and everything will be okay.*

"Of course," Cassius agreed. "We have..."—he checked his watch—"twenty hours. He wants us ready for the trade at midnight tomorrow. He made sure to say he wanted to get a full day's sleep before dealing with us. He promised Carter was relatively unharmed and would remain so."

"But?" There was always a but.

"If we're late, he's going to carve Carter up slowly until sunrise, then throw him into the sun. We took something he wanted, so he'll take something we care about. Typical criminal, making his intentions known."

Beside Cassius, Leith paled and reached for a seat. Cassius helped him sit down. Raphael was snarling from his chair, and I snapped my fingers at him.

"None of that. It doesn't help anyone. Right now, anger helps no one."

"Just trade me! I'm not going to sit here and let—"

"It wouldn't work," I said, cutting him off again. "Do you really think we'll get Carter back if we gave you to Sinclair?"

"What do you mean?" Cassius asked from the other end of the table. "His MO normally says he wants as little violence in his direct perimeter as he can manage."

I hadn't been expecting to have to give an explanation. I had just been trying to shut Raphael up before the man got himself killed or taken. Cassius was going to make me think it through, though, so I started working it out.

"But we're already past that, remember? He's off his MO. He's tried to kill me in my own home, breaking several Laws from my protection as an Executioner, to my protection as a naga. Anyone who threatens me or trespasses on my property can and will be met with immediate deadly force. He knew that when he had his fae and witch torture Paden for information about where I was hiding." I drummed my fingers on the table. "He doesn't intend to give us Carter because he has witnesses that he broke Laws punishable by execution. He knows, even if I get Carter back and he leaves with Raphael, I'm going to hunt him down, even if it means driving the four and a half hours to Las Vegas and doing it on his turf."

"It would never end for him, and everything he'd built would crumble around him while you carved a path to the heart of his empire," Cassius said softly, but I didn't miss the small note of pride. I always knew I was his favorite Executioner, but it wasn't always obvious.

"Exactly. Cassius, this is a trap. He's going to try to kill all of us. The only reason I'm not worried about Paden is Tom and Jeremy, the damn fae and witch, went after him without Sinclair." How I suddenly remembered their names I didn't know, but they were so stupid for a moment, I wanted to laugh. "What do you want to bet that he kills the fae after he kills us, then walks away with Raphael and takes him back to Mygi for the rest of his twenty-million-dollar prize?"

"It's very likely, probably the safest bet we can make," Cassius whispered. "Why didn't we consider this earlier?"

"Because we had a different important conversation," I reminded him. "There's no getting Carter back without bloodshed. People are going to get hurt. The only thing we can do is make sure people don't die."

"We outnumber him," Raphael pointed out. "Three to two. Four, if you include Carter. He's a vampire, so he should count. I've never met him, but..."

"Two to two," I corrected. "You won't be going, and Carter will be leaving the moment we give him an opening. I'm not risking either of you. Stop trying to put yourself out there."

"Excuse me, but—"

"Enough with the Catholic guilt," I snapped. "I'm tired of it. Two capable, powerful people are going to do their jobs for you. Let us."

We glared at each other until Cassius coughed. Now that my fae ex knew what Raphael was, the entire thing was embarrassing. He gave me a pointed look.

"We'll discuss options. We have the rest of tonight and tomorrow to figure out the best idea. We're not letting you go near Sinclair, Raphael. I'm with Kaliya on this one. We're not risking the core of the mission, which is to protect and free you from Mygi and anyone they may hire. Carter is an unfortunate side effect we're going to have to work with. Don't think Kaliya and I will leave him out there to get hurt. We're going to do what we think is best for the safety of everyone at this table."

Raphael stood up and stomped off. I watched him leave, his large back tense.

"He hates this," Cassius said, frowning. "Catholic guilt?"

"I picked him up before he could make it to Mass. He's so...intense about his humanity and not wanting to be a 'freak' or a 'monster.' It's classic Catholic guilt of a new supernatural."

"He's been supernatural for ten years—"

"He never came to terms with it. He just kept running from it. He's a new supernatural. He's capable of making stupid choices."

"You're being very cold about this, Kaliya." He sounded sad. "He's just trying to do what he thinks is right."

"I'm being rational. It's a coping mechanism."

"Ah. I would have thought you were acting harshly because you were avoiding more personal feelings and dealing with fear you're not used to having."

I bared my teeth at him, my fangs down. He was right, obviously, but he didn't have to call me out in front of Leith.

"We still need to talk about what happens after we deal with Sinclair," he said, moving back to the professional conversation. "Mygi Pharmaceuticals and the Tribunal."

"I thought we would handle it when we get to it. I don't want to focus on that problem and fuck up this one. None of it will matter if Sinclair gets away with Raphael and one or both of us are dead."

"Point made, but I think we need to start considering it. It's going to be the first thing we have to do when we've secured Carter and dealt with Sinclair's threat."

"Do we have any chance for backup?" I asked, thinking about our coworkers.

"Most likely, no, but I'll send out word and see if anyone can get here in time to help us. It's worth trying, but they're all busy with their own regions and investigations."

"Worth a shot," I repeated back to him. "So, you have a location written down over there?"

"Yes, along with a small list of demands, such as no enlisting the help of more people who work with the Tribunal. He knows I'm in town, so I have no element of surprise."

"When trouble happens in my region, you're always the Investigator I call. It's expected you would show up when Sinclair attacked my house. He's smart enough to know since I got away, you would be showing up."

"I would have come down after your first call, anyway; I just had to speed up the timeline a little. My uncle was annoyed I was running off to help you again. He thought I was over this."

"Is there being over your job?" I asked, crossing my

arms. "He does know you're the only Investigator with a base of operations in this region, right? Who else would I call?"

"I made sure to point that out to him, and I'm glad you called me. I know you better than the others do and know how you think."

"You know how Sinclair thinks as well."

"Yes, and I think on that note, you and I should continue this conversation in my office." He stood up and gave a pointed look at Leith, who raised his hands and stood up as well, leaving the room. Once he was gone, Cassius looked at me with an expression I was certain any future children he had would hate. "They're nosy."

"They are, but they do it because they want to support you. Where's Annie-Lyn, by the way? I haven't seen her at all."

"She's in the shadows, cleaning up after us. She's not in the mood for company."

"Ah. Tell her I said hello, and I hope she's happy." Annie-Lyn was a dark fae with the ability to disappear into the shadows. The idea of dark and light courts went the way of the dodo centuries ago, but the clans of the fae were still strong, still unique. Annie-Lyn's clan was probably once a strong force of the dark court.

"She would appreciate you taking the time to say something to her," Cassius said with a sharp, knowing smile. She must have been in the room. There weren't many magics that could hide someone from me. Annie-Lyn was one of them, but I trusted her not to stab me in the back or while I slept. Cassius's smile was a stark reminder that some of my friends were dangerous. He knew where she was, but then, there was no fae magic he couldn't see through.

I followed Cassius to his office, checking the corners, wondering if I might catch a glimpse of the little girl fae.

"Stop looking for her," Cassius ordered. "She's uncomfortable that we're talking about Sinclair and doesn't want everyone to see her scared."

"Of course. Actually, her hiding around in the shadows got me thinking." Once I closed the door to his office, locking us inside, I made a little flourish to represent magic. "Do we know anything about Sinclair's shadow magic abilities? I've never seen him use any."

"He doesn't have any," Cassius answered. "He's never shown the ability to use that particular set of vampire powers. It's not common for them to be able to do those magics until they're close to a thousand years old, so we can count ourselves lucky."

"That's right," I said, snapping my fingers. "Age problem. Maybe we can kill him this time, and he'll never get that powerful." As with most supernatural species, age equated to power. The longer one survived, the more powerful you could consider that person.

"If we kill him now, we're going to have to send someone to Las Vegas to deal with the power vacuum," Cassius pointed out.

I nodded, finding a seat. There was a lot to think about, but I kept coming back to one thing, one problem.

"Twenty million isn't worth this," I mumbled to

myself, crossing my arms as I sank into the comfortable leather chair.

"There could be a lot we don't know."

"That really bothers me." I huffed, tapping my foot and playing with my lip piercing with my tongue. "Sinclair has money. Is there some more private deal with Mygi I don't know about? This isn't just his reputation. If anything, he's ruining his reputation. People liked working with him because he was a criminal who was... criminal. He could pull it off and get away with it."

"What if it's Raphael? What if there's something about Raphael he's willing to kill for?"

"Another reason to keep them far apart," I said, raising an eyebrow at the fae taking his seat. "I'm not kidding with this, Cassius. I know it might be a good idea to fake a trade under different circumstances, but I can't risk it."

"I know." His voice was soft and forgiving. "We're going to figure this out. We might need to put him in a safe house he can't get out of."

"The only thing we have close to that right now is your house—which he could potentially steal a car from—and the prison, but we don't have time to make a run there before Sinclair wants us at the meetup location. Normally, I lose a day going out to the prison."

"I never go..." Cassius shrugged. No Investigator ever did.

They let Tribunal guards, low ranking people, handle the prison and the prisoner transport. Executioners only ever went when someone escaped or was due to be executed because new information revealed more about their crimes. As it stood, I was the only person higher than the guards who worked there who visited on a regular basis and only because I was close.

"So, the prison is out of the picture."

"We'll leave him here under the supervision of your staff. He's not a danger to them. All that Catholic guilt stops him from being much of a threat to anyone."

"You seem frustrated."

"He's strong enough to tear heads from shoulders, but he doesn't. He evades, blocks them, wrecks their rides, but he could have defended himself a bit better when my house was attacked. He didn't." Yeah, I was frustrated. Raphael had power, and he wasn't using it for anything worthwhile, and I figured if push finally came to shove, he still wouldn't do what was necessary. And if he did, he would probably hate himself even more, and dealing with him would be impossible.

"It's not wrong to want to avoid violence," Cassius said diplomatically.

"He was going to join the human military. He doesn't get to..." I trailed off, clamping my mouth closed and shaking my head. I wasn't going to call him a hypocrite. I understood this was all shocking for him, and he needed time to adjust, so I kept my insults to myself a little while longer. "You're right, it's frustrating. Can you believe it? I finally meet someone who's compatible, and he's totally against the life I lead. He's here because he knows we can protect him and teach him, but he doesn't..."

"Like us. He doesn't like supernaturals, and he doesn't like the laissez-faire way you treat killing."

"I kill because it keeps me alive," I hissed. "I don't think that's inappropriate. I think it's realistic."

"It is. I've never been as violent as you, but I know the life you lead is for a reason. You don't need to convince me, Kaliya. I have my problems with some of the things you do, and you're someone people need to get used to, but there's nothing wrong with you."

"Really? Because every time he opens his mouth..."

"Do you really care about his opinion?" my ex-lover asked, raising an eyebrow. "You never cared about mine. Not really. If I ever got you to apologize for something, it was because you felt you did something wrong, not because I convinced you that you did. Not because I looked at you differently for doing it."

Do I care?

I was at a loss for words for a moment before sighing.

"Yeah, I do care. I don't want to, but I do. I want him to like me, to understand me. I just met him. I barely know him, but I care that he looks at me and sees a killer. I care that I could never hurt him, even if I don't want him, but he tried to shoot me the evening we met. Biology blows a lot of dick."

"I can see that," Cassius mumbled. "Or it wants you to blow more..."

"Was...did you just..." I pointed at him, trying to find the right way to ask the question. "Sorry I didn't go down on you enough. The fangs make it a little precarious."

"Oh, I know. I was trying to make a joke."

"I wish I could say it was funny, but it just made me very uncomfortable," I said to him, trying for a blank face.

"What makes you more uncomfortable? Me making jokes about our deceased relationship or the physical urges you must be feeling for Raphael that make you want to have one with him?"

I bared my teeth.

"I don't want a relationship with him."

"You want to have sex with him. Let's not lie about that. When we started sleeping together, you gave me an incredibly detailed explanation why I didn't need to wear a condom and that pregnancy wasn't a worry."

"I was attracted to you. Sometimes, I wonder why when you're like this."

"You were attracted to me, but it was never strong. I see the way you watch him walk in and out of a room. I see how you take him in and watch his eyes. I'm not blind."

"Are you jealous?" I crossed my arms.

"No. I pity the man. He's obviously not ready for a woman as strong as you in his life. He's in for a bumpy ride. I wish I could tell him it would be worth it in the end, but..."

"That's just mean." Deciding I was done with the conversation, I stood up. "I'm going to take a drive. I want to get eyes on the only location I know of that Sinclair has here. The one I broke into. Maybe I can get eyes on him and Carter."

"They probably aren't using that location anymore."

"I know, but it would make me more comfortable

knowing they aren't, instead of never taking the chance to find out."

"Be safe," he ordered. I nodded and started walking out.

"Kaliya?" he called softly. When I looked over my shoulder, he sighed. "If you ever need help with...him... just let me know. I don't want you feeling like you have to deal with this alone. You don't. You don't need the other nagas, either. Whatever you decide to do with him in the end, I'll support it."

"Thank you."

I didn't say goodbye to anyone on my way out, grabbing the keys to Cassius's most casual car, a BMW like mine. When I was driving away, I caught Raphael standing in a window, watching me leave.

Whatever I decide? Can I just leave him with you, Cassius?

CHAPTER TWENTY-THREE

It wasn't much of a drive from Cassius's home to the house Sinclair rented. I drove the streets slowly, glad I was in one of Cassius's cars and not mine. Not because they were destroyed, but because I only had two vehicles, and most supernaturals in the Phoenix area knew them. I was a little less recognizable in the rest of Arizona and in New Mexico, but in the city, I couldn't go anywhere without being noticed.

His windows were illegally tinted, and I knew he had a high-level charm on the car to keep it from garnering human attention, strong enough to throw off many supernaturals as well. He was a powerful fae with a lot of money. Maybe I should have taken his advice and help with my own security sooner. *I'll let him do whatever he wants when this is done and I can fix my house.*

I pulled up across the street from Sinclair's little rented suburban home. The lights were off; not too strange since supernaturals generally tried to blend in with the neighborhood, even if they kept a night schedule.

I licked my lips, tasting the cold metal of my lip piercing. The air gave me no scents worth paying attention to. I locked the car and walked toward the house. I had a feeling since Sinclair had made his terms, I wasn't in any danger. He would honor them because Cassius would never move forward on a deal, and Sinclair wouldn't get anything if he killed me right now.

Because the street was dark, I wandered around the house, not worried anyone was going to call the cops. I checked the windows, peeking in as I entered the backyard. I went back around front, doing the same to the other side of the house. Confident there was no one inside, I tried the front door and found it unlocked.

Definitely abandoned since they figured out I had found them. Well, maybe they left something behind I could use.

With confidence, I walked inside and flipped on a light. The place was clean, no signs of a struggle if they had Carter here at one point—I knew Carter would struggle unless he was unconscious or dead. I tasted the air again and only caught the fae with a hint of human, which had to be Sinclair. Vampire scents were strange. They smelled like their most recent meal, a very faint human, thanks to physical contact. If they hadn't fed for a long time, or they were careful about their feeding, they had no scent at all. Many were able to keep a scent on them to keep from pissing off other people. Others were good at never allowing themselves to get a scent, so they could continue to work in secret without being trackable.

I caught a hint of the witch I had killed as well, letting that satisfy me. At least one of them was dead. They had brought the body back here. I caught the distinct note of death in the air, that decay. It left a bad taste in my mouth, but not because I had done the killing. It was just a gross smell.

I wandered through the house, looking through drawers and under furniture. I wanted to be thorough. If I didn't check this house, it would have bugged me for weeks. I would have considered it a missed opportunity and would have never known if I could have saved Carter before the trade. But there was nothing and no one. They were gone, and so was any trace of them except their lingering scents.

I sat down at the dining table, thinking about what Sinclair must have thought when he learned I had stolen the intel. It had been a bold play on my part and a direct challenge to him. It must have infuriated him, which could have driven him to take Carter. Hostages weren't normally Sinclair's thing—too bold, too messy. People just tended to disappear, never to be seen or heard from again. Nothing anyone could prove was him at the end of the day.

I didn't move for a moment as I heard a creak in the living room, just out of sight. I reached down and pulled my gun but didn't cock it. I just wanted it ready.

"I knew you would come back," Sinclair said as he entered my line of sight. "You've played this game well,

Kaliya, but I think we both know how tomorrow is going to end up."

"Yeah. We give you Raphael, you give us back the vampire who belongs to the Mistress of Phoenix." I sounded like it was an easy solution.

"Really? You're ready to shoot me right now. We both know that won't kill me, and that's the only reason you haven't. You want me dead. You've wanted me dead for years."

"If I could, I would, but you're right. You can't kill me either, though. Guess we're at a bit of an impasse."

"You're correct. We're stuck in the same situation we've been in for...a few decades?"

"Several decades," I corrected.

He nodded slowly. "Yes..."

"Tell me, professionally, is twenty million worth this?" I was curious. I wanted to egg this man into telling me his wonderful little secret, whatever was bothering him enough to go this far this time.

"Twenty million is a lot of money."

"You run Las Vegas. Twenty million is what you can extort out of the casinos in a night," I retorted. "I've looked over some of the finances."

"Other people's," he pointed out.

I rolled my eyes. Everyone knew he was at the top of the food chain. He got a cut of everything supernatural, and sometimes human, that happened in Sin City.

"Yeah. Okay, Sinclair."

"See, this is why I'm tired of dealing with you. This Mygi job is going to get me beyond this pettiness with you, Cassius, and the Tribunal. I'm going to get out of the little circles I have to constantly run around you and move on to greater opportunities. I recommend you let me go, Kaliya. Your people need you alive, don't they?" He smiled at the end, and I hissed softly.

"Don't you dare bring them into this."

"Why not? You bring them into everything you do just by being you. You're a de facto leader, are you not? Yet you make enemies and fight against powers you have no chance of beating. I would think after so long, you would know you can't beat me." He rested a hand on his chest, an arrogant gesture of power and style.

"If you knew I was coming to check this place out, why are you here?" I asked, tired of the little game Sinclair was playing.

"Because I wanted to convince you to just accept the trade tomorrow. Don't try anything. There's no reason for so many people to get hurt. Carter is safe, for now, but don't do anything to jeopardize it. It was so easy to take him, you know. My fae just convinced the humans living in the nest he wanted to visit his new boyfriend and he walked right out with Carter like it was nothing. We could have killed him out right, but again, no one has to die. This can be very easy."

"Why do you care?" I snapped.

"He's a vampire like me. Of course I care," he retorted. "You think I liked seeing one of my own kind help you against me? I know the Mistress of this city doesn't like me, but I've never actively worked against my own kind."

I thought about Leith, Annie-Lyn, and Terry—fae, fae, and werewolf. I thought of Paden—fae. Me, the naga, and Cassius, another fae. Raphael, the maybe-human. He didn't even have another vampire working for him on this mission.

Because he intends on killing his colleagues.

"Really? That's the line of loyalty you draw?"

"Why do you think the vampires on the Tribunal are upset with me but don't come after me? They could, you know. They could have brought their nests down on Las Vegas and have wiped me out a century ago. I don't screw over my own kind, so it remains a problem with the Law and the Tribunal at large, but not a problem for them specifically, no matter how much you or the others want them to finish me off." He was still smiling. "I thought you would have put that together already. Maybe Executioner is the better role for you. Maybe I was wrong about that."

"What did Mygi really offer you?"

"Twenty million dollars. Ten for taking the job, ten for completing the bounty," he answered, an obvious but easy lie. There was no way I could refute it without giving away my own hand.

You want Raphael, though. The money isn't worth this. Are you going to betray Mygi as well? Damn it, Sinclair, give me something I can work with.

"Well, I should really go," he declared, checking the elegant pocket watch he had tucked in the front pocket of his vest. "This has been interesting, but I tire."

I snorted. "Dawn is hours away."

"I tire of you, like most people in your life," he retorted, tucking the watch back away.

It's almost funny when people I like a little make fun of me, but damn, I want to rip his fucking head off.

"No witty remark?" he asked, giving me a curious look. "Tell me, Kaliya, if it weren't for me being involved, would you care at all about this man? Raphael Alvarez?"

"Probably not," I answered with my own easy lie, but it was less obvious. Sinclair had no idea I could mate with Raphael and that he was important to my species. He had no idea my fangs dropped constantly, wanting to sink into the skin of the Catholic too full of guilt for my taste. "I just want to win."

"Ah, such childish motivations." He shrugged.

"Why do you care so much? Like I pointed out, twenty million is chump change. There's no reason to go as far as you have for that much money. Hell, I could give you that and ask you to walk away."

"Your confusion as to why I'm doing this shows me just how little you truly know. I guess I shouldn't be surprised. You have an investigative mind, but it never gets you anywhere. Not in your job, not in your personal life. You've never been able to find your way out of the dark, and I hold all the cards you so desperately desire."

I stood up in a rush of anger and surprise, showing that, yes, there was a gun in my hand.

Sinclair stepped back behind the wall. I licked my lips and realized the fae was close. There was no good way for me to go after Sinclair; he had backup, and I didn't. He could have killed me, but my initial suspicion had been right. He was going to wait until he had everyone where he wanted them to finish off this dirty mission he'd taken.

I walked out of the house on my own two feet, unwilling to run or move quickly. I didn't want to show any signs of fear. When I reached the car, my hand was shaking as I opened the door. When I sat down, I let his words sink in.

He can't know anything about that. There's no way.

I looked down at my passenger's seat and saw a note, which definitely didn't do anything good for my anxiety. Picking it up, I read it quickly.

I propose a different deal for you. Raphael for your vampire friend and information about who murdered your family. Same time, same place.

I folded it and shoved it into my pocket, my palms sweaty.

There was no way. Is this his trump card to walk away without a scratch at the end of this? Does he think I'll let him go for this?

The only thing I knew for certain was I couldn't tell Cassius about this. Not any of it. He wouldn't allow me near Sinclair, then I wouldn't be able to get anything. I also knew why Sinclair hadn't said anything inside. He taunted me about not knowing anything, but he left a silent offer because I wouldn't have let him leave the house alive if he had given me this offer in person.

My hands were still shaking as I drove away.

I can't entertain this, right? There's no way. He's bluffing and has nothing, but he wants to throw me off because he's gotten in too deep.

I was nearing the point of hyperventilating, so I pulled over, leaning on the steering wheel as I tried to calm down.

Over one hundred years of searching and now, Sinclair suddenly had information on who killed my family. His face never went on The Board. For the decades I played fucking footsy with the vampire, I never had any reason to believe he knew anything about the group that came into my home that night and slaughtered my family.

He's old enough. He could know.

My hands were still shaking as I thought back to what got me this deep into the mess around Raphael. An obscure connection between two people and Mygi Pharmaceuticals, who probably had nothing to do with my family...but maybe?

Maybe. I lived my life on maybes. I made decisions to meet people, work with them or against them, hurt them, and kill them on maybes. Just maybe the next time would give me answers. Maybe next time, I could learn something.

Maybe.

I pulled the note out of my pocket and reread it. I knew Sinclair's handwriting. I had helped Cassius more times than I could count look through the vampire's files, journals, and other personal property for any sign of wrongdoing.

Cassius was safe. So was Raphael. Carter was in the man's hands, and I had no idea if I was going to get him back alive.

Covering my face, I leaned over further. I was parked on a quiet, dark subdivision street, hidden for a moment. I was thankful no one was taking any notice of my car because I needed to think.

CHAPTER TWENTY-FOUR

When I made it back to Cassius's house, I was jumpy. For some odd reason, Raphael was waiting in the garage.

"What are you doing? Checking out the nice cars?" I asked, trying to act casual. The note in my pocket felt like it was on fire. My fangs ached as I saw the rough not-human man leaning on the wall, looking over me and the car I just got out of.

"Where did you go?" he asked, no inflection giving away any emotion.

"I wanted to check out a place I knew Sinclair had been earlier this hell of a week," I explained. "They abandoned it. There's nothing for us there."

"And you went alone?" He started to frown. "What if something happened to you?"

That caught me off guard. I locked the car and walked past Raphael to put away the keys before I could bring myself to answer.

"Would you care?" I dared to ask back. "I thought I was some heartless, soulless killer. Figured you would think the world was better off without someone like me."

My words hit their mark, causing his eyes to go red and black.

"That's..." He growled, and I watched as he struggled to string a sentence together. "You know, I might not like any of this, but that doesn't mean I want one of the few people who have helped me in the last ten years to get themselves fucking killed!"

"You have a funny way of showing it!" I wasn't even sure why I was lashing out at him. I didn't really get the point of being angry at him. He didn't owe me his sympathy or his concern, and I should have been grateful he spared some for me. Not many people did.

Instead, I found myself lashing out, pissed off he would even bother. That after the few days I had known him, I didn't know what he was thinking, but I was chained to him unless I found someone better or just different.

"What the fuck is your problem?" he demanded.

"I...I don't know." I searched for something he had done that annoyed me. "Maybe it's that you stomped off while I was trying to explain to you that you can't be human anymore."

"You said I lost my humanity."

"And you took it as something completely different than what I meant. You're in a world where it's not just humans and animals anymore, Raphael. You don't get to go back to the life you thought you had. You've lost that humanity, not your fucking moral compass. That much is clear." I waved a hand at him. "Then there's the judgmental bullshit I've gotten about the shit going on. Sorry, but I don't fucking need it or your concern, or anything else from you right now. Try to do something nice for once, and my life has fucking imploded, and my few friends are getting hurt."

I stomped off, dealing with the conflicting feelings I had toward the note and the ache in my fangs. I went straight for Cassius's office, knowing he would be there, but stopped short.

I thought I had decided on the drive back, but I stood there and realized I was a long way from making any sort of decision.

I could give away Raphael and get the information I needed to find who killed my family. Maybe. It would at least get rid of the fucking stress of having him around and the implications of him being here, in my space.

Or I could keep Raphael and hope to get a break in the case later.

With a heavy sigh, the ache in my fangs won. I opened the office door and walked in to find Cassius deep in papers, reading through stuff. At a glance, I realized it was the photos of the Mygi intel I copied from Sinclair.

"Sinclair showed up."

His head popped up, his eyes narrow and suspicious, but also full of concern. When I didn't say anything more, he got up and walked around his desk, grabbing my shoulders and looking me over.

"Are you hurt? Did he try to attack you?"

"No and no. We chatted. He figured I would go back to see if he left anything useful."

"You chatted?" Cassius seemed confused, but I knew he was just processing. His mind was probably working out the thousands of ways the conversation could have gone.

"He offered me a deal. Not to my face. When I got back into the car to leave, after he left, there was this." I fished the note out of my pocket and had to force myself to give it to Cassius. It was so hard showing it to him, knowing I was giving up on taking the trade the way Sinclair intended. If I wanted Sinclair's information now, I was going to have to capture him and somehow get the information out of him, which could prove impossible.

Cassius read the note several times. I watched his eyes flick across it, his expression growing darker each time.

"Thank you for showing me this," he whispered. "I know it was hard for you."

"I had a chance to get rid of Raphael, so the other nagas wouldn't expect me to become a breeder. I had the chance to get intel from Sinclair."

"Do you honestly think he knows anything?" Cassius asked, almost disbelieving.

"You know I don't leave stones unturned. That's what gets me into trouble most of the time. I'm giving you this to stop me." I needed someone rational. If it were just me, I would be questioning whether to take the deal until I was at the meeting place.

I knew I was willing to give up everything—Cassius,

Carter, Paden, even Raphael, who could help me save my kind. I knew I needed one of my friends, the most powerful of them, to stop me from doing something terrible.

It's finding justice for my family, though. Who passes up on an oppurtunity to do that?

"Adhar should stop trying to make you feel bad for not wanting to take that route in life," Cassius whispered, stepping away from me. "He's an ass for treating you like that."

"It's okay. He treats all the other male nagas like that too. We're either having kids, or we're doing it wrong." I shrugged. "Either way, this is me making my choice and sticking with it. Does it surprise you that when I first saw it, I thought about not showing you?"

"I'll never be surprised by your dedication...no, that's not right. I'll never be surprised by your obsession with finding out who killed your family." He sounded sad, and that sadness leaked into his eyes.

"It sucks when the only thing you can bury is pieces," I mumbled, looking away from him, thinking about the closet in my secure office. The few boxes I had there.

"Let's not talk about it right now. With this, we know Sinclair is desperate." He lifted the note with two fingers and waved it around. "He's hoping he can get one of us to betray the group to get what he wants."

"It doesn't change anything. He's going to try to kill all of us, and we're going to try to kill him." I tried to say that with confidence, but the little voice—the little desperate, obsessed voice—told me I wanted to take

Sinclair alive. If I couldn't trade him for the information, I had to get it some other way.

Cassius must have seen something on my face or came to his own realization.

"Capturing him would be hard, but it might put you at ease. We know some of the best torturers in the supernatural world. Maybe we can get the information he's offering. It would also save us if the information is a dud. You wouldn't have to feel guilty for handing over an innocent man to him."

"Yeah, but...if it's not easy, we just go for the kill. I'm not going to let him escape. He knows where I live. He could completely disrupt my life. I mean, he already has..."

"I don't think he came to Phoenix to disrupt your life," Cassius said with some diplomacy. "I think you jumped feet first into this situation, and now, you're paying for it. It's fine, though. You're going to live with me until your home is secure again."

"Yay..."

"We need a plan. What if you pretend to betray me and Raphael?"

"I'm not doing that," I groaned. "Stop bringing it up."

"When you left, Raphael asked Leith to bring him to me. He was upset you were risking everything to protect him when you didn't owe him anything. He's a man who likes to fight his own battles. Sound like anyone we've met?"

"Fuck you."

"We're past that at this point," he retorted. "He

waited in that garage, angry I let you go out alone. I told him if he was foolish enough to think you needed a bodyguard, he hasn't figured you out very well."

"Thanks for sticking up for my honor and everything, but I don't need it."

"He sees a woman who is taking dangerous risks and wants to help her because she's taking those risks for him. Are you really going to lock him in a bird cage and not let him make his own decisions?"

"I thought you were on my side," I snapped.

"I was until you gave me this," he said, waving the little note. "Kaliya, you're picking him over intel you would have thrown me under the bus for five years ago. I have a feeling I won't need to worry about Sinclair getting away with him because you'll be tracking Raphael's every movement. Biology. It's in your DNA to keep him safe."

"And not killing Sinclair like I need to," I reminded him. "If I'm stuck there, protecting a guy who is wholly unprepared for this world, Sinclair could get away."

"You have no faith in my abilities, then," he said, giving her a deadpan look. "Really?"

I fell into a chair and glared at him.

"I don't like it. I don't want him there. I want him to stay here and—"

"Stay safe? Is he never going to be able to go outside without a bodyguard?" Cassius asked softly.

"I fucking hate you."

"Raphael made me feel like a hypocrite for keeping him here, yet letting you wander off. I'm just passing on the terrible sensation to the more deserving recipient because you're the one who's making all the decisions concerning him."

"He's the target! We can't...Cassius..."

"Naga pairs have fought together for centuries."

"Not when they're human!"

"He's not."

I had to admit defeat at that point, throwing my hands up as I realized Cassius wasn't going to budge. He was right, and I was wrong. I was treating Raphael like a bird in a cage who couldn't handle the real world or protect himself.

He's been doing it for five years, and I have just under twenty-four hours to teach him as much as I can about vampires and fae.

Can I trust him to keep himself out of too much trouble?

"I see the wheels turning, Kaliya. What's the plan?"

"We need to teach him. A lot. I don't want him going in ignorant. We have...twenty-two hours. Let's get started. We'll get some sleep during the day. I've already taught him a little. We'll see what he's retained and go from there."

"Okay. I take it this will be things he can use to defend himself?"

"That's right. How to kill a supernatural 101." I got out of the chair and started stretching as I walked. "He's going to be a little upset with me."

"Why?" Cassius inquired as we left his office.

"I yelled at him when I got back. He...he asked where I had gone and asked what if something had happened to me. You know, that typical male, controlling bullshit."

"Ah, yes, that typical male behavior." I heard the sarcasm but chose to ignore it.

"Yeah. I lost my temper for a moment, then stomped away."

"Ah, yes, that typical female behavior," he muttered. I stopped and turned on him. He kept walking as if he hadn't said anything.

We found Raphael sitting in the dining room, watching Naksha bathe under her sun lamp. He looked up when he saw us, then turned back to the snake. He seemed to like her, or at least was interested.

"What are you thinking about?" I asked, going around the table. I stood awkwardly next to him, wondering if he would acknowledge my existence.

"How the woman who sang to this snake is also the woman with the bad temper," he said. I huffed and looked at Cassius, who shrugged, completely unwilling to help me with this.

"It's the same woman, and I'm right here, prick. You can't deny that you haven't been a bit of an asshole since we met."

"I know. I wanted to apologize," he said suddenly, sitting up and turning his body to me. It left me standing awkwardly in front of him, and he stretched those long, muscular legs out on either side of me. "You were right. I've been acting...badly. You're trying to help and probably saved my life at least twice now. Every time something reminds me that none of this is human...it upsets me, and I get angry and lose control. I spent five years doing this on my own. I don't want to be locked away now, while you two take all the risks. Then you went off alone. I would have hated myself if anyone who helped me after so long was killed because of me."

"I know you have abilities, so we're going to spend the rest of our time before the trade training you and getting prepared for the trade off. We're going to fake swap," I said, sighing. "And sorry for being bitchy with you. There's...more going on than just you. There's a lot Cassius and I need to take into consideration when we're making plans."

"I just want to be a part of them. I'm a grown ass man who's being treated like a child."

"You are a child," Cassius said evenly. "But that's okay, so is every newly Changed werewolf and newly turned vampire. Welcome to your second childhood. It's much shorter than the first and goes as fast or slow as you want it to."

"Basically, learn fast, and people will start treating me with a little respect again," Raphael said. "And they won't think of me as someone they can take off the street and torture."

"Exactly. Plus, I already started your training. We can pick up from there."

"Definitely." An excited light came into his eyes. I wanted to fucking melt, and I hated it.

"Swords? She always likes practicing with swords." Cassius was already walking out of the room. I didn't need to confirm his guess.

25

CHAPTER TWENTY-FIVE

I spent the rest of the night sparring against Raphael and Cassius. We rotated, giving everyone a chance to take a breather as the others continued. Raphael was still as bad as he was a couple of nights before, but it was something.

"Cassius, can we use the gun range right now?" I checked the time and saw it was five in the morning. We had enough time to get more practice in.

"We can. It's magically soundproofed," he answered. "Raphael, let's hope you're better with guns than swords."

"I hope so," he mumbled, wiping sweat off his brow. "The fact that you all still use swords is fucking strange, but if that's the way it is…"

"A lot of supernaturals have close abilities and strengths that need a counter if you aren't incredibly sturdy like them. Vampires can become very strong. Werewolves and werecats don't care what you hit them with unless it's silver or a fatal blow—" Cassius was saying.

"And they can bat your head off like it's a tennis ball on a T," I added, cutting in. "Swords, daggers, spears. Old weapons are still very useful in our world. I'll get you something silver from The Market if I can once this is all over. It won't help you tonight, but it's good to keep on you. Silver bullets as well, but I only break those out when I know I'm dealing with one of the Moon Cursed."

"Moon Cursed? Another way of saying werewolves and werecats? Are there other types of were...things?"

"No. No one really knows where they came from, but it's just the two, locked in a semi-aggressive stand off since they came onto the supernatural scene," I said, shrugging. "You learn to get used to not having answers in our world. Not everything has a reasonable explanation."

"I'm noticing. So tonight...fae are poisoned by iron, and a fatal wound with it will kill unless they can find someone who can or will heal them in time. Vampires will die, no matter what, if you set them on fire or leave them in the sun. Everything dies if you cut its head off."

"Or rip it off," I said, looking at his large arms. My fangs were already down, and the idea of sinking them into the mass of his bicep was an urge that made it very hard to focus. "It's disgusting and rough, but you have the strength to do it. Don't forget that."

"Yeah." He practically shuddered.

"You flip SUVs like they're made of paper. It doesn't take much pressure per square inch to break a neck and tear a head off. And you have to remove it. Vampires can heal from a broken neck once someone readjusts it and gives them blood." I put the swords away as we talked. Cassius was picking out several guns from his personal arsenal to take to his indoor shooting range in the basement of his multi-million-dollar mansion.

"Yeah..."

I tried not to sigh. He was still adjusting and wasn't giving us a hard time. He was probably just uncomfortable, thinking he could use his strength for that.

The problem was, I needed him to be a bit more blood thirsty...well, a lot more blood thirsty. I needed him willing to do whatever was necessary to survive.

"I'm ready," Cassius said, holding out two guns for me. One was a neat little Beretta, and the other was an M4, two of my standard choices. He picked up two more and handed them to Raphael, who held them with practiced ease. Cassius grabbed the two he chose for himself and led us to the basement shooting range.

"You know, most rich people would put bowling alleys down here," Raphael said, looking around the large space.

"Most rich people don't need to shoot a lot of people fairly often," Cassius replied as he put his weapons down at the first station.

I hit a few buttons and called targets to come down in the back. "Have you ever practiced with firearms before?"

"It's what I did in my spare time. Go to a local

shooting range and keep working on my aim. Guns have proven pretty useful over the last five years."

"Good. Then you know the deal. Don't point it at anyone else here. We'll shoot back, and we're faster than you."

Cassius didn't bother with earmuffs, and neither did I, heading to my station. One of the things everyone had to get used to was the loud bang of a gunshot or several in quick succession.

We loaded and took aim while Raphael was still making his way to the third station. Cassius's range had six stations. He often brought people down to help them, so they could defend themselves while they were out in the world. I knew Leith, Terry, and Annie-Lyn were all fantastic shots.

We all fired around the same time, emptying our handguns, a variety of different ones between us. When Cassius hit the button, the targets came forward, and I grinned to see all mine in the center ring of the target's body—kill shots, every one of them. Glancing at Cassius's, I saw the same thing. I knew he was equal to me with firearms.

But when I looked at Raphael's, I was genuinely surprised.

Heads shots, all within a few millimeters of each other, making one big hole.

When he noticed me staring at his target, he sheepishly rubbed the back of his neck.

"I know headshots aren't practical in a real situation, but they keep my aim sharp."

"Whatever works," I said, taking his target down and holding it where Cassius could see it. "Um, for future reference, headshots on supernaturals are a good idea. Body shots can easily be healed by certain species. If you can hit the head, go for it. Most can't heal from a severe brain injury."

"However, firearms are generally ineffective with supernaturals," Cassius cut in. "The speed at which many of us can move, our defensive abilities, and more can render the weapon ineffective. They'll also try to get close because it nullifies the problem of ranged attackers. Werewolves and werecats can't carry anything while in their cursed forms, so if you see one of those, figure they will rush you or run. Most animalistic supernaturals want to be on top of you."

"Anything with hands will start with guns or magic, though. If you're the better shot, they'll close the distance," I said, building on what Cassius was talking about.

"Why...why is everyone so violent in this world?"

"Because we live a very long time and are very invested in living our lives for as long as possible. It's easy to make enemies when you have an eternity to do it," I answered. "You piss off someone a hundred years ago, and they'll still be coming after you a century later or making your life difficult by rivaling you in business or politics. Most likely, you insulted them or took something from them they had decided was theirs. Or maybe you were just in the wrong place at the wrong time. Maybe you were too nosy at a party and suddenly know something you shouldn't. If we were all human, conflicts like these would resolve in a few years, and everyone would move on. We're talking about people who make their plans for decades, if not centuries, depending on how long they've been alive. We make enemies at about the same rate as humans."

"So, in the end, everyone hates everyone," Raphael said, breathing out. "And this is what I get to look forward to for…forever."

"No. You age, so only…ninety years, tops unless medical science figures out a way to make humans immortal, then you say your prayers because we're all in trouble."

"The very concept of humanity as it stands becoming immortal…" Cassius visibly shivered. "Let's not consider that."

Raphael found a place to sit, staring at both of us.

"You're both immortal," he pointed out, not shocked. "How does that work?"

"It's different for every species. Remember, immortal doesn't mean invulnerable. I'm actually very fragile. My bones break nearly as easily as a human's," I said, thinking about his incredible strength. If he ever lost control, he would break me in half. "Cassius is a little more durable."

"No, I mean like…" Raphael waved at the two of them. "The aging and stuff. How does it work?"

"Oh." Cassius stepped closer and summoned a chair. Sitting down across from Raphael, he launched into an explanation.

I hated this. We were supposed to be getting ready for tonight, not playing teacher. We could play teacher and student *after* getting Carter back and killing Sinclair.

"Well, fae children aren't raised in the human world. We're raised in our worlds, of which there are a few, and time moves differently there. It could take a young fae a normal eighteen human years to reach adulthood, or it could take a hundred human years. When we come into our full powers, we essentially stop but not completely. We're immortal from a human perspective. In several thousand years, I'll look older than I am now."

"How old are you?"

"I'm not telling you that."

Kaliya wasn't surprised. She didn't really understand how old Cassius was and she used to sleep with him.

"Ah. Kaliya is a hundred and seventeen. Is that considered old or young?"

"Young for her kind, old for others."

"Okay, what?" Raphael frowned. "If most everyone is immortal, then..."

"Average life spans," I said. "Werewolves have a hard time living through their first twenty-five to fifty years after being Changed. Werecats normally live several centuries. Vampires fluctuate wildly, but as long as they control their urges, which becomes easier every generation, the longer they tend to live. They all have a breaking point, though. Some just haven't met it. Fae are impossible to judge because they can disappear into their own realms and live for a year and miss fifty here. Many supernatural species are like me. We grow up here in this world, and we hit maturity. That depends on the species, but it's generally by twenty-five. Then we...stagnate. We exist in our prime. Aging after that is minute. Some nagas look older than me, a couple look younger. Depends on how well you take care of your body."

"Meaning, while immortal, stress can cause the body to age a little, like Kaliya's hair. There's one naga who looks quite old, right?" Cassius looked over his shoulder at me.

"Yeah, and he is. He's second generation, one of the first true born naga. He's been through a lot, and if you ever see him, you'll assume he's a fifty-five-year-old Indian gentleman. He's just as spry as he was when he looked twenty-five, though, so don't toy with a supernatural just because they look old."

"Age is power," Cassius said. "You'll notice a lot of supernaturals won't tell you their exact age, but you can begin learning how to guess, based on things they keep around them. A ten-year-old vampire is much less powerful than a five hundred-year-old vampire."

"Carter is a young vampire, and Sinclair is a...middle-aged one?" I figured, mulling over the numbers. "Sinclair can wipe the floor with Carter's face, and there would be nothing Carter could do about it."

"Okay. Older supernaturals are more powerful." Raphael nodded slowly. "I think I'm starting to figure this out."

"Give it a few years of actively trying to learn, and you'll know what you need to live day to day in the supernatural world," I said, thumping his shoulder. "Now get back to practicing. I want to see you try something a bit more powerful than that Glock."

"Okay." He jumped up, and I watched him grab an M4. He loaded it with practiced skill as Cassius moved a target into position for him. Once the target was in position, he began firing in bursts of three. He hadn't had any military training when he was taken, but he obviously had some practice, some idea about how to handle the weapon. When he lowered it, I nodded in appreciation for his aim.

"Did you ever practice with these?" I asked.

"Yeah, had a couple over the years. Bought them illegally and lost them every time I had to run, but if I had the cash at any point, I tried to keep one in my place. Didn't have enough time to settle in Phoenix to find out where I could get one without the paperwork," he explained.

"Good. Well, I think you're going to be as ready as you can be for tonight. We don't need to teach you how to fire a gun. Cassius? Anything you want to go over with him?"

"No. I think we should all get some sleep."

Leith cleaned up the mess we made, even breaking down and cleaning the firearms.

"I'll leave several of these out for you to choose from later," the butler promised as we walked out.

"Thanks, Leith," I said, waving as Cassius closed the door. "Well, now we just get some sleep."

"Wait...do we have any sort of plan?" Raphael asked.

"Yeah. We're not going to let Sinclair take you. We'll

show up and lay down the Law," I answered. Cassius caught my eye, and I quickly looked away. I wasn't going to betray anyone here. I'd made my choice. The possible intel would have to wait. If Sinclair lived through the night, I could get someone else to interrogate him for whatever he thought he had.

"So, we get there and open fire? Talk it out? That doesn't tell me anything," Raphael huffed as we walked up the stairs to the main floor.

"We'll probably talk to him for a moment, see if he really wants things to get bloody. He'll probably try to taunt us—Sinclair likes to push people to the edge. We open fire once we have taken in the situation and figured out a way of freeing Carter without getting him killed. The best thing for you to do is stay not dead and shoot at the bad guys." I smiled and started toward my room. Cassius disappeared to his suite, but Raphael was on my heels.

"Wait, Kaliya. Really, that's it?"

"That's it. Cassius and I have done this before. It's not fun, and no, it isn't easy, but it's...procedure. We know the steps to the dance. The only trick is pulling them off at that moment and knowing how to adjust for different possibilities. Go get some sleep."

He nodded slowly and stepped back from me. I noted the door he entered was my neighbor to the left. They put him in the friends' wing of the mansion. Cassius had two wings—one for friends he liked and another for guests he didn't really want there but had to entertain. His personal suite was most of the top floor above us.

I went inside and picked out my clothing for the evening, wanting to look over what I had. I noticed Leith had brought in all the stuff I brought from my house, including the weapons that hadn't been stolen from my bag like my phone. He'd carefully laid them out, which gave me a good idea of what I could take. It took me another two hours to get any sleep. When I woke up, I knew exactly what weapons I was taking with me to kill Sinclair.

I also knew exactly what *my* plan would be.

CHAPTER TWENTY-SIX

"Don't forget anything!" I called out as I loaded the SUV Cassius pointed out. It was ten at night, and we had an hour's drive to the meetup point. We were pressed for time, in my opinion. I wanted us there early, able to get a feel for the location.

I had barely slept, but anticipation was keeping me anxious, and I was already prepared for the night.

On my back was my talwar, a piece of home and heritage I couldn't part with. At my waist was the katana I had been given decades ago by a friend. It comforted me, reminding me I was trained for deadly nights like the one I was about to face. Along my belt were throwing knives and shuriken, carefully treated with my venom. It would take more than a small scratch for it to work, but it was insurance if I got a good hit that wasn't fatal. On my left thigh was a large hunting knife and on my right thigh, my Beretta. In the SUV, under my seat, was an M4.

It was a small armory.

"Do you have enough weapons?" I turned to see Raphael, wearing thick black jeans and a dark red shirt, almost maroon, topped off with that leather jacket. His eyes were the perfect, medium shade of brown, not the unearthly red, so I took my chances to be a bit playful with him instead of annoyed.

"You never know when an ex might show up to a party." I shrugged, giving him an innocent smile.

"That's worrisome," Cassius muttered, walking around our giant not-human charge. "But to answer your question, Raphael, no, she probably doesn't think she has enough weapons."

"I could also get those fancy boots with daggers in them," I pondered. "Maybe I could start wearing long sleeves and use my arms more. There's a lot of real estate to carry more."

Raphael started to chuckle. In all honesty, the mood was terribly light for the night ahead. For me, it was a point of habit. I didn't like getting stressed out when I had so many sharp objects. The job was the job, and I did my best to survive the world I lived in. So far, my record was going fairly well, and I wasn't too worried.

Unless tonight goes completely sideways, this should be fine. Not easy, but fine.

"It's probably going to go sideways," I mumbled to myself. "Just have to stay positive."

"What?" Raphael was still standing there, giving me an odd expression.

"Get in the car," I ordered, ignoring his question. He didn't need to hear my internal thoughts.

Though it might be a good idea not to voice them out loud. I'm not alone in my own house.

The three of us piled in, and Cassius pulled out of the garage.

"Does everyone have what they want for tonight?" he asked, his hand hovering over the garage door button.

"I'm ready," I answered.

"Let's get your friend back," Raphael said confidently. I was glad to see he wasn't freaking out. If he stayed calm, everything would go smoother. If he started freaking out, that would be bad. I didn't think he would freeze, but I was a little worried he would hesitate at a bad time.

Hopefully, he can channel that kill-or-be-killed attitude he had when I met him...when he tried to shoot me. Maybe he'll go hard tonight and let the Catholic guilt eat him alive tomorrow when it's all said and done. He seems to know what's necessary at the moment, even if he'll have a problem with it afterwards.

Cassius nodded and closed the garage. Leith waved at us as the door closed. I knew Annie-Lyn and Terry were camping out inside, waiting for morning.

"Cassius, a couple of questions," I said as we started driving. "I know it's something you don't really talk about, but can you take people when you shadow step?"

His face went from calm to severe in a blink of an eye.

"I'm not in the habit of shadow stepping," he snapped. "You know that."

"What is it?" Raphael asked.

"Something certain fae can do, particularly those with darker bloodlines, like Cassius, but he's fucking weird compared to most fae."

"Really? Are you going to pull open my family tree and show him?"

"No, I asked a simple question, and you got huffy. It's important. Raphael also asked a simple question, and I thought he deserved an answer." I narrowed my eyes on my fae friend. "Every supernatural with a toe in fae politics knows your bloodline. It's not some big secret."

Cassius sighed. "Yes, but it could prove fatal to those not of the right fortitude. It's why I don't do it."

"Tonight, if things get crazy, pick Raphael or Carter and try to shadow step them to our way out," I ordered. "And I mean crazy where they'll die anyway, so the risk of the shadow step is minimal at best since it would be their last chance."

"Okay. If it's their last chance."

"What's Cassius's bloodline?" Raphael sounded like a curious ten-year-old boy. When I looked back at him, he shrugged. "I would rather learn about one of you than talk about my impending doom."

"You're smart," I complimented, nodding sagely. "Always good to keep from getting stressed out before these things even get started. Cassius? Can I tell him?"

"I'm the grandson of Oberon and Titania. Born of Brion and Isla, their two eldest children. I was their youngest child. I'm one of the few fae who has a strong claim over both light fae and dark fae abilities and can use certain abilities from either."

"His grandparents were the original Fae King and Queen. They broke up and had dozens of other children with humans, creating the clans and the idea of light and dark fae, Oberon and Titania each passing on different types of abilities," I said, launching into fae lore. I thought it was interesting. "Even though they had a touch of human blood, they were considered pure fae, thanks to being direct children of Oberon or Titania. From there, everyone started inbreeding to keep the lines pure, and the fae population exploded."

"It wasn't all sex, and it wasn't considered inbreeding back then," Cassius snapped. "They created some fae clans out of animals as well."

"How..." Raphael's mouth was kind of open, and I resisted the urge to close it for him.

"Magic. Magic kept it from being gross inbreeding," I said. "Or so the fae say."

"My parents..." Cassius looked downright furious now. "They weren't siblings."

"They had the same parents."

"They looked completely different and had wildly different magic. If they were related, their magic would have been similar." Cassius huffed. "Fae don't really have DNA. We're magical beings. The original fae weren't related because everyone was so unique. Now, children seem like their parents, but not back then."

"And you were their youngest? How many siblings do you have?"

I winced, slashing my hand across my neck at Raphael. *Stop! Stop, damn it.*

"None," Cassius whispered. "Both were dead by the time I was born. I was the last child my mother had before she passed on. My father disappeared later."

"Oh, shit. I'm sorry."

"It's...it's fine. Someone would have told you eventually if you're going to hang around us." Cassius sighed.

"Sorry, I didn't think he would ask more," I said, trying to ease the tension and take the blame for it. "I shouldn't have..."

"He should feel more comfortable, knowing one of the more powerful fae is helping him," Cassius said, his face becoming stoic.

"I like teasing you about the bloodline thing..."

"I'll remind you that everyone in your species is descended from the same one thousand nagas, and the only new genetics you've gotten have been from humans," he said, narrowing his eyes on me. "And there's only nine of you left now. I wonder how closely related you are."

I nodded, admitting defeat. He had a point. Supernatural species didn't exactly play by the same rules. It was a point he'd brought up before, every time I teased him about his parents. Though, I had known him before his father had disappeared. The joke became less funny since then.

"You are both fucking weird," Raphael mumbled in the back. "All this is fucking strange."

"Yeah. Supernaturals can be a bit mind-bending a lot of the time," I agreed. "Want to know more crazy shit?

We're going to be in the car for a while, and there's no reason for you to be ignorant."

"She gets talkative when she's about to kill someone," Cassius said blandly. "You can tell her no, and she'll try to sit quietly in her seat."

"Sure," he said in defeat.

"There are other realms," I explained brightly. "Fae have realms, most of them small pocket dimensions, but there are bigger ones. The Market? The fae black market? It's actually the exact same in every city, but it exists in multiple places at once. It's similar to the Tribunal Chambers, a pocket dimension that can be entered wherever a door is made. Most of the Tribunal members have a door in their residence and jump in it whenever they're needed. It cuts down on the traveling."

"See, that doesn't bother me. Humans have been trying to prove the existence of the multiverse for a long time now," Raphael said, shrugging. "Honestly, it's a little comforting."

"Really?" I raised an eyebrow, wondering why he thought so.

"It means a lot of the supernaturals can go back to where they came from."

"Ah, that's a problem. Werewolves and werecats are just humans with a nasty, transmittable curse. Vampires are…kind of the same way. Once human, but they're more like…magically reanimated dead. Witches are humans with a magical spark and a keen mind that allows them to bend the forces of the world around them. They try to be fae and fail every time, but they've got considerable skills as well."

"What do you mean by they try to be fae?" Raphael yawned, and I realized he was finally getting more comfortable with the wildness of the world he was now living in. Being bored was better than being scared—always better.

"They make powerful, complex spells to try to do what a fae can do with a snap of their fingers."

"They normally just blow something up," Cassius mumbled. "But they are *very good* at blowing things up. They also dabble in things a fae can't or won't do."

"Yeah, summoning demons and angels and other shit we try to pretend doesn't exist, even as supernaturals. There are creatures that live on other planes that don't belong here and *can't* belong here. Like demons and angels. None of us want them around."

"There are more besides them, but because humans have such a deadly fascination with them, they're the most common beings popping up in our world, trying to break dimension barriers," Cassius said.

"Are they...like Gabriel and..."

"Raphael, the angel your parents obviously named you after? Like archangels? Abrahamic lore?" I shrugged. "Don't know. Never met either type. Don't want to."

Cassius pointed at her. "She actually has the right idea here. If you ever hear anyone say 'summoning' with 'angel' or 'demon' following it, please tell one of us. It's an executable offense, and we'll need to shut it down before it gets too far."

"Um. Okay. Sure. You know, why don't we pick up all this tomorrow? I think I just want to focus on tonight."

"Fine," I sighed heavily. "I'll sit here and be quiet."

"Try to be quiet, you mean," Cassius mumbled.

We sat in the car silently...well, almost silent. I played around with the radio until we lost any of the good stations. Then I started messing with Cassius' phone to get some music going. My foot tapped. I kept moving around in my seat, trying to get comfortable.

I was never very good at not being restless before a kill. Even when I was doing more covert work, I got antsy and hyped up. The adrenaline started for me too early and wouldn't stop until it was all said and done. Talking, keeping things light, those kept my mind busy before events.

And I didn't want to think too hard on my plan. I didn't need either man in the car to know something was coming, and if I stewed on the plan, Cassius would know something was off with me and be worried. He knew me well enough to know what would be unusual behavior.

Plus, I had been enjoying talking to Raphael. I liked seeing his eyes light up as he learned new things, even if the light was somewhat dimmed by caution and a healthy, reasonable dose of fear of the unknown that most humans had.

"Okay," Cassius said softly, turning off the long, dark road we had been on, going far south of Phoenix. "We're nearly there."

I looked around. We were in the desert, all right. If anything happened, the likelihood we would get human attention was next to nil. Cassius was now looking at a state-of-the-art GPS map that was heading to the coordinates that Sinclair had given us. It had us turn off the small road we were on and head further into the desert, further away from civilization and help.

When Cassius parked ten minutes later, I was the first out of the car. We had beaten Sinclair to the place, and I was fucking glad to have a chance to look over the area, though it didn't prove to be much. In snake form, there were tons of options to hide and get out of the way of anything, but I couldn't do an entire fight in snake form, and the amount of cover we had for a fire fight was abysmal.

"He picked a good location," Cassius said, getting out of the SUV. "Sparse and away from any potential problems."

"Yeah, I think I hate it," I said, crossing my arms.

"Agreed." Cassius was frowning.

Raphael was the last out and stood next to me, looking over the desert, probably trying to scope out what he could kill someone with.

"What's so bad about it?" he asked.

"There's nothing here. He doesn't have to try to hide any of his deeds. There're no witnesses unless one of us gets out alive," I explained. "And he's probably going to try to kill all of us except you, so...it's bad."

"We don't have to do this. You could just give me to him, and I'll find my own way out. Take your friend and go. You've both helped me a lot, but you don't owe me shit."

"Shut up," I snapped. "We're not giving Sinclair anything he wants. We never will. If he wants you, he'll have to fight tooth and nail for you."

I pulled my door open and sat down, waiting with my feet dangling out of the SUV.

When I could see headlights in the dark, I hopped out but left my door open.

You never know when you might need to make a hasty getaway. May as well keep the option open.

"Oh, one last thing," I said as the SUV drew closer. "Don't let Sinclair look you in the eyes. He might be able to mesmerize you, which is how vampires relax and subdue their prey. It'll make you compliant for him to feed from. You won't be mind controlled, but you'll start finding good reasons to do what he asks. It doesn't last long, but it could last long enough to do damage."

"Oh, that's really helpful to know since he's nearly here," Raphael said with a snort. "Can do. Don't look vampires in the eye."

In other circumstances, I would never let Raphael get close enough to Sinclair for mesmerizing to work. My plan, however, needed it.

Cassius is going to call me a fucking hypocrite after this.

CHAPTER TWENTY-SEVEN

It was quiet when the new SUV cut its engine and turned its headlights off. My eyes adjusted quickly to the dark, my vision relying more on thermal input than light. I knew there were three bodies of varying warmth coming out of Sinclair's car, meaning my old friend didn't bring a replacement for his witch. The two cooler individuals had to be him and Carter, and the last, bouncing up and down, was the fae. I glanced to either side as Cassius and Raphael came up beside me. Perfectly for my plan, Cassius stood on my left, his body temperature also fluctuating like the other fae while Raphael was a blazing inferno compared to the rest of us.

There wasn't anything else alive within thirty feet of us. I would have known. Everything had run off when we drove up, and the appearance of another vehicle this far out would scare off anything that was trying to come back. Wildlife was skittish like that.

I could see Sinclair holding the back of Carter's shirt,

forcing him to come forward. Carter didn't look any worse for wear, no signs of any beatings or torture, but that only gave Sinclair so many points. He had still abducted a vampire who was a good friend of Cassius and me and a member of the Phoenix vampire nest. He'd probably starved Carter as well, and going twenty-four hours without blood at Carter's age was like going a week without food for a human...a month for me. I had no doubt Carter was weaker than he normally was, which was saying something because he was a young vampire. He wasn't all that strong to begin with.

"Carter!" Cassius called. "How are you?"

"I'm—"

A hand clamped over Carter's mouth. Sinclair glared at our group while the fae, Tom Lennon, held Carter.

"Now, now. You haven't earned the privilege to speak to him yet. You have something I want, I have something you want. You can talk to him once the exchange has happened." Sinclair was back to his professional persona, not the murderous piece of shit he had been at my house. It was the same face he had given me at the rented home in Scottsdale, his normal face.

But now I knew there was something lurking beneath the surface, something that hadn't been there in the eighty or so years I'd dealt with him.

"Tell me, do you really think we'll keep your crimes a secret?" I asked loudly.

"I think you're morally grey enough to do whatever is necessary," he answered, smiling. "You've always been...

bad for the people around you. Friend or enemy doesn't really matter."

How right you are.

"We have no intention of trading. I'm willing to let you and Tommen walk if you hand over Carter to us," Cassius said, his posture telling me he was ready for a fight. Tommen, Tom—Cassius knew this fae.

"You have no authority over me, *Lord* Cassius, the one without a Clan," Tommen sneered. "You ran from power when it was offered to you after your piece of shit of a father walked away from us. Your entire family has proven to be nothing but worthless. Oberon and Titania would be ashamed."

"Be careful," Cassius whispered, his voice carrying on the wind. "They might be ashamed, but they haven't taken my power, and my line is far more powerful than yours."

"Not that you ever use it," Tommen said, spitting in the dirt. "Sinclair warned me you might try to help the nagini once she got involved. I don't know why he's worried."

"Let me warn you of something then," Cassius said with a smile. "If you think Sinclair is going to share any of the spoils with you, you're a fool."

"I don't betray my business partners," Sinclair said blandly, almost bored with the conversation. "Your offer is denied, Cassius. I'm not here to make deals. I'm here to see if my offers were accepted or rejected."

"Reject—"

In a blur, able to move faster than anyone there, I

pulled my hunting dagger from my left thigh sheath and brought it up to Cassius's neck. In the exact same moment, I pulled my Beretta from my right thigh holster and pressed the muzzle to the side of Raphael's head.

There was silence as everyone realized what I had just done.

"Start walking," I ordered Raphael softly.

"But..."

"He has something I want," I snapped. In my head, a small voice called me a hypocrite. I told Cassius we couldn't do this. I fought with him over it. But now, there was more on the line. "I'm not letting it get away from me."

Raphael stepped forward, and I kept the gun aimed for his head. Cassius was smart, not moving. I had the blade pressed directly to the skin of his neck, and we both knew who was faster. If he made any move, I would give him a very serious injury.

"Send Carter," I ordered, looking across the rocky desert at Sinclair. He nodded and handed something to the young vampire, who walked fast. Tommen released the light bindings he had put around Carter's arms and legs, giving him the ability to run.

Raphael walked, though, confused, scared, and I felt terrible for each step he took.

"Kaliya, why?" Cassius begged. "There were other ways."

"I made my choice," I answered, hoping he understood the meaning, hoping he put the pieces together. I could have it all if he understood what I wanted. I pressed the dagger against his neck harder. I hadn't treated it with venom for this reason. If Cassius or I moved at all, it would slice him open, just a little. A little more pressure and I could kill him without having to work at it.

We watched Carter draw closer, running as fast as he could. He held up a USB when he was close enough for me to see it.

"This must be for you," he said.

"Get in the car," I ordered sternly. We didn't have time for chit chat. I needed him to get ready to leave. Once I heard the door close, I lowered the gun pointed at Raphael and the knife I had on Cassius. Now was the time. It had to go perfectly right. "Raphael, now!" I roared.

He turned and made it three steps before light bindings whipped around his legs.

"Cassius!" I snapped, lifting my gun to fire at Tommen. Sinclair was moving fast for Raphael, his face not angry or upset—just determined.

"I hate you," Cassius growled at me. He pulled up his rifle and started firing.

Sinclair was fast, and grabbed Raphael, yanking him up. A shimmer appeared between us and them, right as Raphael's eyes turned red and black. He couldn't break the bindings, though, his muscles bulging.

"Damn it!" Cassius snapped. "He threw up a field." He kept firing, unloading all his ammo into the shimmering wall between them.

"Cassius, shadow step!" I yelled. "Now!"

"I can't!" he roared. "I can't go through light magic with dark magic!"

I cursed and started running, holstering my Beretta. Beyond the shimmering wall, I saw Sinclair catch Raphael's gaze and grin. Raphael sagged.

I pulled my talwar out and sliced the shimmering wall just as Sinclair struck, sinking his fangs into Raphael's neck. The iron of my blade broke the wall, leaving Cassius able to move.

"Get Raphael!" I screamed, running for the pair. Light bindings grabbed my ankles, sending me to the ground, and I sliced them off with my sword, glaring at the fae as I stood. A roar filled the night, and I turned to see what had happened, fae already forgotten.

Raphael slumped to the ground, pale and weak. Sinclair stood over him, his eyes now looking like Raphael's, black ink filling his veins and taking over his face and neck. His fangs were longer than I had ever seen, coming down nearly an inch, and his other teeth were razor points as well.

"This is power," the vampire murmured, clenching his fist.

I dropped my sword and lifted my Beretta again. I fired the entire magazine into the vampire, who only smiled as the wounds healed, and the bullets fell harmlessly to the ground.

When Sinclair started walking for me, I backpedaled, making sure to grab my talwar as I tried to keep the space between us. Behind him, I saw Cassius erupted into vision in a pop of black smoke. He grabbed Raphael, saying something as he took one step, holding him, disappearing in another small pop of black smoke—shadow stepping.

"So, this was the plan, huh?" I asked Sinclair. "You vampires get stronger when you feed off supernaturals, but it's not allowed. You wanted to feed off him and see what kind of power he gave you."

"Oh, I knew what kind of power he would give me. There were some things Mygi told me over the phone, not in writing. No chance of it leaking to other vampires and having to fight too many for the privilege," Sinclair explained. He wasn't running at me, still going at a normal, vampire walking pace. That meant I was still the fastest person around and could outrun him. I kept trying to back up to the ride, though. I could hear Cassius and Carter arguing about whether to leave me or not. Who was on which side, I didn't know.

"That was nice of them. You know, I thought when vampires fed off supernaturals, you didn't get the powers of those you fed off of."

"Raphael is different, special. I intend on keeping him. You're not leaving with him, Kaliya."

"But I am," I said, turning and starting to run. That's when I saw the light bindings raise up and grab the SUV. Cursing, I hauled ass and sliced them. One grabbed my ankle, and this time, I couldn't catch the fall, landing hard on the ground, face meeting rocks.

The very satisfied roar behind me sent chills down my spine. Someone reached down and grabbed the back of my shirt, yanking me up to my feet. I saw Cassius, his eyes a swirling mix of white and black—light and dark. His lineage was the stuff of legend, even though he wasn't as powerful as his parents. Turning, I saw that he summoned dark bindings, and they grabbed both Sinclair and the fae.

"Why didn't you do that earlier?" I demanded.

"Because it's hard for my kind of fae to use our big abilities in this world," he reminded me, sounding tired. I looked at his face and saw it looked a little washed out. "There's no human blood in me to anchor me here like Clan fae. Those won't last long. Get in."

I nodded as the last of the light bindings broke off our ride. Cassius jumped behind the wheel and hit the gas before I could even close my door.

I turned to the back seat, looking over the two people back there. Carter's eyes were wide. Raphael's were half closed, but he was alive.

"How's everyone feeling?" I asked.

"What the hell was that plan?" Raphael muttered.

"Cassius was supposed to save you faster," I explained.

"You said to be ready to use it if it's the last possible option," Cassius snapped. The SUV bumped hard and sent all of them close to the ceiling.

"I meant, use it when I told you to," I hissed back. "Why did it take you so long to figure out it was a ploy?"

"Because..." Cassius didn't finish the statement.

Because he doesn't trust me to make the right call when it comes to my parents' killers.

"Well, it's fine. Sinclair is just on the vampire

equivalent of steroids, and we need to get out of here. But other than that, it's fine. Carter, are you okay?" I searched the young vampire's face. "I'm sorry this happened."

"It's fine." The SUV hit another hard bump, and we all bounced. "He didn't hurt me or anything. Look, maybe I can do what he did, and—"

"If you feed off Raphael, I'll kill you," I said evenly, meaning every word. "Not only because I think it's wrong, and it's illegal, but also because we don't know what he just did to himself. I'm not letting you act stupid. He has a whole lot more information on this than we do."

"Okay." Carter nodded. "Then can we switch seats? I haven't fed since that fae broke into my light proof room and grabbed me."

"Sure," I said nicely. I shifted to make it easy and got into the back. Carter carefully walked over me and fell into the front seat. When I shifted back, I looked out the back, seeing only two small dots for headlights. "They're gaining on us," I said softly. "Cassius, can this thing go any faster?"

His foot hit the gas, but the lights kept getting bigger.

"To outrun it before we reach the city? I don't know, but I can make sure they don't drive us off the road," he answered.

"That will have to do," I said. "Raphael?"

"I'll be fine," he mumbled. "Just need a few minutes for the punctures to heal and the blood to replenish."

"Has a vampire fed off you before?"

He shook his head.

"I'm sorry," I whispered, touching the bite gently. "He heals faster than you."

"He's also a vampire," Cassius said from the front. "He already had a better-than-average healing factor. He's full of rich, fresh blood, and it's supernatural with its own quirks. There's no telling what he can do now."

That was terrifying.

I watched as it gained on us, heart racing. The getaway should have been the easy part. It should have been the part where everyone took a moment to breathe.

"We need to talk about your communication skills when we're done," Cassius said from the front seat.

"Yeah," I agreed. "I really thought you would get it sooner."

"Shadow stepping with other people is stupid and dangerous, and you're lucky Raphael is alive."

"What did you tell him before taking him?"

"He told me to hold my breath," Raphael said with a groan. "How close are they?"

"Too close," I answered.

"Do you have the thing you wanted?" He didn't sound mad. I was a little grateful for that.

"Carter? You have that USB still?"

"Yeah." He held it back, and I grabbed it, shoving it into my pocket for later. "What is it?"

"Intel on who killed my family, on whoever is trying to wipe out my kind. Sinclair told me he had it, hoping I would go for the easy trade. I really didn't consider he would get a bite out of Raphael and actually get his powers," I explained. "That's not normal."

"Nothing about this entire situation is normal," Cassius snapped, but it was missing the bite he normally could put in his voice. Did that short distance shadow stepping really take it out of him that much?

I didn't have time to care about it. Sinclair's SUV was pulling closer, and I watched as the vampire crawled out onto the roof. My eyes had adjusted enough to the night to pick out some new changes to the vampire. His red eyes were glowing. His muscles seemed bigger, and the black veins were now visible on his hands. His face was nearly all black and his teeth? They looked like they could scissor off a limb.

What the hell is he becoming?

I didn't get much more of a chance to think about it. He leapt off his SUV as it drew closer and landed on the top of ours. Black nails sank through the roof like butter. Carter was the one screaming as Sinclair peeled off the roof.

CHAPTER TWENTY-EIGHT

I was shocked speechless. Unable to say anything, I grabbed Raphael and yanked him down, keeping him out of Sinclair's reach. Unthinking, I tried to put my body over his head.

"Hold on!" Cassius yelled. He slammed on the brakes and tires squealed. Raphael and I hit the back of the seats in front of us. My head spun as it hit a metal frame piece inside the seat, but I was quick to look up and check on Raphael, hoping he was okay. He didn't seem worse for wear, but I didn't have much time to really ask him how he was doing.

The SUV spun, control fading as it tried to stop, the wheels still screeching on the road as Cassius kept his foot on the brakes. I grabbed Raphael's jacket, pulling him closer, keeping my body over his as the SUV finally made its way to a stop.

"How is everyone?" Cassius asked. "Kaliya? Say something."

"I'm okay!" I said as loudly as I was able. "How're you and Carter?"

"We're fine. Carter hit the dashboard, but he'll be okay," Cassius explained back to me.

I looked over Raphael, lifting off him. He groaned as he sat up, looking at my face.

"You..."

"Don't think too hard about it," I said, swallowing as he realized I had thrown my body over his to protect him. Biological instincts were funny things like that. "Where's Sinclair?"

"On the road about fifty feet in front of us," Cassius answered.

"Get moving again—"

I didn't get to finish that. The fae rammed his SUV into our backend, and the entire vehicle spun again, sliding on the road, debris flying everywhere.

"We need to get out," Raphael yelled.

"On it," I snapped as it came to a stop. I forced my door open and staggered out onto the road. I helped Raphael out and checked Carter over once he was next to me. Cassius stood in the road, glaring at the fae in the other SUV.

"Cassius, we're going to have to fight this out!" I yelled. I knew it wasn't going to be easy, not while trying to protect two people and getting everything out of the deal while Sinclair got nothing. That was why I had avoided it and decided on a getaway instead. I could always hunt Sinclair down after the fact, especially since I had leave to kill him at any point.

Now, I didn't have much of a choice.

"Let me feed on Raphael. Maybe I can fight him." Carter was looking at Raphael with a ravenous expression that made me uncomfortable.

"No," I said, looking around. Sinclair wasn't in front of us on the pavement like Cassius had said. I pulled the katana from my back and stood ready. Glancing at Cassius out the corner of my eye, I saw he was still waiting on the other fae, ready to fight against his own kind in some kind of grudge match I wanted no part of.

I wasn't as ready as I thought I would be. Coming in from the darkness off the road, Sinclair slammed me into the side of the SUV, snarling viciously. I screamed as my back hit the metal and glass tore into my back. My grip on the hilt of my katana failed due to the sheer force and pain of the impact. I tried to kick and push the deadly sharp fangs from me, but I knew I was going to fail as they snapped again, grazing the skin of my neck. I decided to bite back as Carter and Raphael struggled to pull Sinclair off me. I sank my fangs into him and depleted the small amount of venom I had been able to replenish since killing the witch. Sinclair roared and dropped me, but even through my double vision, I could tell there were no signs my venom was effective.

Raphael's blood. He's immune because he fed on my fucking possible mate, and there goes my most efficient way of killing someone.

Sinclair turned, and I saw a large knife sticking out of his back. Without hesitation, I jumped, grabbing the hilt and wrapped my legs around Sinclair's waist. I yanked out the blade, ignoring the black blood that poured from the quickly closing wound. Before I could stab the back of the motherfucker's head, he reached back and grabbed my arm. I couldn't tell what happened after that but knew he threw me, and I was in for a hard landing. I shifted into my snake form, hoping that would help me, but I wasn't a cat and didn't know how to land on my feet. It didn't help that I didn't have any.

I bounced off the ground several times before I was able to check if anything was broken. I wiggled and moved, trying to catch my breath before shifting back into my human form. I panted when I was shifted back and looked up at the road. He'd thrown me probably twenty feet and now I watched Carter and Raphael play cat and mouse with him. Raphael was still pale, but he was looking better every second, his eyes red. Beyond the car, I watched Cassius and Tommen duel, their swords clashing as their powers warred. They were trying to bind each other, Cassius trying to shadow step to gain an advantage while Tommen was consistently throwing up shields.

I knew who I needed to help.

I grabbed a throwing knife and tossed, aiming for the vampire's head. It sliced open the side of his neck. My aim must have been off because I was dizzy.

"Hey, motherfucker!" I called.

Sinclair turned on me and snarled. Every time I saw him, he looked more monstrous, more not vampire, or even remotely human. Raphael's blood was changing him, and I didn't understand how or why. Part of me wondered if Sinclair even knew why he was fighting anymore. He wasn't saying anything. He seemed mindless.

Question to ask tomorrow. What in all the fucking realms did Mygi turn Raphael into that could cause this sort of fucking reaction?

I threw another knife and watched it hit the vampire's heart to no effect. Sinclair ignored it as if he was now dead to the pain of a blade. Or maybe it was the type of blade. Vampires didn't have a specific weakness, but I didn't know about Raphael. He hadn't mentioned any sensitivity yet.

I threw every single thing I had. Knives and shuriken stuck out of Sinclair ineffectively. The injuries didn't make him pause, and the venom did nothing. As Sinclair advanced, I walked backward again, not wanting to take my eyes off the beast. I tried to make a large loop to get me back to the road, but Carter and Raphael started talking, and that caught both my and Sinclair's attention.

"I can fight him!" Carter said. "Please!"

"Fine! Just don't make me drop the way he did," Raphael snapped. "Kaliya! Keep him busy!"

"No!" I yelled.

Sinclair spun as the wind brought us the smell of fresh blood, stronger than it had been previously. I ran to get ahead of him as he stalked up on Carter, who was biting down on Raphael's wrist.

Idiots! He's not going to appreciate someone munching on his godsdamn snack.

"Stop feeding and fucking hide!" I screamed as

BOUNTY

Sinclair grabbed the back of my shirt and tossed me aside. "Cassius!" I screamed, trying to stand up and run in time.

I saw my old lover turn, and his eyes go wide. Tommen took the chance to knock him to the ground. Light bindings wrapped around Cassius, and Tommen yanked his hair to force him to watch Sinclair.

I couldn't help anyone. I was transfixed by Sinclair grabbing Carter's head and pulling it off Raphael, who he whacked aside. I had nothing else to throw and there was no way for me to get there in time. Sinclair twisted and twisted.

And Carter's head came off.

I didn't scream in horror. I didn't retch. Nothing felt like it was going to come up, and tears didn't threaten to fall. I watched Sinclair, turned into a bloody fucking monster, rip off the head of a young vampire I had considered a friend.

But I didn't scream.

I turned for Cassius and Tommen, taking advantage of everyone still transfixed by Carter's falling body and jumped on Tommen's back. With a quick snap I broke the fae's neck and let the body drop, releasing Cassius from his hold.

"Get up. We have a monster to kill," I snapped.

Cassius's eyes went wide when he turned to me. I pulled him off the ground to his feet and pointed at Sinclair.

"Focus," I ordered.

"You..."

Sinclair's growl interrupted the thought. I saw my

katana lying by his feet. He wasn't looking at Cassius and me. He was stalking Raphael, who was still trying to get up from the pavement where he had landed. I ran for my katana, ignoring how Cassius tried to call me back.

"Bind him!" I roared, grabbing the hilt and slicing across the back of Sinclair's legs in one motion. The vampire tried to kick me away with a roar, but I rolled away, flicking black blood off my blade. Dark bindings swirled up and grabbed Sinclair's ankles and wrists. I launched myself at him and found myself swatted out of the air like a fly, hitting the wrecked SUV. My vision went black for a moment, ringing erupted in my ears, and my body hurt. I was certain bones were broken. I didn't know if I could feel my legs.

A roar came over me, and two things crashed together. I tried to stand and found someone to grab.

"Kaliya, you need to get up!" Cassius yelled desperately. "Please!"

I struggled to my feet, blinking several times. My vision came back slowly as I stumbled around, Cassius pulling me.

"What..."

"Raphael decided he was healed enough to join the fight," Cassius whispered. "We can talk about it later."

I turned to see the two men brawling. Sinclair and Raphael, throwing punches and grappling. Raphael still had the size advantage, his face nearly covered in black, and it was still growing down his neck. Every vein on Sinclair's skin was black. The only difference I saw between them was that Raphael didn't seem so mindless, so monstrous. He had some control.

Sinclair's mind was long gone.

I wonder if this is what he wanted, or if he didn't know it was going to happen.

"You have to help," I said. "Help Raphael." I tried to push Cassius back toward the fight, but he didn't budge.

"You're bleeding from your ears, Kaliya. I'm not leaving you."

A chorus of roars and a large crash took our attention off each other and back to the fight. Raphael had been thrown into one of the black SUVs. Sinclair ran for him, and my heart raced.

"Go for the head!" I screamed, hoping Raphael heard me, hoping he understood. "Cassius, bind Sinclair again!"

"I'm getting weaker by the minute, and he's breaking out in seconds," Cassius snapped. "You know I can't use magic for extended periods in this realm."

"Try!" I staggered away from him to find my sword. Sinclair and Raphael were beating on each other again, and this time, when I looked at them, I was certain Sinclair was getting bigger. He'd been a fit man but not bulky, only my height. He looked like he was several inches taller now and had been hitting the gym for several hours a night.

Dark bindings tried to grab Sinclair, but Raphael accidentally tossed the vampire out of them.

"Hold him!" Cassius roared. "Hold him still!"

I ran toward the fight as Raphael heard Cassius and understood. He struggled to push Sinclair to the ground, and the dark bindings were taut, straining to hold the vampire. I rushed in, swinging my katana over my head.

I brought it down on Sinclair's neck. It took three swings.

But eventually, Sinclair's head rolled away, and the body sagged. Cassius ran up next and pulled a matchbook from his pocket, striking three at the same time and threw them on Sinclair's body. Raphael jumped away and fell as the vampire's body ignited into flames.

Realizing what needed to be done, I grabbed Sinclair's hair and tossed it into the inferno.

"No one can know," I said softly. I wobbled on my feet and fell on my ass, groaning in pain. I tried to continue talking, knowing I needed to say something important. "We can't tell anyone what Raphael's blood does to vampires. They'll all want him."

"Agreed," Cassius said, panting. "Could you imagine if that was a more powerful vampire? We wouldn't have been able to match him."

I looked back and saw Carter's body. Wherever his head went, I didn't know, but there was his body.

"We weren't able to match him," I whispered. "We weren't able to match him at all."

He's dead, and it's all my fault.

I shoved the thought down and tried to blank out the feelings flying through me. Not now. Not yet. The moment I knew I was safe, I would let those thoughts come.

"You know what this means, right?" Cassius looked at me, then Raphael. "He said Mygi told him about your blood. They must have experimented with this already. They knew what they were getting into, telling Sinclair about it."

"Maybe they thought they could...clean up? I don't know," I said, rubbing my head. "I don't understand anything anymore."

"I have a feeling we're never going to really understand," Cassius said softly, watching the blaze now. "He lost his mind. Raphael's blood turned him into a mindless beast."

"How not normal is that?" Raphael asked, falling onto his back. I could see his chest rise and fall with exhaustion.

"Unheard of," I answered. "If he fed off Cassius or me, he would have just been more powerful, harder to handle but still of his mind. The power would have faded as he needed to heal and shit. Your blood seemed to turn him into a meaner version of you. That..." I shook my head and winced at the pain. "Are you okay?" I asked, trying to ignore my own pain.

"I'll live. I don't know. I saw you hit the SUV, and he was going to crush you or something, and I knew I had to...stop it." He sighed. "Too bad I couldn't stop him from killing Carter. I'm so sorry, Kaliya, Cassius."

"We'll figure it out," Cassius said gently. "It's no one's fault he died. Kaliya's plan could have worked. None of us could have foreseen..." He waved a hand at the fire.

I wobbled and nearly fell over. I touched my side and groaned, feeling the blood there.

"Cassius, how are we going to get home?"

He turned to me. I think he paled. Raphael sat up, his eyes going wide.

"Jesus," the very-not-human gasped. "She needs a hospital."

"I have service," Cassius said, coming to my side. "Kaliya, hold on, and someone will get to us. Okay?"

"Yup. I've been more beat up," I said, but my eyes didn't want to stay open. I wanted a nap—a very long nap. "Tell when me the Tribunal gets here to reprimand us for the mess."

"Okay," Cassius promised.

"Don't let her fall asleep!" Raphael cut in, moving toward me.

"She'll be fine."

I didn't care to hear them argue, so I let my eyes close and let the blissful dark pull me away from the pain.

CHAPTER TWENTY-NINE

Waking up to darkness, I sat up slowly, groaning at the dull ache in literally every part of my body. I didn't freak out. I knew where I was. I remembered everything. There was nothing to be freaked out about.

Everything had gone sideways with Sinclair, and now I was in my room at Cassius's house. Raphael and Cassius made it out with me. Carter...didn't.

That sent a sharp pain to my chest. I hadn't grieved when it happened. I had seen heads ripped off bodies and had been able to disassociate at the moment. Now, it sank in, and tears flooded my eyes. I had known while Sinclair burned, that this moment was coming. As I looked at Carter's body, I had known.

It still hit harder than I was prepared for.

All my fault. All my fault. All my fault.

The door creaked open, and I didn't look up, curling my arms over my head to hide my tears.

All my fault. All my fault. All my fault.

"Kaliya, it wasn't your fault," Cassius whispered.

It's always my fault.

I looked up and wiped my eyes with the back of my bandaged arm.

"He would have never—"

"No, he wouldn't have been involved if not for you, but Sinclair got ahold of your phone. There was a chance he could have targeted anyone in your address book. Your plan to get everyone out was a good one, Kaliya. His death was..."

"My fault," I whispered harshly. "It's always my fault. Everyone I go near gets hurt. Look at Paden. Look at you. Look at my *family*."

Guilt caused me to stop as a sob wracked my body.

It was always like this. Obsession drove me, guided me, and every time it happened, someone got hurt or killed. This time it was Paden and Carter.

And yet, I knew if something else showed up that might lead me to my family's killers, I would do it all over again.

"Kaliya...There's nothing I can say that will make you feel any better. What I can say is the healers promised you would be awake at this time for the Tribunal. They had questions for both of us, and a judgment needs to be made about the situation between Raphael and Mygi Pharmaceuticals. Mygi also needs to answer for Carter's death because, in the end, it's their fault. You were justified, going after and securing Raphael because they made a bounty saying he was human. They decided to hire Sinclair, and it was that monster who killed him. No one blames you, except maybe Imani."

I cringed at the name of the Phoenix vampire Mistress. She was never going to forgive me for this one.

Then another realization hit me.

"She should have been protecting him better," I mumbled. "He was a member of her nest. Where the fuck was she? She knew the meeting place to get Carter back. Why didn't she send us any backup?" And I was never going to forgive her for that either. Carter had been one of her nest and she had failed him too.

"I don't know," Cassius answered. "I'm certain we can get those sorts of answers at the meetings, which we will be in all night."

"Fuck. I need to shower," I said, pushing the sheet back. Looking down, I realized I was naked. Bruises covered my body, but nothing felt broken or maimed. I had feeling in my toes, and my head didn't pound like someone was hitting it with a hammer.

"No, you don't. The last healer did a cleaning spell on you," he said gently. "A brownie with a bit of medical training."

"Fantastic." I really hated that. I licked my lips, wondering if the scents were still in the room. Sure enough, three fae, other than Cassius, had been through, along with a variety of other species. A werewolf and a werecat were the two that stood out. "Who all came in here?"

"A few of the Tribunal came to look in on you. They

sent someone to make a door to their chambers in my house for this to go smoothly."

"How long have I been out?" I demanded.

He concentrated for a moment, and I waited patiently on the answer.

"About twenty hours. It's nine. You took the most damage. I just needed to sleep in my chambers to regain my strength." I had figured as much. Cassius's room was a pocket dimension that gave him access to his family home in one of the fae realms. For the few fae like him, it was important to have that connection. "Raphael ate through every red meat kept in my kitchen, much to Terry's dismay, then he was back to normal. You were the one tossed around by Sinclair the most without the healing abilities to handle it."

"I was also the most skilled. You decided to play footsie with the other fae. Tommen," I bit out.

"We should have focused our forces sooner," he agreed softly. "He made me upset and effectively kept me out of the more important fight, and I think he did so on purpose."

"Probably, but he's dead now," I reminded Cassius with a grin. Something made me happy. Sinclair and both his little motherfuckers were all dead now, I was still fucking among the living, and no one was going to take that away from me...not yet, anyway. And so were Raphael and Cassius.

My heart wanted to split in two again for Carter, but Cassius had a very real point. There was still work to be done. Mygi and the Tribunal waited.

"Meet me outside," I ordered him. "Are they expecting anything formal?"

"Would you wear it if they did?"

"No."

"There's your answer," he said, chuckling softly as he walked out. I figured he was glad for the semi-normalness of the banter.

I'll be okay. I'll bury Carter and make sure nothing like this ever happens again. No one will ever know what Raphael's blood does to vampires, and I'll kill anyone who tries to take him. Carter won't have died in vain.

Shit, I should have asked Cassius about Carter's body.

I jumped out of bed and quickly got dressed, rushing out even though my knees hurt, and my back pulsated with a dull ache. I hurried to the kitchen, hoping to find him hanging around there since it was normal. I was lucky to see him accepting a drink from Leith.

"Carter's body," I said loudly, leaning on the counter. "What—"

"It was accidentally destroyed after you were unconscious," he answered, giving me a look. He'd burned it, then. No one would ever know. "Imani already marked tonight as the official grieving period for him. There's a small event going on at her home. We're not invited."

"Of course not. We should do something, then. Later, just us," I said, my mouth a little dry. Cassius nodded solemnly. As if he could read my mind, Leith put a coffee down in front of me. I grabbed it and sipped, smiling to see Leith remembered how I liked it. "Which door did they steal to use to get into the Chambers?"

"Closet door across from the dining room in the hall," he said, pointing in the direction.

I walked away, ready to handle this mess with the Tribunal. There was still paperwork and all that good work of being an employee for the supernatural governing body, and I was certain if any representative from Mygi was around, there was still a chance Raphael could end up with them.

"Kaliya, wait. They're talking to—" Cassius tried to grab me as I drew close to the door.

"Don't care," I said, grabbing the door handle and yanking it open. They very rarely made doors that didn't have necessary guards. I guess Cassius and his staff were special enough to warrant the liberty to come and go as they pleased for this.

At the far end of the room were the Tribunal members in attendance, sitting in a long line, perched high up like a row of judges, and in a semi-arc around an empty circular opening, was the floor where criminals normally sat to plead their case. Chairs lined the walls and looked over the pathway to that spot.

There were a few reasons the Tribunal would meet in full—public trials, showcases of Tribunal power, and the force they had, a chance to witness the all mighty rule they claimed to be in the supernatural world. Those were very rare. I could count on one hand how many had happened in the last century, and I had only been to one of them.

Private trials were done under the cloak of secrecy, or more usually, indifference. Standard cases of this or that criminal behavior and a verdict needing to be passed, so the Executioners could go off and do their jobs after the Investigators finished theirs. I went to those. I flew to the closest permanent door to the Tribunal Chambers and sat in while people rambled on until a verdict was passed—capture, kill on sight, or innocent.

Finally, there were meetings like this one. Semi-formal, there would be no judgment passed on one person this day, only a decision made about a troubling situation. They had to mediate different parties to a sound resolution that couldn't be ignored. Judgment by the Tribunal was always final. It wasn't always perfect or right, but it was *always* final.

Which meant I only had one real chance to make my argument heard without pulling out my trump card to win this fight. I had to make a good first impression.

"Executioner Sahni, I'm sorry, but we're—" Isaiah, the male vampire of the Tribunal, began.

"Sorry, I was told I needed to make a report, so here it is," I said, walking further into the room. There was a man standing in the center circle, and I licked my lips, playing with my lip ring. Everyone on the Tribunal knew what I was doing. They all made it a point to know as much as they could about every species that agreed to their rule. Standing there was a fae, well dressed and somewhat older looking.

"Are you the CEO of Mygi Pharmaceuticals?" I asked, standing next to him.

"I am. You must be the nagini—"

"Good. You need to contact Mistress Imani of the Phoenix vampire nest some time tonight. Reparations are owed in the death of Carter Wilkenson, vampire of her nest and dear friend of mine. I'll be doing so as well since his death also comes back on me."

"Excuse me, do you know—"

"On a scale of one to ten of how important you think you are, I don't give a fuck if you're an eleven," I snapped. "Your incompetence and the incompetence of your company has led to the death of a promising young vampire."

"I and Mygi had nothing to do with—"

"A board member of your company went rogue and hired a vampire who went by the name of Sinclair. Notoriously dangerous, he stood in front of this Tribunal multiple times and was able to get away with several crimes, including murder. Now, you can bring the board member in front of the Tribunal, and he can answer, or you can just take a small hit to your finances and reputation."

"Executioner Sahni, must you be like this every time you come into these chambers?" a woman asked, not sounding angry, more exasperated and unsurprised.

I looked up to smile at Alvina.

"How's my favorite Tribunal member?" I asked sweetly.

"I've seen better days. Less busy days. Kaliya, we wrapped up a Trial less than a week ago. How have you found so much trouble in so little time?"

"I'm good at these things," I said, shrugging nonchalantly.

"Can we get back to—" The Mygi CEO tried to cut in.

"Can someone tell him I'm more important than him?" I asked loudly, waiting for any of the Tribunal to step in.

"Brother," Alvina purred. "This is Kaliya Sahni, Tribunal Executioner, nagini, and one of the two leaders of her species. When she comes onto the floor, we give her the respect she is due."

"You like her," the fae King muttered. I met the gaze of Cassius's uncle. Alvina was his aunt, but she was nice, and I didn't judge Cassius for that relation. This one, however... "The same can't be said of all of us."

"Oisin," I greeted coolly.

"Where is our nephew, and why hasn't he come in to put you on your leash yet?" he asked.

"I left him standing outside the door. Maybe he knows I don't like leashes." I smiled wickedly. "Actually, I know he does. I made sure to tell him that when we were fuck—"

"Again, you come into these Chambers and disrespect—" Oisin was officially pissed, in record time, too.

"Silence," someone ordered quietly. There was enough quiet power behind the words, I stopped talking. Oisin turned slowly toward the right end of the table, his left. I followed his gaze and found Hasan sitting at the end. "I'm gone for only a century, and the

Tribunal is getting into petty arguments with an Executioner. What in the world has happened?" He sighed heavily. "I grew tired of this years ago, so let's please stay on topic. We were hearing from Lord Ardghal about Mygi's interpretation of events and what he believes should be done about one Mister Raphael Dominic Alvarez. As far as I can tell, he thinks we need to hand the unknown supernatural over to him, and he has good reasons, as he has the science available to continue trying to discover what Mister Alvarez is." Hasan stared down at me, looking annoyed and bored. "I take it you have different opinions. This is your chance to share them."

"Raphael escaped from Mygi five years ago for a reason. He was experimented on against his will. I've seen the scars on his body from those experiments and the numerous times he escaped from attacks Mygi committed on him in private in the name of recapturing him." I spoke directly to Hasan. He seemed bored, but I had a feeling he was anything but. His keen eyes didn't match his lazy body language. "Over the last few days, I've noticed several...anomalies that don't match up with how a respectable organization should behave, concerning any new supernatural of any species. Raphael had no education. He knew of species already out to the public, but he was never told that supernaturals were holding him. He was purposefully left ignorant."

"Ardghal, can you explain this?" Callahan demanded. I knew the werewolves would have issue with it, possibly the vampires and Hasan as well. All of them were species who required education of Changed or turned humans. It was vital.

"No," he snapped in answer.

"Continue, Executioner," Hasan said, waving a hand.

"Also, it was relayed to me by Investigator Cassius that Mygi told you the story that Raphael was dangerous and uncontrollable. That he would expose us through his actions as a whole to the humans. I can tell you if he's made it five years without humans figuring out what's going on, they won't. He's done well to hide from both supernaturals and humans after him. The unfortunate incident when he...became what he is now is just that. An unfortunate incident. There have been no signs of it coming to pass again—"

"You've only known him for a few short days," the fae beside me cut in.

"Does that matter? In a few short days, his entire world has opened up as I and later, Cassius, have educated him as best we can—"

"He's a danger to everyone here. You don't have the facilities or the expertise to control him if he goes into another rage and kills several people. You know it. I know it. The Tribunal should know it. Don't pretend that because he hasn't done it yet means he'll never do it—"

"We can say the same for every single supernatural in this fucking room, asswipe," I hissed back. "A werecat rolled over an entire werewolf pack in Dallas only a few weeks ago. We sent her home with a slap on the wrist, if that. Vampires lose control and need to be put down when they get blood high. Werewolves fall to the Last

Change." I glanced at Hasan. "So do werecats, I believe?" He nodded. When I turned back to Ardghal, I made my point. "Would you lock up every supernatural just for the possibility of it? Because every supernatural has a line that needs to be drawn, or we're animals that need to be put down."

"It's safer for him to come back to Mygi."

"So you can chop his hand off and see if it'll heal back on without any help again?" I asked. "Because I've seen that scar."

"You have no right—"

"I think I have every right—"

"Stop arguing at once!" Isaiah screamed from his seat. "You are both behaving like children arguing over a toy. The Tribunal will reconvene in one hour. Both of you have valid, important points about the situation and good positions for your stance. Be ready to make final arguments when we return, please."

I was left stunned as the entire Tribunal stood up. It was part of protocol. If one of them called a break, no one argued. The member obviously needed a moment to think.

But it left me pissed this time. Ardghal was smiling at me, already plotting.

I wasn't letting anyone take Raphael from me. They would know that soon enough.

CHAPTER THIRTY

I stormed out of the Tribunal Chambers and found myself back in Cassius's hallway. He was still standing there.

"You could have come in to back me up," I snapped.

"I don't make a habit of storming into the Tribunal Chambers uninvited. We were to wait until they were ready to speak to us." He looked over my face. "What's changed?"

"One-hour recess, then final arguments," I grumbled, walking around him. I was still holding my coffee, but it was cold now. I headed into the kitchen and handed the cup back to an expectant Leith. "Sorry. I need another one."

"Don't give her another one until she's explained to me what she's talking about," Cassius said, storming in after me. "What do you mean they expect final arguments in an hour?"

"Me and Ardghal, that fucking uncle of yours, got

into it about whether Mygi gets Raphael back. Needless to say, it was a mess. I didn't even get to properly report on how the last few days have gone. Hasan asked for my stance, and I gave it to him, but that piece of shit fae kept interrupting me. Isaiah called a recess."

"Who all spoke?" Cassius asked. "I need everything, Kaliya, if I'm going to be any help."

"The witches were dead silent through it all, as they tend to be. They keep their opinions private until there's a vote. Callahan was somewhat unsettled by the fact Mygi made no efforts to educate Raphael while he was there. Alvina still loves me, and your uncle fucking hates me."

"If Callahan was upset, Corissa will have strong words about it, even if she's in the minority. They generally work together. Pack mentality," Cassius pondered, nodding. "And there's Hasan. Werecats have strict social protocol for the creation of more of their kind."

"Yeah, new werecats become like pseudo-children to the werecat that Changed them, and it's really weird," I agreed. "He looked fairly...bored through the entire thing, though. I don't know him, but I could have sworn he was interested but didn't want the others to know."

"Hasan doesn't like when the other Tribunal members think they can play him, so he's always been a bit distant," Cassius explained. "He's there because someone has to represent the species most hurt by the actions of the larger groups. I'm certain he would have left the Tribunal permanently ages ago if he could get away with it and know the werecats would be safe."

"Would he be an ally? Should I work to play to his vote and see who falls in line?"

Cassius shrugged. "That's up to you."

"Come on, Cassius. You know I'm generally just told to point and kill something. You've always been a lot better at this than me, which is why I normally hand this part over to you."

"You're the one who just woke up and decided to barge in there, guns blazing," he reminded her. "But I'll be in there with you for final arguments. I'm not letting you go in alone for that."

"Should I go? It's about me," Raphael finally spoke up. I turned to him and nodded.

"Yeah. They should see that you have some control over yourself, and we're not trying to hide you. Maybe one of them will recognize what you are, even if they didn't remember based on a description of you and your powers."

"They should allow you a moment to speak as well, even if these are final arguments. I don't think they'll be against hearing a few more people. I'll try to get a word in before the end. Kaliya, you should consider that thing we talked about."

"Only as the last resort. There's not much to consider. If all else fails, I'll pull out the trump card, and none of them will be willing to fight me about that."

"You could stop all this right now—"

"What?" Raphael stood up, looking between them. "What does he mean you can stop this?"

"Naga Law and none of your business. It's a dangerous move, something Cassius and I were about to go talk about." I was even more against it now than I was when I told Cassius that Raphael was eligible. I had seen the look in Ardghal's eyes. He wasn't the type of man to give up.

"We'll take this to my office then," Cassius said, waving me to follow him.

"Wait, I really think I should know—"

I turned on Raphael and put my hand on his chest, stopping him from coming any closer.

"It's naga business, of which I am one of the de facto rulers. You can know if I want you to know, and it's very possible it wouldn't work, which is why it's my last resort. I have just under an hour to figure out other options. You'll give me that," I said evenly, trying to ignore the furious ache in my fangs. Being healed must have overactivated my venom glands because they felt full and tight like I needed to milk them again. Touching Raphael, though, feeling the broad, hard planes of his chest, feeling the insanely warm natural body temperature he was...I wanted to bite him now more than I had before, even with the thousand questions swirling around him.

I pulled my hand away before my mind could wander too much.

"We'll be right back," I promised. "This is just something I don't share with outsiders. I'm sorry."

"What would it entail? This protection thing you might be able to do?"

"Everything," I said softly, turning away. I walked out, letting Cassius follow me. Once we were in his office, he locked the door, and I fell into my favorite chair.

"Why, Kaliya? Why won't you do it now?"

"Mygi wants him back so badly that they're willing to kill for it. They're willing to justify to the Tribunal the torture they put him through for years. They have enough political sway, I know I won't be able to get them completely shut down. We'll be lucky if they walk away with a slap on the wrist."

"I understand all those things, which makes naga protection over him even more im—"

"Dangerous. It makes it more dangerous," I said, looking up at him as he passed me. "Cassius...what do you think Mygi will do when they find out some unknown supernatural species can breed with nagas? That's groundbreaking. My own people might even be okay with him going into that lab again, to find out if we can make more of him to..."

"Oh, Kaliya," Cassius whispered, sitting down slowly. "You're being paranoid—"

"I know Adhar. He's not a bad man, but he's a desperate one. He'll want Raphael picked apart and studied because maybe it'll find him the mate he's never had. As far as we've always known, nagas can breed with other nagas or humans. Humans are harder to have children with than a pure naga pairing. What would that mean for Raphael? He presents human, smells human, looks human...until he isn't. This rocks the foundation of my species to the core, and I *can't* trust my own kind with him." I looked away, feeling the weight of rule on my shoulders, a rare problem, one I avoided with a passion. This was my call to make, and I was going to do the best I could with it, even if it meant setting back the nagas by potentially decades. "I have to keep this from them, so I have the chance to find answers without outside help I disagree with. I have to do this on my own."

"Not on your own. If we can find a way to protect him, I'll lead a formal investigation into what he is. I'll feed you information to do with what you will, even if it means fighting battles you shouldn't."

"You just said I was being paranoid. Now, you're deciding to help."

"I told you I would support whatever decision you made, and I'm doing that. You don't trust Mygi, the Tribunal, or the other nagas with Raphael. That means he's going to stay with you or me because I know you trust me."

"I do."

"Then we're going to work this out. Let's look through the Laws and see if we can find some protection for him."

"Mygi is trying to make it sound like what they did to him doesn't matter," I said softly as Cassius floated a book to me. I flipped it open and sighed. "There's going to be nothing in here to protect him. Without knowing his species, we don't have any laws that would cover him from their activities. He's not dead, therefore, they didn't really do anything wrong. It's so fucked up."

"I know," Cassius agreed.

"And because he is an unknown supernatural, going to Mygi will seem like the safest option. They can study him and try to give him answers. The Tribunal will probably be watching them closely, so the fucked-up experiments would probably stop, but...I can't send him back there."

I kept flipping through the pages, not really looking at them. My mind wandered.

Naga protection might be all I have. Declare him a compatible mate and tell them to shove it. Take him home and kill anyone who tries to come on my property, the way every naga does it. Seven hundred years as a Tribunal species has given us certain allowances, since we only joined and accepted the Tribunal authority to have those protections granted. They granted the demands because we were one of the first to join who wasn't one of the founding species.

The Laws don't stop anyone from trying to kill us, but they give us legal protection to fight back without anyone being able to demand reparations.

I frowned.

"Can Raphael declare his species and become a protected species of the Tribunal?" I asked myself. I flipped through the book of Law and found the portion about new species' admittance into the governance of the Tribunal.

It required one of two species leaders to declare

intent. If the species was democratic or had shifting leadership, there was a trial period for any of those in the species to fight for the right to lead and remove the application.

None of that mattered for Raphael, though. There was nothing like him in the world, not that we knew of.

"Kaliya? You were saying something?"

"I think Raphael should go in front of the Tribunal to ask to become a protected species," I said, looking up, the idea settling. I had a good feeling about it. "He could be a species under the Tribunal, then apply for protections under the Endangered Species Law, like the nagas and kitsune. Mygi wouldn't be allowed to come near him without his permission. He would be allowed to defend himself with deadly force."

"You can't declare a species you don't have a name for, and he's not the leader—"

"There's no requirement in the Laws for a name of the species," I said, pointing at the book in my lap. "None! Because everyone assumes every species already has a name. So what if Raphael's doesn't, so far as we know. And for leaders? I'm the de facto female leader of the nagas because I'm the only one. Why can't Raphael be considered the de facto leader of whatever he is because we don't know if there are others?"

"You're mad…" Cassius said, standing up, furiously flipping through the pages of his copy. I watched him read through once he was on the right page. "It might just work."

"It just might," I said, grinning. "Cassius…he

wouldn't need either of us. He would have protection on his own. He would be able to go and do as he pleased within the confines of the Law, and the Tribunal could treat him the same way they treat every supernatural, except he'll be endangered and have all the same protections I do."

"They would have to give a placeholder species name...but..." Cassius nodded quickly now. "Go get him. Get him in here. We're going to start working this out. Kaliya, this is genius."

"I have my moments," I said, grinning wildly. I ran out of the office and stopped in the hall. "Raphael! We might have an idea!"

He was coming down the hall seconds later, taking long strides.

"We can protect me from Mygi without breaking a bunch of Laws? I don't really want to have to fight it out for the rest of my life."

I grabbed his arm and pulled him into the office. I didn't want any Tribunal people who might be wandering Cassius's house to overhear. I hadn't seen any yet, but I had a feeling they were there. Relocking the office door, I let him go and grinned at him.

"We can't stop people from attacking you, but we can fight to get you legal protection and certain privileges reserved for only a few species."

"What do I have to do?"

"You'll have to put in a formal request to the Tribunal to become a species that submits to its authority. That means you'll be completely beholden to the Law, but you'll also be granted all the protections of it. If someone outside your species attacks you, you can defend yourself. Mind you, you'll have to pay reparations for the death if one occurs. But I think we can go a step further. I want you to ask for protection under the Endangered Species Law."

"What?" I knew I had lost him by the look on his face.

"Some species are given special dispensation to kill at first sight for trespassers or attackers with no legal ramifications. No reparations, no talking it out with the Tribunal to see if you accidentally committed murder. Nagas are one of them. If anyone comes on my property without my permission, I'm allowed to kill first and ask questions later, and no one can try me for murder."

"It's based on the werecats," Cassius added. "They have land magic, a territorial thing they do where any supernatural that crosses into their territory can and probably will be killed on sight. Other species asked to be allowed to protect themselves like that, but they have to have good reason or unfair wars over land would pop up. Generally, a werewolf pack and a vampire nest can't fight over a city just because they want to. Both the pack and the nest would be put down for such an egregious display of bad behavior. But species low in numbers, under undue threat of extinction, are given permission to defend themselves like werecats do."

"Werecats aren't protected under the Law, but no one is going to stop a werecat from killing anything on its territory," I said, shrugging. "It's your choice, Raphael, but this is the best we can do. This isn't a world where the fighting ever truly stops. There's always something or someone that wants to kill you, but this will allow you to fight back every time. If someone tries to capture you, kill them. If someone comes into your home, kill them. No guilt, no possible repercussions. They know what they're doing when they go after you if this becomes a thing and goes public."

"I..." Raphael sighed. "This is really it, isn't it?"

"Right now, you're an undeclared species with no protections from the Tribunal. Without those, The Tribunal and Mygi can put you in a dark room and experiment on you until their hearts are content. The Tribunal makes it a point to treat species who aren't loyal to them badly, as a way to say, 'join us, and we'll stop this.' It's cruel, but it got several very dangerous species in line. Pocket populations, mostly, like you. The Tribunal had no legal right to tell Mygi to stop, even if they wanted to." Cassius closed his book of Law. "It's the right decision, Raphael. By agreeing to the rules, the rules also protect you."

"This sounds like something that came up in my human rights class," he muttered. "Everyone has rights except those people who aren't 'us.'"

"That's exactly what this is," I agreed, feeling bad. "But it's worked for our world for a long time. The Tribunal is eight hundred years old, and it's the first attempt supernaturals have ever made to have a centralized ruling power to keep us all in line. While it keeps us in line, it also protects all of us from exposure."

"What would happen if I exposed it all?"

"Don't consider that," I whispered.

"Why not?"

"They would order me to kill you, and I..." I couldn't say that I would. I couldn't say that I wouldn't try. "An Executioner would put you down, and you would be written off as a deranged mad man with no idea what you're talking about. The species who don't want to go public shouldn't be forced to."

Cassius caught my eye.

"It worked for someone else," my ex-lover pointed out.

"Hasan is a Tribunal member, and he was fighting to keep one of his own alive. They wouldn't be able to write him off as an idiot, either. Not if his entire family went public and took the Tribunal with them. Raphael is one man. His case would be the same as everyone else's." Hasan had threatened to expose everyone if a werecat was put to death. It was what brought him out of hiding only a few weeks ago. I had been at that Trial.

Fuck, it was the business trip I was on just before this mess started.

"Fair points," the fae conceded. "I just wanted to make sure you weren't going to start considering his idea. It would also look like a ploy because someone else just held the Tribunal hostage with that very threat."

"Exactly." I nodded, sitting on the edge of his desk. "So, Raphael, your choices are to make an attempt to submit to the authority of the Tribunal and be given protections or run for the hills and go back into deep hiding."

"Would you two keep helping?" he asked softly. "No matter what I choose?"

"Yes," I answered. "I'll always help you. That's a promise." It was the only one I could give.

"I'll ask them for the protections, see if I can do this the right way before doing anything else," he decided. "How do we do this?"

"Let's get to work," Cassius said, a smile in his voice.

CHAPTER THIRTY-ONE

One minute before the recess ended, I walked into the Tribunal Chambers with Cassius and Raphael behind me. Ardghal was already waiting, and so were most of the Tribunal members with the exception of Hasan. Cassius led Raphael to sit down, and I took the floor beside Ardghal. Since we were the last two speaking to the Tribunal, we would have to be the first two. It was protocol.

Five minutes after the recess technically ended, everyone was still waiting on Hasan. While no one voiced a complaint, I could see annoyance on the faces of a few of the Tribunal members, especially the werewolves. I could imagine they didn't like waiting around on a werecat. Then again, Hasan had been an enemy of Callahan and Corissa once, eight hundred years ago. The two most powerful werewolves of their time and the oldest werecat on the face of the earth, they had been the leaders of the werewolf-werecat war.

There was old animosity there but it wasn't my business.

When Hasan came in ten minutes late, everyone stared at him. He walked slow, seemingly unperturbed by the looks, and sat down in his seat without any sort of rush.

"Sorry. One of my children and I were speaking." He turned to me and tilted his head. "You never told me you were trained by my son."

"Excuse me?" I wasn't sure where he was going with this. I knew what he was talking about, but I didn't see how it pertained to anything.

"You were trained by a werecat named Hisao. I'm certain you know his reputation."

"Hisao the Assassin. Yes, I know his reputation. I also knew he was your son. I just didn't think it was worth mentioning. He found me doing something stupid and took me under his wing. When he finished training me, he pointed me to the Tribunal to apply to be an Executioner. I got the job. Was there a reason you were speaking to him about me?"

It wasn't exactly proper to question a Tribunal member like that, but he was digging around in my personal business, so I felt I had the right.

"My son makes it a point to know about everyone who excels in his line of work. I inquired about you because you made a very distinct impression earlier. I wanted to know who I was dealing with."

I hated that. Hisao knew me better than most people. He was the one who found me after I ran away from

Adhar. I had decided I didn't want the life Adhar thought was right for me, keeping me locked away, even though I'd already had a taste of the world. He wanted me to find a breeding mate and start having kids as soon as I could. I had to be respectable and demure—perfect.

Hisao had watched me grow from an awkward, angry teenager into what I was today. He'd seen my hair go white of all things.

And he was telling Hasan, Tribunal member, about me.

"He says you have a knack for troublemaking. You have a general lack of regard for authority. Let's not forget, you sometimes take the Law into your own hands." Hasan considered me. "He also has a high amount of respect for you."

"That's very kind of him."

It was Ardghal who decided to cut into this before Hasan was finished.

"Can we get started? I don't want to waste my entire night with this affair."

Hasan turned to the fae and snarled. It sent shivers down my spine.

"You hold no power in this room, young man. I don't care who you're related to," Hasan snapped. "For that, Kaliya, you may start with your final argument first. I see you've brought Investigator Cassius and...that must be Mister Alvarez with you."

"Yes, sir. I would like to call both Lord Cassius and Raphael Alvarez to the floor to speak to the Tribunal of their own accord before I make my final argument against

Mygi taking custody of him," I declared. "Will you allow it?"

"We'll allow it, but only for Mister Alvarez. He's due his moment in front of us since we're passing judgment on his future. I'm going to assume Cassius has the same things to say that you do," Callahan said, glaring down the table at Hasan. "You need to remember that you don't speak for the entire Tribunal."

"You would have let her go first if Ardghal had cut into your conversation," Hasan countered. "Forgive me, though. It's been a long time since I've sat with equals on this bench."

"Forgiven," Corissa said quickly, resting a hand on Callahan's shoulder. "Let's not get into arguments over this, friend. This is a serious matter that deserves our full attention."

I caught the male witch rolling his eyes and wondered if the witches, for all their silence, always had such strong opinions about the other creatures on the Tribunal.

"Well, let Ardghal and I clear the floor so Raphael can speak."

"I can't believe this," the fae beside me muttered, shaking his head, a dark look on his face.

I hurried toward my guys. Cassius was tense, but there was nothing I could do to relax him.

"Sorry, it looks like this is just going to be Raphael," I said softly. "Raphael, you know what to say. Just...good luck." He didn't look worried as he stood up, adjusting the blazer of his suit. Cassius had gotten him one, and gods, it looked good, but I couldn't sit there drooling over him all night. "You feeling good about this?" I asked as he started walking down the stairs to get to the center floor.

"No, but I know if this goes wrong, you and Cassius have my back. If there's one thing I've learned since this started, it's that you two are some of the best people I've met in ten years, and I'm glad to have that support," he said, swallowing. "How bad can this get?"

"They won't be able to take you anywhere tonight, no matter what, but depending on how this plays out, your future could get a lot more dangerous." This wasn't the first time he'd asked, but I gave him the same answer each time.

So could mine.

He walked past me, and I fell into the seat next to Cassius. We watched in silence as he stood alone in front of the Tribunal. One of the vampires waved for him to begin speaking.

"I'm certain Kaliya and Cassius can tell you everything that's happened over the last few days. I just want to make it clear, I don't want to go back to Mygi. What they did to me was against my will, and I have no intention of going back to their laboratories. If it's decided tonight that I will, you will be forced to fight for it." Raphael started walking, and I smiled. He was starting off strong. Since the Tribunal didn't know what he could do, they didn't know how serious his threat was. They would have to treat it seriously.

"I would like to avoid conflict, though. Before coming here tonight, Executioner Sahni and Investigator Cassius walked me through some of the Laws of the supernaturals. So, under the Laws you enforce and rule through, I would like to put my species in for consideration to join the Tribunal's authority."

"Excuse me?" Oisin snapped. Hasan started to laugh at the end of the bench. Callahan and Corissa were staring at each other with wide eyes. Isaiah, the male vampire, was sputtering, while the female vampire was frozen in shock. It was one of the witches who decided to speak up since Oisin didn't continue his questions, and Raphael made no move to repeat himself.

"You wish to submit your species to the Tribunal," the woman said in a whispery voice. "Bold. Brave. But we don't know what you are."

"There's nothing in the Laws that say a species name is required," Raphael answered. "I can call myself anything, and since I'm the only known member of my kind, it would be the proper name. I would also be the leader of my kind."

"I'm going to assume your plan doesn't stop there," the male witch said with a note of amusement.

"No, it doesn't. I would like to also submit my species to be protected under the Endangered Species Law."

Hasan laughed harder.

"Hasan," someone said, looking down at him. "Are you okay?"

"Executioner Kaliya," he called out, waving me to come back to the floor. "I'm going to assume he knows about that portion of the Laws because of you."

I jumped up to my feet and nodded but didn't move down to the floor.

"Yes, sir. I felt he deserved every chance to live among other supernaturals that we have granted to each other. Because he's alone, the decisions are alone his to make."

"He's a danger!" Ardghal screamed. "To himself, to us."

"As I said earlier," I roared over him. "We're all a danger to each other and to ourselves. There's no reason he should be denied the chance, and if that means he must represent himself in the eyes of the Tribunal, then that's what it takes. You don't make choices for any species except your own, Clan Leader Ardghal. You are not the Fae King or a member of the Tribunal! That would be your brother, and I certainly hope you aren't using your familial relationship to him to sway this in your favor."

"And you are just the last pathetic remnant of a dying race. I'm not sure why anyone finds you relevant to this conversation," he snapped back.

"ORDER!" Isaiah screamed. He always had the piercing, angry way of bringing the room back to attention. "Both of you will sit down."

"I think we can make a ruling right now," the male witch said, a smile on his face. "I think it's fairly clear what we should do."

"Agreed," the female witch said airily.

"I've made mine," Hasan added. "But I'll have some conditions."

"I think we are of the same mind, feline," Callahan said from down the table to the werecat. "Corissa?"

"Put it to a vote," the female werewolf said, sighing. "Let's see how this plays out."

Callahan stood and looked at the two parties who had yet to say anything. "Do you need more time to deliberate?"

"No," Alvina said, looking at Oisin when it came to him.

"No."

"Vampires?" Callahan turned to the last party. Both shook their heads, indicating they were ready to vote. Callahan cleared his throat. "We'll start off with the big problem. Raphael brought the pressing matter of joining the Tribunal before us. Raphael, do you understand that none of your species will ever hold a seat on the Tribunal?"

"Yes."

"Good. All in favor of the species of Raphael Alvarez being subject of Tribunal Law?"

Hasan, the witches, Alvina, and one vampire raised their hands. Corissa and Callahan voted last, also agreeing.

"So, we have it. Come tomorrow night, we'll sit down with you and discuss individual Laws governing your kind. Do we grant protection under the Endangered Species Law?"

The same hands raised, giving Raphael the protection I wanted him to have but couldn't safely give him.

"Hasan, you had conditions. If they're agreeable, we'll hear them and pass judgment."

"Raphael Alvarez, uneducated in the supernatural world. You will stay with Executioner Sahni or Investigator Cassius for a period of one year. You may move back and forth between them, but they will be in charge of you for one year, and anything you do will go back on them. Mister Alvarez, is that agreeable?"

"Yes sir," Raphael said strongly, looking back at Cassius and me. "I can handle that."

Hell, that was the best condition I'd ever heard. I was more than agreeable, nodding down to him. Cassius was also quietly nodding, giving his consent.

"In addition, Investigator Cassius and Executioner Kaliya, you will be point on the investigation into the identity of Raphael's species. There's no such thing as something coming out of nothing. Even the oldest supernatural species have their origins, whether it be curses, other worlds, or hidden abilities in magics. Everyone comes from something, which means Raphael must. You will find out. You will have a yearly review until the truth is found." Hasan looked at us evenly.

"Agreed," I called out.

"Agreed," Cassius repeated.

"Wait. Sahni is an Executioner. She cannot formally participate in an investigation," Oisin said sharply. "You know that."

"Fine." Hasan seemed annoyed at that. "Cassius, you will be point on the investigation and Kaliya, you shall be the Executioner we all know will be involved, anyway. Don't break any rules while you're at it."

"Yes, sir," I said, smirking.

"Hasan—"

"They've agreed," the werecat growled.

"Then I wish to add my own conditions that Raphael submit himself to Mygi—"

"You're lucky none of them have pressed charges against Mygi," Alvina pointed out. "Don't push your luck, brother.."

Oisin sat back in his chair, looking incredibly displeased, but I knew we had it. Raphael was coming home with me, and there was nothing on this earth that could take him away from me now.

Wait. No. There's nothing to take away his freedom. He's not mine.

"As for Mygi..." Callahan turned to the CEO. "You do realize the only reason you're walking away from this relatively unscathed is because of your reputation prior to this incident, correct? Even if you weren't breaking the Law, what you've done is to be frowned upon. Don't presume to be protected in this Chamber again, Ardghal."

"He does good work for our people," Isaiah said softly. "This is a regrettable situation, but we must allow him to redeem himself."

"Of course," the male witch said, waving a hand. "But dispensation like this shall only be given once, or I'll personally move to have Mygi hand over their research to a different company and let them continue the good work. This entire situation has not only been regrettable but embarrassing. And our own Executioner and Investigator had to bring it to light for us. Mygi had ten years to tell us they found an unknown supernatural species and didn't. You'll notice, he hasn't even offered to help the new investigation." The witch smiled. "Don't think we'll forget that, Lord Ardghal."

"Of course, sir," Ardghal said, his face not quite blank enough to cover his rage and disgust at having to answer to anyone but Oisin.

"You're dismissed," Hasan said with a growl at the end. "You better hope I hear no stories of werecats in your labs, Ardghal, like the ones I'm certain Raphael will tell us about his time there."

"Of course, sir." Ardghal moved fast, and I couldn't blame him. It was one thing to embarrass yourself, another to piss off a few of the Tribunal members. Both were easy to do. Having witches and werecats looking for a reason to kill you was a good reason to be scared.

Callahan looked down at Raphael and continued the topic at hand.

"And so, the Tribunal has passed judgment. Raphael, your species will submit to the rule of the Tribunal and be granted all protections under the Tribunal. You will also be added to the Endangered Species Law, denoting your right to defend yourself and others of your kind. This Law includes mates and children. This can all be discussed tomorrow night while we document everything you can tell us about what you are and what you can do for the Tribunal Archives. You will spend one year under the supervision and tutelage of Executioner Kaliya and Investigator Cassius. It would be a wise choice to take that seriously, as they have gone above and beyond to help you. They will continue helping by trying to find more information about what you are, so work closely with them as you might find the answers you need. You are dismissed for the evening."

I raced down the stairs, grabbed Raphael's arm, and pulled him out of the Chambers, Cassius following us, ignoring calls from his uncle and aunt. Once we were out of the Chambers, I grinned.

"We fucking did it! Raphael, welcome to the supernatural world." I laughed, the feeling of victory making me giddy.

"Thank you. Thank you for everything, Kaliya," he said softly, leaning against the wall.

"Any time," I promised.

32

CHAPTER THIRTY-TWO

"Let's find something to eat," Cassius said, gesturing to the kitchen. "We can discuss tomorrow over—"

"Cassius," someone purred. "I'm so glad to see you're okay."

I turned to see a beautiful fae standing down the hall. She had silky silver hair and large moon grey eyes.

"Love," Cassius gasped. "What are you doing here?"

"I got tired of waiting for you to send word," she explained as Cassius walked to her and wrapped his arms around her. It seemed terribly intimate. "Now, are you going to introduce me to the famous Kaliya Sahni and this human you've helped save?"

"Well, he's now Raphael Alvarez, leader of his supernatural species."

"King of one," Raphael joked. "You are?"

I knew.

"Lady Sorcha. It's an honor to finally meet you."

Cassius hadn't told me he was marrying the fae

Lady that defied the world and learned to work iron in ways none of the others could. It was said she was immune to it, even though it was toxic to the fae species.

"And you," she said, smiling. "We have much to talk about."

"We do," Cassius mumbled. When Sorcha and I looked at him, he realized his fiancée meant we were going to talk about him. "Oh, no. Raphael, let's go get a drink."

"Yeah..." Raphael looked between Sorcha and me, realizing two very dangerous women were about to become friends.

"I love when men realize we're the dominant sex," Sorcha said with a sly smile. "Cassius knew before I met him. I was pleasantly surprised." She looked at me expectantly.

"You're welcome. You came at the perfect time, actually. Cassius is going to have to make Phoenix his permanent home." I didn't know this woman except by reputation, but after the week I'd had, I was willing to go with anything. Friends seemed like a good idea.

"One of you will have to explain this..."

We talked as we walked down the hall. We found the guys drinking in Cassius's office already, and Leith was running around with Terry, trying to prepare food.

I watched Raphael most of the night, more at ease than I had ever seen him. Even though just twenty-four hours ago we'd been fighting for our lives, I felt good.

There were still a lot of questions I had to answer—

about him, about my reaction to him—but at least I now had some time to get those answers.

When someone lifted a glass in Carter's name, I lifted mine as well.

Hopefully, no one else is going to have to die before I have them.

I sat up straight.

"The USB," I said quickly. "Where is it?"

"Hold on." Cassius went to his desk and pulled it out of the top drawer. He brought over a laptop as well. "Get to it. I was hoping you would forget about it for a night, but oh well."

I turned everything on and plugged in the USB. I tried to open a file and growled as the laptop blue screened.

"Well, Sinclair got the last laugh, it seems," I sighed, turning the laptop. "It was a virus."

"Ah, well. We had suspicions he didn't know anything," Cassius said sadly.

"Yeah...Well, there's always next time," I mumbled, closing the laptop. I looked up and met his eyes, something unspeakable passing between us.

Carter was gone, and he was gone in vain.

But tomorrow was another day and now Cassius and I had a new mystery on our hands. We had no answers and it didn't seem like Mygi Pharmaceuticals was going to help. Looking at Raphael, a rush of fear ran through me. He was both my possible mate and a new supernatural species that needed my help.

I had to do better. I had to work harder. I had to be the best.

I sipped my drink as I stared at Raphael, promising myself that I wouldn't rest until I uncovered the truth.

For both of us.

∾

Keep reading for more information about the next release, special news, and more.

DEAR READER,

I hope you enjoyed your first journey with Kaliya Sahni! Lots of questions, not a lot of answers, but don't worry, as the series goes, Kaliya calms down... a little and answers will come. Kaliya Sahni will a 6 books series, so I hope you're ready for the ride!

If I still have you, head over to my website to get the latest updates on the next book in the series. Head over to my website and sign up for my mailing list! There are exclusive teasers for those who are signed up: Knbanet.com/newsletter

Also, I have a Patreon, where I write a monthly short story or novella. You can check that out here: Patreon.com/knbanet

And remember,

Reviews are always welcome, whether you loved or hated the book. Please consider taking a few moments to leave one and know I appreciate every second of your time and I'm thankful.

THE TRIBUNAL ARCHIVES

The Kaliya Sahni series is set in the world of The Tribunal. Every series and standalone novel is written so it can be read alone.

For more information about The Tribunal Archives and the different series in it, you can go here:

tribunalarchives.com

ACKNOWLEDGMENTS

I'm very bad at giving really public praise. I shower people in praise in private. But that's not everyone's love language and that's okay.

So this little page shall now be dedicated to everyone who helps me get these books from the concept to the release and beyond. From my PA, to my editor and my proofreader, to my wonderful friends helping me through the hardest moments. To my husband, who doesn't read my books, but loves that I write them and is willing to listen to me talk about them for hours.

And to you, the reader, for without you, I wouldn't have anyone to share these stories with. I'm a storyteller at heart and you have given me the greatest gift of listening.

I love all of you. Thank you for continuing to go on this journey with me.

ABOUT THE AUTHOR

KNBanet.com
Living in Arizona with her husband and 5 pets (2 dogs and 3 cats), K.N. Banet is a voracious... video game player. Actually, she spends most of her time writing, and when she's not writing she's either gaming or reading.
She enjoys writing about the complexities of relationships, no matter the type. Familial, romantic, or even political. The connections between characters is what draws her into writing all of her work. The ideas of responsibility, passion, and forging one's own path all make appearances.

- facebook.com/KNBanet
- instagram.com/Knbanetauthor
- bookbub.com/authors/k-n-banet
- amazon.com/K.N.-Banet/e/B08412L9VV
- patreon.com/knbanet

ALSO BY K.N. BANET

The Jacky Leon Series

Oath Sworn

Family and Honor

Broken Loyalty

Echoed Defiance

Shades of Hate

Royal Pawn

Rogue Alpha

Bitter Discord

Volume One: Books 1-3

The Kaliya Sahni Series

Bounty

Snared

Monsters

Reborn

Legends

Destiny

Volume One: Books 1-3

The Everly Abbott Series

Servant of the Blood

Blood of the Wicked

Tribunal Archives Stories

Ancient and Immortal (Call of Magic Anthology)

Hearts at War

Full Moon Magic (Rituals and Runes Anthology)

Made in the USA
Middletown, DE
22 January 2023